CONTENTS

Borough of Bones 1

Chapter 1 3

Chapter 2 12

Chapter 3 17

Chapter 4 19

Chapter 5 33

Chapter 6 40

Chapter 7 50

Chapter 8 63

Chapter 9 73

Chapter 10 79

Chapter 11 87

Chapter 12 96

Chapter 13 102

Chapter 14 114

Chapter 15 123

Chapter 16 130

Chapter 17 137

Chapter 18 143

Chapter 19 150

Chapter 20 159

Chapter 21	166
Chapter 22	172
Chapter 23	184
Chapter 24	189
Chapter 25	199
Chapter 26	205
Chapter 27	212
Chapter 28	218
Chapter 29	225
Chapter 30	232
Chapter 31	236
Chapter 32	246
Chapter 33	253
Chapter 34	263
Chapter 35	267
Chapter 36	274
Chapter 37	279
Chapter 38	286
Chapter 39	293
Chapter 40	305
Chapter 41	312
Chapter 42	317
Chapter 43	331

BOROUGH OF BONES

Book 2 of the Zone War Trilogy

by
John Conroe

John Conroe

The Demon Accords:
God Touched
Demon Driven
Brutal Asset
        Black Frost
Duel Nature
Fallen Stars
Executable
Forced Ascent
College Arcane
God Hammer
Rogues
Snake Eyes
Winterfall
Summer Reign
The Demon Accords Compendium, Volume 1
The Demon Accords Compendium, Volume 2
Demon Divine
C.A.E.C.O. (Summer, 2019)

The Zone War series:

Zone War
Borough of Bones
Web of Extinction (coming Fall, 2019)

Cover art by Gareth Otton.

CHAPTER 1

Curiosity kills the cat. I've heard that one before. Not quite true in the Zone. Drones ignore cats. Now, a feral dog or coyote, or maybe a horde of rats might do for a cat, but not a drone. I also didn't think curiosity had killed the lady in the bathtub either. Second floor bathroom of a little house on Cooper Street, northern Manhattan. She looked like she had tried to hide in her slipper tub but a small drone, probably a Crab, had climbed up and shot her twice in the face with small caliber rounds. Based on the brownish stains on the white tub behind her head and the way her skull was turned to the left, I'm guessing she had her eyes closed at the end. Bits of torn and rotted cloth still draped her skeleton, but rats, roaches, and who knows what had cleaned up the rest of her. Curiosity? No, I think she stayed in her house too long, then tried to hide from a computerized killing machine. Like hundreds of others after the drones attacked. Generally an unsuccessful tactic with the Zone drones. But curiosity was certainly a problem for all three of us. Myself, Sergeant Eros, and, the curious one, Sergeant Primmer.

Just a day-long training exercise into the north end of the Zone, that's all it was supposed to be. Major Yoshida insisted on us using upper Manhattan for some reason, and as it's generally a little less populated with drones than the lower end, it made sense.

So it was me, Rikki Tikki, the two military snipers, and their two experimental Kestrel drones. I had argued for

3

using the Decimator that Yoshida had sent to help me when I fought the Spider, but that was a complete no-go. The advanced Decimator was still being debugged and Yoshida's pet scientists were still trying to figure out the best training for its onboard AI. So we were *attempting* to duplicate my success with Rikki with the Kestrels. The powers that be had allowed me input into setting up the lesser drones, but they still seemed pretty clunky. No real problem solving, slow learning.

Anyway, I digress. Rikki was scouting a one-block area around our position, which was a residence in the Inwood neighborhood, Cooper Street. The two Kestrels were parked outside, perched on the small roof between the two bedroom dormers, mostly hidden from sight. Drone activity was very light and we had successfully infiltrated without detection. It had been very slow going, as teaching others to do what I did was proving to be much harder than I ever thought it would. I've heard that the act of teaching often provides as much instruction to the teacher as the student, but I never understood it. Now it was crystal clear.

Things that I do without thought had to be carefully considered and broken down into the hows and whys. Eros and Primmer were only my second set of trainees. The first two had gone pretty well, but I think those two snipers had been carefully handpicked for success. Each had previous Zone experience and both had been sponges, soaking up everything I said or did. Most importantly, they had been egoless in their desire to learn. This second set was different.

Eros was actually okay, but Primmer was... difficult. They were older than me, both sergeants, with years of experience as soldiers. So listening to a young civilian seemed to be an issue, especially for Primmer. Also, they were both new to the Zone and lacked a certain respect for it. Sure, they had undergone the Zone Defense orientation sessions, but watching video, no matter how graphic, didn't provide the same lessons as firsthand experience.

Wow, again with the digressing. Okay, so I'm on the second floor of the home, scoping out the immediate area from a south-facing window, when I hear two sharp reports downstairs. Gunshots—small caliber.

My brain interpreted the information even as I found myself on the stairs, headed down. I saw Eros pulling a bleeding Primmer behind the heavy dining room table that was now lying on its side, even as two more gunshots cracked, blasting splinters of wood from the table. The shooter was a Crab bot, maybe even the one that had killed the homeowner ten years ago, standing on its six legs in the hallway to the kitchen, its .22 caliber gun twisting back and forth as it tried to get a shot at my trainees. No idea how many rounds it had left.

The bot heard me on the stairs and scuttled around, bringing its gun up toward me, but I ducked back out of sight. Below me, I heard its metal-tipped feet clicking on the hardwood floor as it moved further into the living and dining rooms.

Reflexes kicked in and I grabbed the round woven area rug from the stair landing, holding it by the edges, ears straining. The little killer decided its tactics in a second, the ticking of its fast feet telling me it was rushing into the dining area, which was at the bottom of the stairs.

I spun the rug out like a Frisbee, like a fisherman on a tropical island casting a net, then instantly went for my suppressed .458 Socom just as quick as the rough fibers left my hands.

The rug caught half of the little Crab, which was only the size of a toaster oven. Enough to throw it off-kilter. Which was enough. My first shot wasn't even aimed, just point fired as the compact rifle was coming up. It hit one of the back legs, knocking the drone off its feet long enough for the second, better aimed shot to smash the robot killer into oblivion.

The bot still twitched and scrabbled, but the gun and central processing portions were destroyed. Dropping the Socom on its sling, I grabbed my kukri and jumped down the last flight of stairs and chopped the bot to pieces.

"What happened?" I asked when the drone was fully incapacitated. Sergeant Eros was applying a nano bandage to Primmer's left thigh while Primmer was injecting himself with a pain blocker from his kit.

Eros didn't answer, leaving it to Primmer, whose face was pale with pain. "I was reconning the basement and this thing was down there, sitting up in a windowsill. It looked completely deactivated."

"I told you both to stay on this floor."

"Clearing the house should have been our first priority," Primmer said.

"Only if we were staying, making it our base of operations. I told you—leave doors shut, blinds down, disturb nothing. A Crab can sit quiescent for months, years maybe. Now we need to go... or we're dead. Can you walk? At all?" I asked, putting aside the mistakes that had been made, now less important in the face of our imminent deaths.

"I'll have to, won't I?" Primmer asked, grimacing in pain as Eros pulled him up to his feet. We were wearing all of our kit, distributed about our stealth suits, so we only had rifles to carry in our hands.

"Get ready to exfil. I'm going to check outside," I said. Eros was already ripping apart a dining room chair to make a crutch.

Stepping to the door, I listened and watched, but the only thing in sight was Rikki hovering three meters above the street, facing me.

"Status?" I asked.

"Twelve aerial units inbound from the south. Three aerial and two ground units moving from northwest and northeast."

A soft buzzing announced the arrival of the two Kestrels from behind my Berkut. *"Orders?"* they asked in unison.

"Engage northern inbound drones under tactical direction of unit Rikki Tikki," I said, simultaneously pulling a trio of MSLAMs from my pockets, activating each, and tossing them to the ground as their legs unfolded.

"Rikki, direct emplacement of Mobile Selectable Light Attack Munitions along elevated positions of the most likely drone approaches from the south," I ordered as Eros helped Primmer hobble out the door.

"You're letting the drone place them?" Eros asked. Primmer looked like he wanted to comment, but pain was occupying most of his attention.

"Rikki is tracking the inbound units. He will continue to direct the MSLAMs even as they change vectors. Let's go," I said, moving out into the street, rifle up and pointed ahead, a fresh magazine in place.

"We're on Cooper. We head north, turn up W 207th,"

7

then follow Seaman till we're out of the Zone. About two klicks, give or take, and we'll be right by the barrier where the auto guns can provide cover. Sergeant Eros, take point. Rikki will be overhead. I'll take rear. Primmer, haul ass as fast as you can."

"Where are the Kestrels?" Primmer hissed out between clenched teeth.

"They're going to engage the northern inbound units."

"But we didn't direct them?" Eros asked.

"I did. I have override," I said, which was apparently the first they'd heard of that. One of my conditions for undertaking this doomed experiment. "Now move. The drones from the south will be here in seconds."

After a single glance at the hobbling Primmer, Sergeant Eros moved up the street, rifle up and ready, head swiveling for threats. Primmer dragged himself after, his improvised crutch scraping on the asphalt as he grimly plodded ahead. I turned and watched behind us for a handful of seconds, then moved after Primmer.

We were too slow. A flat-out run would have been too slow, but it would have been better. This painful crawl was gonna get us killed.

I pulled out my last two MSLAMs and dropped them onto the street after programming both for motion-detected detonation.

MSLAMS are, in my opinion, one of the best recent creations of the US military. Combining simple robotic functions with a multi-use explosive device was fantastic. But they were only going to help a little.

"Command detonating middle approach munition now," Rikki announced from above our heads. Immediately be-

hind us came a loud explosion.

"Detonating western munition now."

A second explosion announced the demise of another mobile mine.

"Fire off the last one," I said, knowing the drones had missed the street it was on, but hoping it would distract a few.

A shadow moved overhead. Rikki. He'd pulled back to help me cover. Nothing I'd ordered or programmed. His own idea. Seems my Berkut was having more of those lately.

"Ten units survive. Three Wolf UGVs have joined. UAVs coming into line of sight in three, two, one."

Right on cue, a swarm of killer assault drones shot around the corner and filled the air at the end of the street. The Wolves would be right behind them. I fired, fired again, and then got off a third shot before the first Wolf bounded into visibility. At least two of the aerial units exploded into parts before I focused on the bigger, heavier armored ground bots.

Above me, I heard Rikki's onboard 9mm gun fire, it sharp crack a counterpoint to the boom of my .458 Socom. Suppressors were off, noise reduction now pointless, and the concussive blasts from my rifle and Rikki's gun brushed the skin of my face with every shot.

With eight shots left in this magazine, I locked my sight reticle on the lead Wolf, stroking the trigger and sending out chunky tungsten carbide-cored expressions of my regards in its direction. Two rounds on number one dropped it, but the second Wolf leaped to the top of a decaying Volkswagen Jetta, metal talons tearing the automotive sheet metal like paper. That car happened to be the place one of my last MSLAMs had scuttled under. The MSLAM exploded, the bot sending its explosively formed projectile straight up through the car body. There must have been some fumes left in the tank because the result was impressive. A fireball engulfed half the street along with two aerial Raptor drones, the blast flinging the Wolf up end over end. I shot it mid-air, knocking it backward into the burning car.

The last Wolf and what looked like five Raptors burst out of the smoke and carnage, the Wolf leaping up onto the face of a house, actually turning and running sideways for twenty feet along the clapboarded side of the building before twisting back to hit the front lawn of the next house. It took me a nerve-rattling three shots to fully tag it and take it out.

Rikki had winnowed the aerial units down to three and between us, we took them down.

"Fifteen more UAVs inbound from the east, west, and south. Kestrel one has successfully destroyed one of the three aerials in our path. Kestrel two was destroyed by the other two drones, but managed to damage one. The ground units still approach, a Leopard and a Tiger unit."

I reloaded the Socom as I jogged to catch up with my trainees. Primmer was sweating profusely but hustling as fast as he could swing his crutch and drag his leg. His expression was a mix of pain and fear, with fear being the more prominent one.

Sergeant Eros suddenly fired his HK417, ripping off three fast shots of 7.62 ammo, followed swiftly by an additional two rounds.

We got closer and I could see the metal carcass of a UAV

strewn about the street.

"Good shooting. But stay sharp," I said. Eros glanced back with a grin and his left shoulder exploded in a gout of blood.

CHAPTER 2

Rikki and I fired as one, both of us locking onto the Indian Skyhawk that had come streaking out from between two houses. I missed, but Rikki didn't. The Skyhawk smashed through the front bay window of a small two-story.

Eros was already pressing a nano blood clot bandage into place.

"Flechette. I'm fine," he said, leaving the bandage to adhere itself and focusing on his weapon.

"Then let's haul ass."

Primmer never stopped moving, dragging himself like a man possessed up the street, eyes focused ahead, machine-like. We were off Cooper Street and on W 207th and ahead of us was a wall of trees that marked the edge of Inman Hill Park. Stores, coffee shops, and other big buildings lined both sides of the street. My military snipers both perked up at the sight of all that green ahead and I realized they would feel far more comfortable in the forest of the park than this urban terrain.

"Stay in the street. Do not enter the forest. You're both bleeding and the drones will easily track you. We need clear line of sight to engage."

Eros nodded, reluctantly, but Primmer just kept pounding ahead, awkward and jerky yet maintaining a steady pace.

Behind us, I could hear a soft whirring. Then came the crunch-crunch of steel on asphalt. They were gaining—rapidly. Time for another new trick or two. "Rikki, sweep left. Prep for Boomer two."

My Berkut ticked four times fast to acknowledge the command and then shot off to the west, heading to the right of the path behind us.

I pulled a soda-can-sized grenade from my left leg pocket, primed it, and set it down on the street, backing away swiftly but carefully. The cylinder sat still for a second, then sprouted four little legs that proceeded to lift it up about two centimeters off the ground. It beeped softly, letting me—its operator—know that it was armed, then it started a slow creep down the street, headed back the way we came. I turned and ran to catch up with the others, who had moved about forty meters ahead.

As soon as I got to them, I spun around, covering our six, and just in time as a hundred and fifty meters away, a new cloud of drones shot into sight. My rifle was already up and sighted their way so I tapped off two rounds, not expecting to hit anything but just to focus their threat identification protocols. Even as I fired, I kept up a fast backward shuffle.

One drone spun away, clipped by a lucky .458 bullet, leaving only a dozen to maybe a dozen and a half to seal our doom. The little mobile grenade kept up its slow steady crawl down the street, now fifty or so meters away from us.

I fired two more shots at the drones as I continued to tread carefully backward, following my trainees. Both shots missed as the drones engaged in wild looping evasive movements that maybe slowed their forward progress a teeny bit and possibly bought us a second or two, but more importantly kept their focus on me.

The aerial drones shot forward and at least two had laser weapons, as my visor suddenly darkened. The military stealth suits we were wearing were state-of-the-art and the eye protection was rated for most hand and drone-mounted laser weapons. The drones were trying to blind me.

The little grenade stopped walking and crouched down.

"Open your mouths," I yelled ahead to Eros and Primmer.

The Zone drones were already halfway to us when the grenade suddenly jumped a full meter off the ground and then exploded with enough force to knock me backward and down. The XM-2080 Multi-purpose Urban Novel Explosive grenade was *the* thermobaric weapon for the modern warfighter. You could set it behind or send it on a path, ready to fire its air fuel explosive at the first motion it sensed. You could also theoretically throw it, but you better have an arm like a major league pitcher or an NFL quarterback, because the blast radius was much, much greater than a normal hand-thrown ASM hand grenade. And the thing about big blasts in urban areas is the shockwave propagation factor of houses and buildings. The damage effects of bouncing concussive waves off flat walls is enormous.

My ears rang despite the automatic noise dampeners in my suit's hood, while pieces of debris fell all around me. I glanced at the sergeants, saw Eros pulling Primmer back to his feet, and then looked back at our pursuers.

Only four drones were still flying, and all four were wobbly at best, with bits and pieces of the other drones strewn all about the ground below them. That's when

Rikki swept in from their flank, firing six times to kill all four of the survivors. Perfectly executed tactical maneuver we had titled Boomer Two.

I turned and ran, quickly catching up to the trainees and then past them, getting fifteen meters out ahead.

"Where the fuck are you going?" Primmer demanded, even as I slowed and brought my rifle up, fiber optic gunsight locked to my eye.

I held out my left hand out and back in the military small unit stop signal. My ears were still ringing and I really needed to hear. Even when the two professional soldiers instantly stopped and stayed quiet, I was still having trouble hearing anything. Then a pair of pigeons took off from the corner of a building sixty meters ahead and I swung around to cover the spot with my rifle. Nothing happened. Suddenly a gray and brown spotted metal and synthetic monster exploded through the front window of the defunct business, landing and jumping at almost the same time. My first shot missed the Leopard, a big divot of exploding asphalt telling me I was low and left.

Then it was in the air, hurtling straight at me, seventy-five kilos of steel and carbon fiber death coming at me at twenty meters a second. My trigger finger flexed all on its own, with no conscious decision on my part. A triple tap, with the first round shooting under the bot and the last over it, but the middle round was the Goldilocks bullet—just right. Hit dead center where the neck collar met the torso of the mechanical beast.

My supply guy, Egan, somehow found a cache of these old .458 caliber dangerous game bullets from Speer Corporation. With a heavy core of tungsten carbide, they had been deemed an expensive overkill for hunters thirty years ago, especially when *all* African big game hunting was aggressively outlawed, but they were absolutely perfect for armored land drones. The big, heavy bullets either punched right through the armor or imparted so much kinetic energy that they could literally stun a UGV the size of an Indian Leopard, especially with the borderline excessive charge of smokeless powder that I hand loaded under them.

This bot hit the ground two meters in front of me and skidded almost to my feet even as I hopped, skipped, and jumped backward, putting two more bullets into it to keep it down. The killing machine twitched and spasmed, steel claws raking white lines in the faded pavement.

"Tiger unit has circled ahead and ceased broadcasting its transponder signal," Rikki reported from overhead. *"Distance to barrier approximately .7 kilometers."*

Great. More than halfway to safety and we only had to get by the most feared land drone ever fielded.

CHAPTER 3

We hit the corner of W 207th and Seaman Ave, immediately turning right onto Seaman. "Stay away from the forest. It's not your friend today," I said, eyes on Primmer in particular. Neither said a word, just kept moving as steadily as they could. Primmer was pale, extra pale, but Eros only looked a little better by comparison. Still, they were professionals and they kept up the pace. Overhead, Rikki moved in circular sweeps, watching but otherwise quiet. Bird sound in the woods reassured me, and the only other noises were the huffing of exhausted bodies and the scrape of boots and a chair-back crutch.

I moved myself to the middle of the road, between the sergeants and the forest, with Eros and Primmer on the developed side of the street. That was all well and good right up until the buildings stopped and the park took over both sides of the road, right at the corner of Isham Street. A big pit formed in my stomach. This was prime ambush territory.

I was still on the left side of my soldiers, watching the trees, with Eros covering the right side with his HK 417 7.62mm. Yoshida had dug up some great older guns when I insisted on only cartridge weapons, no electro mag rifles. Zone Defense now had a whole cache of these Heckler & Koch rifles.

Suddenly the vegetation on my side thinned and I could see an open area. A second later, I realized it was a set of old ball fields, the tree cover thinning to almost nothing. I glanced to the right, to a forest much thicker than I was facing. And both men were crowding close to that side. The pit in my stomach ballooned.

"Watch the tre—" was all I got out before the Tiger exploded from the upper branches of a big maple.

Leaves, branches, and bark flew as the metal monster launched itself in a close approximation to a real tiger. Time slowed to a crawl, my rifle barrel weighing a metric ton as I tried to yank it around to the Tiger. Small bullets from Rikki smacked into the leaping bot with no appreciable effect.

Eros's rifle fired twice, missing once and getting a glancing shot off the armored back of the drone. Then the Tiger piled into Primmer, rolling him up like a rag doll, razor-bladed jaws clamping onto his neck and shoulder. He screamed, briefly, then grunted as the weight of the machine slammed into his stomach.

Eros waved his rifle around, trying to get a clear shot, but I just started firing, focusing on the gray and black wherever I could. The machine's hind feet came up to its metal underside, the long steel claws sank into Primmer's belly, and the bot flexed both hydraulically driven legs, ripping Primmer into two pieces with a wet tearing sound.

My gun fired and fired till it clicked empty and the Tiger shook in jerky tremors, processors dying, its metal body wearing the bloody remains of my trainee.

CHAPTER 4

"Take us through it again," Yoshida said for like the fifth time.

Wearily, I restarted the same awful tale I had told over and over. The first three times, I hadn't been interrupted, but the fourth time, he started asking questions halfway through. This time, I didn't make it to the first quarter of the story.

"What exactly did you tell them?"

"I said *Stay here, hydrate and eat, but don't touch anything.*"

"Why?"

"What do you mean why? So that they wouldn't blunder into a drone and get killed."

"But you said earlier that Primmer felt he had to clear the building?"

"We weren't staying there longer than a rest stop. You don't overextend in situations like that. Minimal activity, minimal disturbance."

"And you were upstairs?"

"Yes, glassing the area from the bedroom windows."

"And it was okay for you to go up there because..."

"I had Rikki clear it first. That's how I do it. I use the drone as much as possible."

John Conroe

"What if you didn't have the drone, like Primmer didn't because you had the Kestrels outside the building?"

"First of all, I showed them how I do it with Rikki and had them use the same commands with the Kestrels. When our immediate area was clear, I sent the drones outside. Rikki was on scouting duty and the two Kestrels were half hidden, sensors looking for any incoming bots.

"Second, if I had to do it by myself, without a drone, it would take a couple of hours to do it right. It's a painfully slow process. *You* wanted a short in-and-out training run to get them started. So we were going to be leaving that house in like twenty more minutes."

"So Primmer went into the basement and what? Woke up the Crab?"

"I was upstairs. I only know that I heard a pair of .22 shots and then we had to kill the Crab, which had already sent out an alert."

"Why didn't Rikki find the Crab when it scanned the building?"

He knew this, I was certain, but he waited for me to answer. "Crabs are hideaway drones. Mobile long-term anti-personnel units. They find a spot and go dormant. Often they drop an arc of little miniature passive sensors around themselves, on thin wires, then power down to the barest minimum. Almost no EM output. If I had to guess, it was likely hunkered on the sill of basement window, so that it would get at least a little solar power each day. If Primmer stepped onto the stairs without fully clearing them, then he would likely have tripped a sensor. That's why fully clearing a building is so slow."

Yoshida frowned at me, clearly unhappy with my words.

"Tell me how you would have cleared the basement—using your drone."

"I'd crack the door from well behind it. Rikki would be rolled up in ball form, sitting on the floor so he wasn't making any hovering sounds. I'd let him sense the space till he was ready to lift off and hover down. He finds Crabs usually within the first ten seconds. If not right away, once he goes in, he trips their sensors and then they ping him for his transponder code."

"So you find them, then what next?"

"Depends on where they are, what I have with me, and what's available in the house."

"Explain?"

"Well, I've flooded them with water, especially when they're in a basement. But sniping them with a suppressed round is usually the safest and cleanest way to clear them. They don't have much armor, so even a handgun round will do it. One time, I sprayed one with a fire extinguisher, then smashed it with the empty canister."

He frowned again and flicked his fingers through the air in front of him. Immediately his left eye lit up with a reddish light as he scanned some information on his contact lens feed.

"You've turned in only fifteen Crabs in your entire career, and most were early on?"

"You guys pay almost nothing for Crabs. What, like fifty bucks or something? Not worth the weight of hauling them anywhere. I kill 'em and leave them near the doorway so that if I ever come through that building again, I'm reminded I was already there."

"So, it was Primmer's fault?"

I sighed. "No, it was mine. I should have sat on both of them. Primmer was a bit argumentative, always questioning my decisions. I should have realized he wouldn't stay still."

"Ah, but Sergeant Primmer was a professional US Army sniper. He had years of experience and countless hours of training. According to Eros, he didn't listen to his instructor."

"Eros said that?"

"He did. He said that both of them were put off by your age and the fact you weren't even military. But Eros followed the chain of command, despite his misgivings. Primmer didn't."

"Still my fault. Four trainees into the Zone and one is already dead. I can't do this anymore. But then, you're cancelling this program, right?"

Yoshida's eyebrows had gone up as I spoke. When I was done, he smiled, just ever so slightly, then shook his head. "No, Ajaya. We don't give up because we have setbacks and losses. We review, study, plan, and adapt new tactics."

"But they aren't going to listen to me. They don't have any respect for me. I haven't earned it in their eyes," I said.

His own brown eyes widened as though something was occurring to him. "Ah, then we change our orientation program. We show them all the reasons why they need to listen, why they should respect you, why they have to obey. Every single one of them is a volunteer. We go over the risks but maybe we can do it in a more graphic manner. I have some ideas about that. Now, we're done here for the moment. You should head back to your family. Losing a soldier weighs on a leader like nothing else. You did the best you could do, which in my estimation was likely better than anyone else could do. But soldiers are people and people have their own minds. We will use this a teachable moment."

"Why is Zone Defense doing this? Are you looking to clear the northern part of the borough? Trying to move the barrier south? Reclaiming something to show progress?"

His eyes narrowed. "The mission parameters are on a need-to-know basis. But you, my friend, are pretty sharp. Go home, Ajaya. We'll talk about your training program tomorrow."

So I found myself back at the family apartment after securing my weapons at the precinct house around the corner. Aama was there, and for a change, so was my mother. Our recent work with the *Zone War* show, as well as our portion of the proceeds from my dead drone caches that we had shared with Johnson Recovery, had put us in a pretty good financial condition and so Mom wasn't having to work as many hours, teaching language or doing translation work.

I opened the door quietly, hearing their voices immediately. Not sure if I wanted to face them, I headed to my room to drop off the rest of my gear. As I came back out, Mom was waiting in the hallway. Her eyes did a quick eval, scanning me head to toe before focusing on my face.

"What happened?" she asked.

"I, ah... ah, well one of my guys, he didn't—Mom—it's all my fault," I said, dropping my eyes from hers.

Instantly I was wrapped in a tight hug and when I lifted

my head, I found my grandmother standing just behind Mom, worry and sympathy mixed in her expression.

"Was there a death?" Mom asked gently.

I nodded. "He didn't listen, but I should have known."

"Oh sweetheart, I'm so, so sorry. Leading soldiers into dangerous places is practically guaranteed to result in losses. And the Zone is the *most* dangerous of places. I *know* you did everything you could, but these soldiers are all volunteers, all professionals. If he didn't follow your guidance, then there is very little you can do to protect him. I'm sure you've told the story a thousand times, so let's not rehash it. Although, you are very much your father's son, and he would rehash missions over and over till he just about made himself sick."

Mom gently guided our little group to the living room and made me sit on the couch with her next to me. Aama brought me tea, sweet and buttery, then settled on my other side while I sipped it.

After a bit, I told them the story. I did it slower and without as much military vernacular as I had reported it to Yoshida.

"Ajaya, I am so sorry that you lost a man, but listening to you and knowing your habit of understating your own actions, I have to say that anyone who enters with you has the very best chance of living through it—as long as they listen to you. Your own father lost half of his trainees the first mission and almost as many the second. That's when he quit. Why do they want to do this anyway?" Mom asked.

"I think they're trying to reclaim Manhattan, inch by inch. They're focused on the topic of clearing houses and buildings, and I think Yoshida is trying to build a corp of soldiers able to survive in the Zone to get the job done."

"I think they should go back to the EMP weapons and do it that way," Mom said. Aama nodded in agreement.

"The EMPs don't reach all the nooks and crannies of all the buildings in Manhattan. They tried that already, years ago. The first few attempts knocked out quite a few drones, but then results went downhill. Personally, I think the Spiders have found ways to anticipate attacks. Sneaking drones near the wall to electronically monitor communications, tapping into the internet, stuff like that. Harper thinks so too."

"Harper seems to know a lot about drones?" Mom questioned.

"We were in the same class for drone tech," I said, reminding her of the story. And it was very much a story, as Harper had never attended drone tech school. She could easily teach it, but she hadn't lived outside the Zone until just recently.

"Mom, I think I'm going to go lie down for a bit," I said, finishing my tea.

"Okay, dear. We'll get you later when dinner is ready," Mom said after a glance at Aama.

"I might not be hungry," I warned them.

"But you *will* still join the family for dinner, because that's what you need—family."

"Okay," I agreed, taking myself off to my room.

Once I was flopped on the bed and staring at the ceiling, the awful image of Primmer getting ripped in half immediately ran through my head. I tried to banish it but it kept coming back. I tried listening to music, I tried looking at the family business accounts, I even picked up a book I'd been trying to read for a week. But every time I thought my mind was clear, that horrible, bloody image would come screaming back through my mind's eye.

Then something rustled on the floor by my door.

It was the backpack that I carry Rikki in. I had forgotten to get him out. Cursing softly at myself, I jumped up and opened the pack. Rikki, in ball form, hovered up out of the payload section and floated over to his charging station.

"Analysis of mission reports have been flagged as an improper selection of candidate Primmer. Zone Defense leadership has implemented a change in the personnel screening process to eliminate individuals with known authority and chain of command issues. Also, Major Yoshida has ordered new orientation videos incorporating satellite footage from today's mission. None of the written evaluations place blame on Ajaya Gurung," Rikki said in an uncharacteristic burst of unsolicited information.

"Rikki, how do you have access to Zone Defense screening parameters and confidential mission reports?"

"Rikki Tikki has implanted scout viruses in Zone Defense networks."

I was stunned. My drone had taken it upon itself to infiltrate the US military computer network that monitored the Zone. And succeeded.

"What protocol established this action plan?"

"Primary mission: Protect Ajaya Gurung."

That wasn't exactly correct. Primary mission was to protect humans with a focus on myself, my family, and additionally, Astrid Johnson. Rikki had been changing slightly ever since he got knocked out of commission back when I intervened and sniped the Johnson clan out of a Spider trap in lower Manhattan. That train of thought brought a beautiful blonde face to mind.

My personal AI assistant played a snippet of music that announced a message from Astrid. Isn't it odd how you think of someone and suddenly they're contacting you?

"Read message."

"Yo tall, dark, and sneaky. How was your day?" My AI read, using a copy of Astrid's voice.

"Reply. *The worst,*" I said.

The reply came back almost instantly—a chime requesting full visual and audio.

"Answer," I told my AI. Anyone other than Astrid and I would likely have declined the call.

The blank white wall across from my bed suddenly became a video window, filled with Astrid's beautiful face. "Are you hurt?"

"No."

"People injured?" Her face was worried—and smudged with a little grease on one cheek, her long blonde hair tied back in a ponytail.

"I lost a man."

"Oh AJ. I'm so, so sorry."

"Me too. My fault—wasn't watching him."

She frowned at me. "Everyone who enters the Zone is responsible for themselves. I know you did everything possible."

"Not so sure about that. But hey, how was your day?"

Her frown turned to something sympathetic at my awkward topic shift. "We stayed out of the Zone. Made upgrades and repairs to the LAV."

"What upgrades?" Team Johnson always had the best gear and vehicles. Any upgrades were bound to be interesting… maybe even distracting.

"Well, among others, we Installed a Sinoarms Ping A8 on the minigun."

Sinoarms was the largest Chinese defense company and the Ping, which if I remembered correctly, translated as Shield, was an anti-drone automated targeting system.

"With radar?"

"Radar, full spectrum machine vision, and echolocation."

I didn't know there was a version that melded all those sensors, but then, I didn't keep up with armored vehicle accessories like she did, just like she wasn't as fully versed in stealth tech as I was. But we were both interested in each other's tools of the trade, particularly anything that promised more safety in the Zone.

"What's Martin going to do?"

Her middle brother, who was a giant asshat, usually manned the minigun station. The Ping would make him redundant.

"He'll be backup if it fails, but primarily he will supervise the new Zaman sensor suite."

"Wow, the old man really opened up the wallet."

"Seems we got a bunch of easy money raiding some drone hunter's trophy caches. Dad wants to be as prepared as possible for Spider activity. Which is why we also added a Finya launcher."

I could feel my frown form as I listened to her. Civilian armored vehicles were not allowed to mount grenade launchers or any type of missile system other than smoke and concussion grenade launchers and even then, they were restricted to 37mm. They could use machine guns for days, but anything that launched explosive devices was verboten. The military and law enforcement used 40mm systems. The Finya was 37mm, a slight but important legal distinction, and only it launched smoke, rubber sting pellets, foam batons, and a rather underwhelming variety of flash-bang grenade that kept it legal. Nothing that would be effective against drones. Brad Johnson had always been rather vocal about the uselessness of the neutered civilian systems.

"Well, if some idiot left a bunch of dead drones lying around, why wouldn't you help yourself," I said, buying time while I pondered the Finya.

She smiled. "He's not an idiot. A little slow maybe, but otherwise he's pretty nice."

"Nice? Old ladies and friendly shopkeepers are nice. Don't you mean he's handsome, sexy, and exciting as hell?"

"Well, he's one of those solo warrior types, so he's pretty quiet. Also, his face is a dead giveaway for all his emotions. You're completely bewildered by the Finya, aren't you?"

"Your dad always hated those things."

"Yeah, well, we found an abandoned Federal law enforcement agency vehicle while we were making a run into the Zone. Big SUV with a full load of goodies in the back.

Martin recognized the labels on the main stack of boxes. Some special stuff for Uncle Sam's agents. All 37mm, but way, way better than the normal stuff. Like, lethal. Finyas are inexpensive and with this stuff on board, we'll have some surprises for the drones."

"But the first time you shoot them off on-air, the Feds will come down on you."

"Maybe, but we'll be alive to beg forgiveness."

"So how good are these?"

"Please—like I would ever say over open internet. I will tell you that they're pretty surprising. Never heard of the brand, but Martin had and knew the ordinance labels, so he's maybe good for something."

"Well, anything that makes your little recreational vehicle safer is good in my book."

Outside my room, I heard a pair of voices that sounded almost identical—actually were indistinguishable to most people, at least those who hadn't grown up with them.

"Twins home?" Astrid asked. I realized I had tilted my head when I heard their voices.

"Yes—" was all I got out before a knock came at my door. I frowned and Astrid grinned at my expression. "Be nice," she said.

"Come in," I said, turning my head to the door and raising my voice a bit. Instantly the door popped open and my sisters stuck their heads in.

"Who you talking to?" Monique asked.

"Who do you think he's talking to?" Gabby asked her twin with a grin.

"Yes, it's Astrid," I got out and then they were inside my domain and bouncing on the bed on either side of me. Both greeted Astrid but uncharacteristically stayed serious. "Mom told us you had a really, really shacked-up day," Monique said.

"Yeah. Astrid's been distracting me," I said, waiting for one of them to take the bait. Surprise... neither of them *ohh*ed, *ahhh*ed, or made any suggestive noises at my comment.

"That's good. We'll leave you to it," Gabby said, standing back up.

"Just wanted to check on you. Plus Mom says dinner in five," Monique added.

They waved goodbye to Astrid and vanished out the door.

"Who were they and what did they do with my sisters?" I asked.

"They're concerned about you. All that snark and sass comes from love. They worry like crazy every time you go in. Do you have any idea how many calls and messages I get when you're late, or even worse, when you have to spend the night inside?"

"I knew they stayed home and slept in Mom's room, but I didn't know they bothered you about it," I said.

She frowned. "Ajaya Gurung... how could it be a *bother* for me to talk to your sisters when they're worried about *you*?"

Oops, I had just stepped in it. Happens to me all the time. I don't recognize the danger till it's too late. But the key to the whole thing is to recognize that you've fallen into a pit and immediately exfiltrate the hazardous area of conversation.

"I just meant I didn't know they did that."

"Nobody else goes in like you. My family goes in all at once, and we're behind tons of steel armor. The other teams go in at least pairs, also inside armor. You go in all by yourself and just about naked."

"Naked. Is that how you imagine it?" I asked, arching one brow.

She rolled her eyes, but I caught a little grin before she wiped it away. "Yeah, buck naked, cowering, and afraid."

"Let's focus on the buck naked part," I said, ignoring the other stuff.

"Perv. Leave it to a male to go down that road when we're talking about violent death and dismemberment."

I almost said something about members but her head turned and she listened to something offscreen. When she turned back, her face was resigned. "Gotta go. We're running tests on the new stuff. I'll check back with you later, hotshot, okay?"

"Yeah, go kick some ass—" I said, pausing, opening my mouth as if I was going to add my pet name for her, which is Trid. But that would have been too corny. I just smiled instead.

"Bye AJ," she said, giving me a smile that was half amused and half sympathetic. Then the screen disappeared, leaving a white wall.

CHAPTER 5

I had a message waiting on my AI when I woke up the next day. Yoshida. He wondered if I might join him at Zone Defense after lunch.

My wake-up was a good two hours later than normal, as I hadn't really slept much during the actual night time. Dragging myself into the kitchen, I found the coffee pot, mumbling good morning to my mom and Aama while I helped myself. Their conversation had shut off as soon as I shambled in, both turning my way with matching looks of concern.

I take my coffee black, no dilution, no watering down of the caffeine. Today I needed every bit of chemical stimulation I could get from the mug. Collapsing into a chair between them, I sipped my coffee. Something struck me as odd. Oh yeah. "Mom? You stayed home today? Are you sick?"

"No dear. I have stuff to get done, so I took a day."

"Oh. For a moment, I thought you were keeping on eye on me. You know... cause I sha... screwed up so bad yesterday."

"Major Yoshida sent me a message. Said you would likely be blaming yourself for yesterday's tragedy. Said in his estimation, it's amazing that any of the three of you made it out alive. That your trainee made a big mistake. That you did everything you could. Told me the steps you took would become part of the curriculum," Mom said.

Going back into the Zone after the running battle on Manhattan Bridge had been a bit of a battle itself. Mom was instantly dead set against it, and I didn't really blame her. But Yoshida had approached me with this teaching gig and it was at the north end, and therefore somewhat lower risk, and much of the time it was just classroom stuff. It paid well. When she still didn't go for it, Yoshida had approached my mom directly, displaying a level of tact and diplomacy that frankly shocked me. Now that I was actually doing it, he gave her regular updates to keep her anxiety down. But most importantly, he kept his contact with my mom a secret from the rest of Zone Defense. I would have been a laughingstock among the soldiers if they knew that my mom played such an important role. But Barbara Gurung had lost her husband to the Zone, and Baburam Gurung, had, in turn, lost most of his students when he tried teaching Zone survival. So Yoshida understood the family dynamics. He also didn't bullshit my mom. Ultimately it was always my decision, but when you live in a close-knit family and depend on one another like we did, the dynamics are... complicated.

Still, I hadn't expected Yoshida to reach out to my mom about Primmer's death.

"Oh," was the extent of my verbal wizardry. Aama set a plate of *sel roti* in front of me. Luscious rings of fried rice bread. My grandmother made it in big batches, then hid it away, only dishing it out on special occasions.

"Thank you, Aama, but I don't think a reward is warranted."

"Ajaya. You led, you fought, and you brought out everyone you could. That is your duty, and you did it with honor. The Gurung name has been upheld. Of course it deserves a small reward," she said, her English heavily accented but excellent. Mom nodded next to me at the table.

"Did you sleep at all?" Mom asked.

I shook my head, a piece of *roti* already in my mouth.

"Eat some breakfast, then why don't you lie down on the couch and try to rest? The major said he was going to have you go down to Zone Defense later this afternoon. Maybe you could catch a nap," Mom suggested.

I ate the roti, which Aama followed with a plate of beans fried in ghee, then, with nothing else better to do, I decided to go with Mom's idea.

The couch was soft and the morning news was playing on the viewing wall, so I lay and listened to the repetitious cycle of weather, traffic, sports, business, headline news, and human interest bits. The only thing that was remotely interesting was a side piece about a small group of delivery drones that went slightly amok, dropping their packages like little bombs on the recipients. The megacorp that owned them, along with owning a bit of damn near everything else, reported that it was a software glitch, which they found and fixed, preventing them from having to ground their national delivery fleet.

The news anchors, artificially bright, cheery, and attractive, rambled on, repeating the same stuff almost word for word. I drifted off into a strange dream, one where I knew I was dreaming, where retail drones hunted me with heavy packages of clothes that my sisters had ordered.

Part of my dreaming self wondered that any such packages could weigh much at all, as my sisters are petite and had entered that teenage phase where the clothing they chose was even tinier than they were. The rest of my dream self was trying to avoid death by package while shooting back at the drones with a t-shirt cannon filled with shirts bearing the logo of the New York Yankees. Then part of me that was aware that the news was playing realized that the current sports story was about the Yankees' spring training. I woke up almost immediately after that thought and found that a couple of hours had slipped by. And then I remembered Primmer and the way he died.

I sat upright, fast, startling my mom, who was at the dining table working on her AI, probably making lesson plans. "You okay?" she asked.

"Ah, just a bad dream. But the nap helped. I feel a little better."

Which was the truth. Still tired but not as groggy as before, I dragged myself off the couch, showered, shaved, and got ready for the day, trying to think of anything but the Zone and Sergeant Primmer.

Mom had made lunch in my absence, turkey melt sandwiches with tomato soup. "Where's Aama?"

"Your grandmother has her women's craft group meeting today."

Aama had found a group of Nepalese women who got together every week to practice the traditional handcrafting of Nepal. They did a lot of weaving but sometimes tried jewelry making or ceramics. Aama's specialty was weaving blankets, woolen ones that were so tightly woven that they were basically waterproof. In the cold weather months, I usually included a thin one of dark gray wool in my Zone survival kit.

"Okay. That's good. I guess I'll start out for my meeting. Walking part way will do me good," I said.

She smiled slightly, nodding. "Being out in the City is probably a good idea. It's a very distracting place."

As I headed out the apartment building's front door, I almost hit a jogger with the glass door as she ran up the steps. Then I realized it was Harper. She was kitted out in athletic Lycra gear, a slight sheen of perspiration on her forehead.

"Hey Ajaya," she huffed out, a little winded. She had come out of the Zone and immediately taken up fitness like it was her life's calling. You only run in the Zone if you're already being chased, and then you're not likely to live to finish the race. Harper had always moved slowly and cautiously, so she had had a hard time with cardio when we had raced to get out of the Zone. I think she wasn't going to ever have that happen to her again.

"How far today?"

"About ten klicks, give or take," she said, pulling her right foot up behind her to stretch her quad.

"You've come really far, really fast," I said. "And look at your arms! Weights?" I asked.

"I'm taking a kettlebell class."

"Nice. How's work going?"

"Picking up. Word of mouth takes a little longer, but once it starts, it's the best form of advertising," she said, now stretching her other leg. She did look good, muscles toned under the close-fitting gear. Then I forced my thoughts back to her answer to my question.

Harper had a new identity, skillfully crafted and carefully implanted into society's records by her computer genius mother. But no matter how good it was, it wasn't foolproof. So she earned her living by troubleshooting drones and robotic hardware and software, skills which she had in spades, and she avoided most normal online forms of advertising. I had helped her get some of her early jobs, but it was her own quality work that was expanding her clientele.

"*Zone War* is toying with the concept of sending a few drones in with the armored teams," I said. "They've asked me about shielding their units from interference by Zone drones. I've mentioned that I would consult with a friend who might be able to help them. You have any interest?"

She looked at me, the whirring wheels of thought almost visible as she considered the idea.

"It would be a bit of a risk, revealing any knowledge of what goes on in there, but it's probably pretty good pay, right?" she asked, head tilted slightly as she waited for my answer.

"I, ah, let it drop that my contact had done some work with me, like on Rikki. So it gives you a plausible reason for knowing this stuff, and yes, I told them it would be a little expensive. Trinity didn't bat an eye."

"You spoke to Trinity Flottercot about *me*?"

"Without saying anything about who you were. Told her I'd have to run it by you."

She locked eyes with me, a pleased smile on her face, then nodded. "I'll do it. Only, you have to introduce me."

"Yeah, of course."

"Okay, great. Let me know when you set it up. I gotta bounce," she said, sliding past me through the doorway. She got real close, brushing against me, then headed inside with a quick smile over one shoulder.

She seemed to have adjusted pretty well to life outside the Zone, and to the loss of her mother. I think she had made a few friends, but I was pretty sure I was still one of her most important ones. Even if she was usually a bit snarky with me. And she *had* helped me with both Rikki and with questions about the Kestrels when Yoshida pressed me for improvements to his program. I owed her my life, so I would do everything I could for her, but it seemed like some of her smiles went a bit beyond basic friendship. Or maybe not. What do I know about girls? Which made me think of Astrid, and that thought left me with a big smile.

CHAPTER 6

I made it to Defense headquarters on Roosevelt Island a bit earlier than the time Yoshida had specified. With time to kill, I took a seat on the retaining wall near the steps leading into the glass and steel building that used to be Cornell Tech's main campus building, instead of housing the military. Soldiers and a few civilians moved up and down the broad staircase, a couple glancing my way.

My time on *Zone War* had made me a slight celebrity, not recognized all the time, but enough that it wasn't unusual. I sipped my second coffee of the day and watched people walk by.

"Yo Boyle, look... it's a real-life star!" a female voice said to my left. Corporal Kayla Jensen was walking my way, her ever-present buddy Corporal Boyle shadowing her left side.

"Wow, Zone Defense soldiers! Like freaking recruiting posters in the flesh," I said back, unable to stop a little grin.

"There you go with all that talk about flesh again. If I didn't know better, I'd think you were obsessed with my body, Gurung. But you know I don't play for your team."

"Easy, soldier. I was talking about Boyle."

"Oh?" She turned and gave him a considering glance. Tall and raw-boned, with scars on both cheeks, he was more dangerous-looking than anything. "Well, there's no denying he's a dreamboat."

"Fuck both of you," he said without any change of tone.

"Ouch," Kayla said, then smirked at me. "So, you here for show and tell? Heard you had a rough day yesterday."

"Yeah, the worst."

"Nah, Shooter. The worst is the kind you don't come back from. You made it out and that Marine sniper, Eros, was sure singing your praises. These guys and gals are all professionals. You aren't a babysitter. Boyle and I wouldn't dream of going into the Zone on a sneak and peak without you for a guide, right B-man?"

"Truth," the somber Boyle said.

"You done sunning yourself like a lizard?" Kayla asked me.

I nodded.

"Then let's head inside. We're headed to the team ready room. You'll probably find the major there."

Sure enough, we almost bumped into Yoshida as we approached his strike force's section of Zone Defense headquarters. Yoshida, as far as I could tell, seemed to wear two hats: first, he led the ZD Instant Response Strike Force, which Kayla and Boyle belonged to, and he was also tasked with oversight of the Counter Drone research group, the people who had developed the potent Decimator drone that had helped Rikki and myself when we were facing down a Spider-led horde of Zone drones.

"Ah, Jensen and Boyle, you seem to have found my civilian consultant. Excellent. You two head on in. I believe there is some armor maintenance in your very near future," the major said when we found him.

"Yes sir," both answered. Kayla turned to me. "See ya around, Shooter." Her buddy just gave me a nod and they vanished into the team's offices.

"Come on, Ajaya. I've got some things to show you. We've made some progress with your Spider carcass."

The Chinese Spider CThree he was referring to had been designated Lotus and been one of three in the Zone. They controlled and directed all the other drones. Lotus had begun setting traps and my running battle with it had resulted in it falling into the East River with a bunch of big bullet holes in it. The water had pretty much ruined most of it and this was the first I'd yet heard about any progress in computer forensics.

"What changed?" I asked.

He grimaced. "They finally got it completely apart. Damned scientists wouldn't rush their dissection of it no matter how hard I came down on them. They found the equivalent of an aircraft black box. Some kind of backup log recorder. My geeks have just broken the encryption system protecting its files."

"And you're sharing with me?"

"*Some*. I'm sharing *some* of the intel with you. You know me, gotta keep some cards back."

He led me to an elevator that brought us down to the drone labs where the Decimator was built and kept, passing us through multiple layers of completely automated security.

The lab doors opened all on their own as we approached and without any fanfare, we entered the main lab. Three familiar figures were clustered around an AI worktable, looking at streams of code that were being holographically displayed in the air above the table. A huge flat table held the massive dissected metal carcass of the Spider CThree, spread out in orderly deconstruction. An unstoppable shudder ran through me as I looked at it. Then I looked to my left as we approached the Yoshida's braintrust, spotting a big, matte black delta-shaped form floating over a very specialized charging station. The Decimator, Unit 19, was docked at its charging station, hovering on magnetic repulsion fields, with only a few lights lit up on its ocular band. Much as I hated to admit it, Unit 19 was even more aerodynamic than my pet Berkut, plus it was better armored and better armed than my drone. Yet, somehow, Rikki still managed to outperform it in actual combat conditions, a fact that drove Yoshida's people nutty.

The three scientists, Aaron, Eric, and Maya, didn't notice our arrival as we stood behind them, listening to them talk. "These log events indicate the Spider accessed the internet. How?" Eric said.

"It could just clamp onto a fiber optic cable and have at it," I suggested. They all turned, regarding us without real surprise, more focused on my words than our sudden appearance. Weird people.

"Fiber optics? Where?" Aaron asked, something in his voice suggesting I was a dumbass. That *something* seemed to always be there when he talked to me.

"Almost anywhere in Manhattan, genius, but the old Western Union building on Hudson Street is a major hub. Some of those lines are still being used," I said.

"Hmmm. I suppose," he said, turning back to the code on the display.

"So Lotus was on the web?" Yoshida asked.

"It appears that Lotus was on the web *a lot*," Eric said, moving his hand over the display to scroll the code upward.

Yoshida turned to me. "You're not surprised?"

"The Spider CThrees that were released into Manhattan were enhanced and upgraded way beyond their original specs. They've been learning and growing for over ten years while they pursue their single mission—kill humans. They aren't going to let the Zone stop them."

Yoshida and all three scientists were staring at me. "How did you know the Spiders were enhanced?" Aaron asked, suspicious.

"I've been rummaging around in the Zone for ten years. I've been in the hold of the ship that delivered them. I've seen spec sheets," I lied smoothly. The best lies are embellished truths. I *had* seen drone spec sheets in the hold of the drones. Some specs *were* about the Spiders. But most of my knowledge came from Harper's mom, Dr. Theodora Wilks.

"Why have you never said a word," Yoshida asked, his own expression now suspicious.

"I don't carry a camera, and what I've seen was too water damaged to survive. Nobody ever believes half of what I say I've seen. Who here was going to buy my story without proof? Now you have proof," I said, waving at the metal skeleton on the big table.

"Do you know *what* was done to it?" Aaron asked.

"What I saw indicated better chips, much better chips. Also mods to the power and recharge systems, and notes that indicated changes to the neural net. Couldn't really read all of them because the East River had had its way with the paper and ink. Enough to know they were better than off-the-shelf versions."

"And off-the-shelf was pretty darned good ten years ago," Eric said.

"So why was it on the web?" Yoshida asked.

"The log indicates it was visiting multiple corporate sites, maybe looking for ways into the companies' networks," Maya said.

"Seeking more ways to kill humans," I said. "Hey, does that box back up any of its software?"

"No," Aaron said. "Strictly a log of last activity, like the little computer chip in the old manually driven cars, the one that tracked the last five seconds of engine activity before an accident for insurance and law enforcement investigations. Why?"

"Just a thought," I said.

Before Zone Defense learned about my pet Berkut drone, I always had to leave Rikki in the Zone when I got out. If anything happened to him while I wasn't there, I needed a way to back up all of his files, so I built a set of data chips inside him that received near continuous updates as he went about our business. The weak spot in my plan would be finding his dead airframe if he went down. But *if* I *did* find him, I'd be able to resurrect him, or at least give it a good shot. Nowadays, he just backed himself up at his charging station every night, but the chips were still inside and still functioning. I was kind of glad the Spiders had no such feature. Bringing them back to life would be disastrous for everyone.

The major was reading something on a mini-tablet, then typed on it, old-school fashion with his two thumbs. He looked up, glanced at the doors, then turned to his team.

"So we have no real idea of what…" Yoshida started to say but the lab doors opened and the two Department of Defense guys that I knew as Agents Black and White entered, along with about ten other guys in the same black suits that the agents wore.

"What are you doing here?" Yoshida asked, tone outraged. Yoshida had never gotten outraged before, just deadly angry. It was odd—almost forced. An act?

Agent Black, who was white, moved directly for our group, eyes locked onto the Spider's metal carcass. Agent White, whose skin was darker than mine, slowed to look at the Decimator as he followed. The other agents carried metal boxes the size and shape of large volume beer coolers. Really large beer coolers.

"We'll take it from here," Black said, his men moving up and pushing the three scientists out of their way. Immediately, the men in suits started to pack the metal boxes with Spider parts.

Yoshida pushed in front of me, his left hand holding his mini-tablet back my way, the action hidden by his body. I took it from his hand and backed away from the sudden press of people around the Spider.

"That drone is Zone Defense property," Yoshida objected, moving up and bulling into the mix of agents around the disassembled drone. That caused some return shoving and I took the distraction as an opportunity to look at the tablet.

If they get too grabby, say Unit 19, then say Patrol.

He'd known they were coming—maybe got advanced warning from some of his people elsewhere in the building, and he was thinking that they might try to grab the Decimator, too? Some kind of power play was in motion, or... cover up?

"Ah, Mr. Gurung. So you've joined the major's little group?" Agent Black asked, eyes now locked on me. He kept watching me but turned his head and spoke to his agents. "Transfer all computer, video, photographic recordings, and observations evidence to our keeping and wipe the rest clean."

One of the agents nodded and sat down at an AI workstation, immediately moving his hands while both eyes glowed red as he accessed the network on his iContacts.

Agent White was still staring at the quiescent Decimator and he now turned to look my way, his expression thoughtful.

"Bag this thing too," he suddenly said, waving at the hovering drone.

"Unit 19?" I asked, trying to sound startled. Instantly the Decimator lit up, coming awake at my words. Ah, so that's how it was. "P...patrol," I said, coughing a little in a lame attempt to cover it.

Unit 19 shot straight up overhead, then accelerated forward and out the open lab doors like a bullet.

"Oh wow. It took off," I said, trying for an *aw gee* tone of surprise. "Were did it go?"

Agent White was glaring at me, but Black just nodded thoughtfully. "Well played, Major," he said. "Alright, let's get this wrapped up and get out of here," he said to his crew, whirling one hand in a winding up motion.

His men hauled the now packed boxes of Spider parts out, the two senior agents following. Agent White was the last to go, and he turned, pointing his index and middle fingers first at his own eyes then poking them out at all of us before leaving without a word.

"Major, what the hell?" Aaron asked, incredulous.

"There are things you all don't understand. Things above all of our pay grades. That was one of them," Yoshida said, his sudden anger magically morphing into determined action.

"They confiscated the Spider, all of our notes and information, and they would have taken the Decimator too?" Maya asked.

"Yes, and they have the authority to do both. I couldn't intervene," Yoshida said, typing on his tablet madly.

"But if I gave a verbal command, being an outsider and a civilian, there were less consequences?" I asked.

"Theoretically," the major said. "They could also have arrested you, but there wouldn't have been much point. Unit 19 was most likely going to be held as a hostage for our good behavior. Now he's not. I learned that little trick, or a version of it, from one of the best." He nodded in my direction.

Okay, point to the major.

"That's why you didn't let us take Ajaya out of Unit 19's command loop?" Eric asked.

"I'm scary good, but I'm not *that* good. I had you leave him in because 19 did better alongside Ajaya and his Berkut than ever before. I was going to have us run more joint drills."

"I didn't even know I was ever in its command loop," I said.

48

"When we sent it to help you on the bridge against Lotus. If you had given any orders, it would have obeyed. Now... I have to get down to General Davis and lodge my formal protest. It won't do a damned bit of good, but it's expected. Gotta keep up the act. When Unit 19 circles back, download any recordings it might have made of your Spider dissection," Yoshida said.

"Oh! That's why you insisted the charging station be set up right there," Maya said, a note of admiration in her voice.

Yoshida shrugged. "Redundancy is a survival protocol. Just ask Mr. Gurung how much redundancy he uses in his forays into the Zone, eh, Ajaya?"

I just nodded, impressed with his foresight. Unit 19 might have detailed video and audio recordings of the whole Spider analysis.

"I also want you all to dig deep and make detailed personal reports of everything you can remember about the Spider. Everything. Then make copies of all of it, let's say, oh, I don't know... ten. I'll be back after I talk with the general. Ajaya, come with me. I want to walk you out."

CHAPTER 7

"Why would the DoD confiscate Lotus?" I asked as soon as we got into the hallway.

Yoshida waited for a white-coated technician to walk past us before answering.

"There is a whole lot about the Zone that you don't understand, Ajaya," he said, head swiveling to look for anyone nearby.

"Like who actually caused the attack and why?" I asked, taking a huge chance.

His head snapped around my way, eyes first wide, then narrowed and hard. "You're entirely too smart for your own good. Or you have access to information that you haven't shared?"

"I basically grew up in the Zone—I've seen, read, observed all kinds of things in there that conflict with the public version of events. I've guessed even more."

"That kind of speculation can get deadly, Ajaya," he said. "And I never heard you make that comment."

"What comment?" I played along.

"Exactly. Now, let's just say there are power factions in our government that are at odds over the Zone. While the majority want the Zone cleared and reopened, there is a subset that is concerned over things that you should *never* speculate about. Very concerned. This group will use virtually every power at their command to keep things hidden and quiet. And they have a whole lot of power... deadly power, Ajaya. You're already on their radar. Retrieving that PC and sniping the Spider to save the Johnsons brought you clearly into their view. A person who can infiltrate any part of the Zone at will and retrieve almost any piece of information or data is a major threat. Why do you think you are working for me?"

"To keep me controlled and to monitor my Zone activity?"

He touched his nose with one finger, eyes super serious despite the funny gesture.

"Why didn't they push to capture the Decimator? All they had to do was wait, or maybe even have you give the counter command?"

"First, the Patrol command has a whole protocol associated with it. Normally the command would be to Sweep, as in sweep the perimeter, or Recon, to explore a new area. Patrol turns it loose to follow its own inclinations for a short, but variable period of time. It wouldn't listen to a counter command even from me, unless the person who ordered it to Patrol gave that command. Which is very specific—the word Recast. Tells it to return but still under its own autonomy. So if you, the original issuer of the Patrol command, had been able to communicate the word Recast, it *might* have come back but would have observed the continued tension and probably evaded. Probably. I'm not certain because we've never used either command outside of the test area before."

"You've given it way more leeway than I would have expected from the military," I said.

"All relatively new. We've observed how much autonomy you give to your Berkut. These protocols are copied on that."

"You sure it will come back?"

"Yes. Mostly. Say ninety-nine percent certain," he said, then smiled. He constantly surprised me. Super-serious elite soldier one moment, joking the next, then charming my mom right after that. He was even more dangerous than first impressions, and first impressions were impressive.

"You should consider yourself under surveillance at all times, Ajaya," he said, serious again.

"I've found bugs in our apartment. Thought they were yours," I said.

"One was. If you found more, then there are others watching you. White and Black aren't the most dangerous ones, either. And when I say danger, I mean to you, your family, and your friends."

A sudden chill raced down my spine—a shudder at the thought of my sisters, my grandmother or mother or Astrid in the hands of people who had set up the drone strike on their own country. Or Harper... who would be dead instantly if they found her.

"Head for home, Ajaya. We're done for the day, as I have to do what they expect or else *I'll* be under suspicion... more suspicion. I was hoping we'd have more time with the Spider and get more information. But that's life on the tip of the spear, right? Come back tomorrow. We'll work on a new approach to the training. Oh and I'll admit it... your guess was right. We need to show progress clearing at least part of the Zone, or other, more radical approaches might be implemented. The cost in soldiers would be high. I'm trying to avoid that."

"Oh. You should have said something. I can get on board with that. I'll work on ideas for teaching building clearing."

"I didn't want you knowing more than you had to. But I've got a feeling you know more than you should—a lot more."

I just gave him my innocent look—eyes wide and surprised, hands out in a *who me* gesture.

"Yeah. Keep it like that. Now get the hell outta here," he said, tired but clearly determined.

I hit the road, catching a ride off Roosevelt Island with one of the major's team members. She dropped me off north of home—many, many blocks from home, but I wanted to take my time and think things through. So I walked for a while. I could call a car when I got tired of walking, but I needed to process what had just happened.

When I first met Yoshida, he'd been with Agents Black and White, as well as the head of Zone Defense, General Davis. I thought they were all on the same team. But Black and White wouldn't be taking the Spider and all the geeks' computer files about it if they were truly on Yoshida's side. So factions, like the major had said. Harper's mom had told me about the secret network of power players who had orchestrated Drone Night, using the national and global shock at the attack to destroy the world's financial markets and then rebuild them, making themselves ungodly rich *and* the new masters of the universe at the same time.

Dr. Wilks had said that they were entrenched in finance, government, and the military complex. Yoshida had hinted at knowing about various competing factions within the government's power structure. Dangerous ones. Maybe, just maybe, the unified group that had quietly and secretly overthrown the previous power structure was fracturing from within. Yoshida seemed to know about them, or at least hinted at something like them. But the knowledge of the modified Spiders was being hidden away. If *I* had done something *that* twisted and evil, I sure wouldn't want anyone finding out about it.

I stopped into a noodle shop and got a to-go order of Pad Thai, figuring I'd walk and eat. Across the street, I noticed a news vehicle, the reporter and her technicians talking to what appeared to be a really angry woman. No, a really angry *mother*, one who kept pointing at her baby in its stroller and then back at the news crew. Then I saw one of the techs carrying a broken drone while the other one was picking up pieces of the drone off the ground—near the stroller. The traffic was too loud to hear much, but the mom was seriously pissed off. I caught a snippet: "... could have killed her..."

The reporter lady seemed upset, even as she tried to calm the mom. Something had gone wrong with the news drone and it had probably crashed near enough to the baby to first scare and then piss off the young mother.

I'm kind of hyper alert to drones—go figure. Sure, I know when I'm not in the Zone, and that the modern world uses drones for news, surveying, sightseeing, entertainment, and the delivery of everything from an online clothing order to tonight's takeout. Crashes and crash-related injuries had been a thing back eight or so years ago, but the bugs had been worked out, especially in big cities. Most every kind of commercial and government drone had all kinds of backup software to prevent accidents like the kind that had just almost landed that baby in the hospital. So it was odd to see the aftermath firsthand, and also odd to recall the one news story I had heard during my siesta. Two different sets of commercial drones getting shacked up on the same day... seemed like a lot.

"AI, search for recent stories on drone-related accidents. Go back two weeks and filter out any experimental versions, new technologies, or obvious operator error. Create a new file titled Drones Amok."

"Complying," a voice said softly in my right ear.

I kept walking, moving south, paying attention to the activity around, looking for any other odd drone activity. Lots of drones but nothing out of the ordinary. At least at first. That's probably how I spotted the ones following me, or maybe I should say *why* I spotted the ones following me.

There were two of them. Different models, nondescript, no attention-getting graphics or loud advertising. But newer. Commercial drones in the Big Apple get the shit kicked out of them during day-to-day use, and most businesses run them right down into the ground before replacing them.

So as I looked around, concentrating on the ubiquitous drones that filled modern life, two fairly new units lacking any marketing graphics caught my eye, just for a second. And then when I looked around again a few minutes later, they were still above and behind me. One was tiny, the size of a coffee mug, a mini quadcopter, all in white. The other was larger, a hexacopter, dull grey with a camera pod swiveling underneath.

The second time I spotted them, the little one shot across the street and up a side lane, while the big one stopped and hovered straight up, disappearing over a rooftop. The thing was that their cameras stayed pointed at me the whole time both drones were changing direction.

I ducked into a music shop and spent some time looking at guitars that I knew nothing about. The guy behind the counter asked me three times if I needed help. I left before he got to the fourth time. About fifteen minutes had elapsed, enough time for the drones to be long gone. Outside, there was no sign of them, so maybe I was just a little paranoid.

I called an Ublyft, watching the skies until car number 7659 pulled up and opened its door for me. Crawling in, I looked out all the windows as the vehicle pulled out into the city-AI-controlled traffic, but all I saw were the normal business drones of New York City going about their normal business.

Twenty minutes later, I was home, stepping out of the car and seeing nothing out of the ordinary. So yeah, maybe I'm a little paranoid. I've spent half my life in the Zone—sue me already.

The twins were home when I walked in, talking excitedly to Mom and Aama about some boy or maybe even *boys*. They cut off like a switch had been thrown the second I appeared. "Ah, hi everyone."

"How was it?" Mom asked.

"Ah, fine. Zone Defense is a weird place," I said.

"You should fit right in," Gabby said instantly. Her twin's eyes got big and Mom's mouth thinned out into a tight line. A second later, I think Gabby realized she was supposed to treat me with kid gloves or something because she backed up a step and shot a quick glance at Mom.

"We must be cut from the same cloth because they have posters of *you* up all over the place," I shot back.

"They have posters of me?" she asked, her embarrassment forgotten.

"He's making fun of you, moron," Monique said. Only the twins were allowed to mock each other. Anyone else faced their combined wrath. Some days, the Zone seemed easy compared to matching wits with my sisters.

"Enough making fun of anyone," Mom said, but the taut look was gone from her face and I might have seen the twitch of a smile. Family dynamics back to normal.

"I've got some reports to go over. Aama, do you need help with dinner?" I asked.

She snorted. "You are sweet, but we all need to be able to *eat* the food," she said with a smile.

"Aama, that's cold!"

She shrugged and smiled.

I *can* cook. I don't care what anyone says. But matching my grandmother's culinary skill? Nope.

"It's your night to do the dishes, AJ," Monique said. "We did them for you last night."

"Oh. Thank you," I said. Gabby opened her mouth to take a shot but realized it wouldn't work in the face of my gratitude. "I'll be working in my room if anyone needs me," I said, smiling to myself at my sister's uncommon lack of a response. I have to treasure these singular moments when either twin is speechless.

Inside my room, Rikki *woke* as I entered, lights coming on across the area that would be equivalent to a fighter plane's cockpit canopy. "Hey, Rikki. Status?"

"*All systems nominal. Residence secure. Three notable sur-*

veillance incursions during the last four hours and forty minutes."

"Surveillance incursions?"

"Exterior attempts to gather intelligence via UAV. The first occurred at 13:42 hundred hours. Media drone registered to Caliper Productions. Second incursion at 14:10. Unknown unregistered commercial drone attempting to insert micro surveillance drone unit. Third attempt at 15:25. Unregistered commercial unit utilizing onboard sensors against Gurung residence."

15:25. That was just a few minutes ago, about when I got home. "What happened to them?"

"Rikki unit used high output, focused radio frequency jamming on media drone, which performed a return to base response. RF jamming was also successful in disrupting second unit and its micro unit, but units only withdrew to observe from outside RF interdiction distance. To insure defense, Rikki unit initiated a viral software attack, utilizing directed laser communication. Both units withdrew before successful insertion of virus. Third unit unresponsive to jamming attack or virus insertion. Rikki unit suborned uninvolved delivery UAV and successfully intercepted third unit. UAV impacted ground at 15:28."

I ran to the window and looked out. A few people were standing below, watching a man in a suit carry a drone into a black car that immediately took off. By the time I got downstairs, even the bystanders were gone, but there a few bits and pieces of plastic scattered about. Part of a fan prop, as well as a piece of something I thought might be a camera covering.

Back upstairs, I met Mom at the door as I came back in. "Ajaya, everything okay?"

"Yeah, Mom. Thought I left something important outside," I said.

She looked at me for a moment, then nodded. Most moms, at least the moms of the friends I'd had growing up, would have instantly asked what important item was left outside. My mom didn't. I shared a great deal about my Zone activities with Mom, but not everything.

Long ago, we had come to the understanding that some things were far too disturbing to casually discuss. I never described the countless skeletons or tragic scenes of death I regularly encountered inside Manhattan. So when I got vague about things, Mom usually left it well alone. And I didn't want her worrying about surveillance drones watching us until I knew enough to properly brief her.

Back in my room, I examined the crash debris. "AI scan items on desktop. Compare to known drone types."

"*Scanning,*" my AI reported. I turned back to Rikki. "You have the ability to take over other drones?"

"*Imprecise description of capability. Rikki unit is able to disrupt flight software and payload retention of certain common UAV models. Slowing or tilting one or more fan blades causes errant flightpath. Precise application resulted in mid-air collision.*"

"In the past week, how many attempts have you defended against?"

"*Four. Three media units seeking footage of Gurung family members. One unknown unit took station on building directly in line with this structure. RF jamming was successful in driving all units away.*"

"Have you interfered with any other UAV software recently?"

John Conroe

"Negative."

"What is the source of software interference capabilities?"

"Software upload from Spider CThree units."

"When?"

"Two years, seven months, three days ago."

"How many Spider software uploads have you received in the last three years?"

"Seventeen."

"Range and type of upload?"

"Nine IFF protocol changes, five tactical modifications, three offensive enhancements, including the interference protocol."

I *knew* that Rikki had had interaction with the drone network still inside the Zone, as he acted exactly like a double agent, trusted by the network until we blew his cover. So the transponder friend and foe updates made sense, but I never realized the Spiders were uploading packets of code to *my* drone. I mean, I'm not an idiot. I checked his software religiously for changes, but I focused on his core mission programming and some of his flight software.

"What were the other two offensive upgrades?"

"Autonomous coordination of subdrones, upgrades one and two."

"So the Spiders gave you code for commanding other drones?"

"Affirmative."

"How many at once?"

60

"Upgrade 2 increased number from six to ten."

"Other Berkut units can do this?"

"Surviving seven Berkut units had this capability as of last connection by Rikki unit to drone network."

I probably should have been asking Rikki more questions all along, but then again, the luxury of having him at home with me is a new thing. For two years plus, I only saw him when I went into the Zone on missions. And *that* is not the place for a heart-to-heart with your robot pal, talking out loud, where anything that can hear can also kill you.

I tabled the whole uploads thing, deciding I needed to let it ferment in the back of my brain for awhile. "AI, what is the status of Drones Amok?"

"Twenty items for review."

"List and project on the wall, please."

Instantly, a list of exactly twenty reports appeared on the white empty wall of my room.

Scanning down through them, I saw a lot of recent accidents listed, all either taken from news articles or reported on blog sites.

"Additional references to drone accidents found on chat rooms," my AI said.

"How many?"

"Three hundred twelve."

Twenty official or semi-official reports along with another three hundred plus unofficial, and who knows how many unreported drone accidents there were.

"Please run a similar search for the six-month period prior to the Drones Amok search."

"Complying."

Over three hundred accidents in two weeks? Something was going on, and I was pretty sure it originated inside the Zone.

CHAPTER 8

"All right, listen up," Yoshida started after stepping out in front of the twenty-four soldiers sitting in the same auditorium where we had once planned the rescue of the Bonnen brothers.

"You've all volunteered and passed the screening process for a new Zone initiative," the major said, clearly comfortable in front of so many professional warriors. Personally, I would have been pretty nervous. Public speaking hasn't really ever been my thing.

"To reiterate what this is all about, you lot are going to form an initial cadre that will infiltrate the Zone on foot and clear buildings one by one. Our mission is to take back Manhattan and we'll do it street by street, building by building until we've cleared every damned drone in the Zone. This is a long-term project and we expect it to build in momentum as we go forward.

"Now, let me address the elephant in the room—the death of Sergeant Paul Primmer. I've looked over Sergeant Primmer's records and I can tell you with certainty that he was a hell of a soldier. Brave, capable, and successful—decorated.

"But he died in the Zone, and I can tell you with absolute conviction exactly why that happened... he made a mistake. In the Zone, you generally don't get to survive even one of those. Primmer's mistake was overconfidence, or maybe you could call it contempt. He didn't listen to his instructor, and it cost him his life and almost cost the lives of the men with him."

Yoshida paused and looked over the group of very quiet operators. I was standing in the back, along with Sergeant Rift, who was waiting to go over the most recent upgrades that Yoshida's people had made to the current stealth suit model.

The major was making eye contact with each and every person sitting in front of him, row by row, and when he reached the last person at the very back, his eyes moved up and met mine.

"You are all professional, experienced operators with multiple successful missions into some of the most dangerous theaters of operation in the world. But none of you have ever been in the Zone. I have, and I count myself lucky to be alive. Eight times I've been inside, on foot. The first seven of those were complete failures, with people wounded or killed on each and every mission.

"The eighth was different. We penetrated ten blocks into the north end, moved through an apartment building, and exfiltrated without incident. Along the way, we set nine passive traps for drones. Subsequent missions by several members of my team found and neutralized four land drones in those traps, while setting an additional fifteen collection devices.

"So what was the difference, you might ask? I'll tell you —I took an *expert* with me. And I did *exactly* what he told me to do, no more, no less. I took out my ego, stuffed it in my gear locker, and treated the mission like it was my very first. In many ways, it really was. Your instructor has survived hundreds and hundreds of trips in, out, and all around Manhattan. He's spent enough nights inside to qualify for gold status in most hotel membership programs. He's also at least a decade younger than I am, and he's a civilian to boot, and you've seen him on *that* show that we all love to hate," Yoshida said, his right hand coming up to point directly at me.

Every head swiveled around to stare at me. "Look at him... hardly out of high school, although he *does* have a degree in drone technology. Most of you are going to be tempted to take him under *your* wing rather than you under his. The rest of you are likely ready to discount half of what he says. Do either of those things and you *will* die... horribly. Ajaya grew up in the Zone. He and his family survived Drone Night firsthand. Then he learned sneaking and peeking from a highly decorated SAS sniper... his father. He has had more success in the Manhattan Drone Zone than all of the *Zone War* teams combined. He's quiet, humble, and has the highest score ever recorded in our simulated Zone shoot house. He will take you into the Zone, train you in surviving it and, probably, bring you out—if you listen *exactly* to what he says. Check your egos people, because the drones in Manhattan will eat you for breakfast. Questions?"

A wide-shouldered woman in the third row raised her arm. "Corporal Copeland? How much of his success is because of his pet drone?"

"Don't ask me—ask him! Ajaya?"

Every eye came back to me. "Having Rikki improves my speed, my chance of survival, and increases my drone kill counts by probably two hundred or more percent. Without a scout, everything takes four to six times longer, at the very least. In the two-plus years I've had him, my success ratio has skyrocketed. Probably collected as many kills and recoveries with him than in all the other years before I got him," I said, meeting her eyes.

"How many years is that?" she asked, frowning.

"Since I was twelve. I'm twenty-one."

Another hand went up, a lean lieutenant in Marine battle dress. "Yeah, Stokes?" Yoshida asked.

"Do we get drones?"

"Yes, we will be using Kestrels. Ajaya is helping us modify their programming, and they've been successful. Not quite up to his Berkut, but improving with every training mission and every foray. We've rebuilt our simulator and you'll all be going through our computerized version of the Zone, first by yourselves, then with Ajaya leading you, and then multiple times with your assigned drones, all before we ever send you into the Zone."

Stokes' hand went up again. Yoshida just nodded at him. "Can we see it? The Berkut?"

"You know, that's actually a hell of an idea. Ajaya, care to introduce them to a Death Eagle?"

It was spooky, but the major must have foreseen exactly this moment happening. He had asked me to bring my drone to the auditorium and prep it for something just like this. Called it Show and Tell.

"Rikki, please execute OpFor," I said. Short for Opposing Force. We had already started on some training scenarios.

Rikki dropped from his perch high above, directly over the class of hardened combat operators. His gun started shooting with his first motion and by the time he slammed to a stop two meters above the tallest soldier, he was out of ammo. The blanks all went through his suppressor so the actual shots were pretty quiet, but for hardened combat soldiers, they might as well have been full sound. Most of the class hit the ground, dove into empty seating rows, or, in a few cases, simply stared in horror at the flashing, smoking gun barrel. The empty brass casings rained down all around them for a couple of seconds after he finished.

I threw Rikki another block of ammo and he flipped over, ejecting the empty case in my direction while catching the full one in mid-air. Then he shifted forms, delta wings sliding out and fans moving to full forward propulsion. Like an arrow, he shot across the room, banking up and around the side wall, the back wall, the other side, and then strafing down the middle of the auditorium from the stage in front, his gun firing the whole time. He stopped directly over my head, spinning in place to face the class, ejecting the now empty ammo cassette right into my upturned right hand.

"That, class, is a Russian Berkut," Yoshida said. "Rikki, what was your kill count?"

"Nineteen on the first pass, Major Yoshida. Then four were terminated on the second pass with additional insurance shots placed on sixteen of those that may have sustained survivable wounds."

"There, you heard it... you're all dead. In about three seconds."

"And we're supposed to fight that?" another soldier asked.

"Well, generally it's better to avoid them, but yes, if you have to, or if we put together a mission to hunt them. Ajaya, how many Berkut have you killed?"

"Well, three, not counting Rikki. My dad got the kill shot on Rikki," I said.

"I thought your dad died in the Zone?" a female soldier in

Army green asked.

"He did," I said.

"By a drone?" she asked. I nodded.

"What kind?"

"Berkut. This one," I said, pointing straight up. Her face screwed up with confusion, as did several of the others. "This Berkut attacked us at close range. We both shot it, but Dad's was the kill shot. It scored a round on him, and bone fragments nicked an artery that we didn't know about and he bled out internally. I rebuilt and reprogrammed the Berkut to become Rikki."

Shock filled most of their faces, although a few showed disgust. "You *kept* the drone that killed your father?" the army lady asked, incredulous.

"His idea—before he passed. Also my mom's. The airframe and some of the internals are the same, but the rest is all rebuilt. Personally, I was going to destroy it, but eventually I saw the wisdom of making something good out of something bad. Just so you know, Rikki wouldn't shoot at any of you except that he verified both ammo cassettes were blanks and that this was a training simulation. He's programmed to protect humans and kill drones. And he's killed hundreds of drones."

"You personalize it," another soldier, a Special Forces Green Beret, noted.

"Yes. I named him and I call him a him. There's nothing human in the Zone. Just bones. Everything else wants a piece of you. The drones are obvious, but then there are dog packs and hordes of rats that will swarm you if they can. So I named the drone that keeps me alive," I said with a shrug.

"It's a killing machine, designed to hunt and terminate humans. How does it actually keep you alive?" Green Beret asked.

"*This* Berkut is much different from the stock models. Upgraded chips, extensive reprogramming, advanced learning. And it turns out that it's as efficient a design for killing drones as for killing humans. But mostly Rikki is my eyes, ears, and EM detector. Plus he can still connect to the drone network inside the Zone. For a long time he was a double agent, trusted by the other drones. He masked any anomalous readings I gave off, sort of convincing any nearby drones that I was a data and sensor error. The network doesn't trust him anymore, but he can still listen in on their networks, although the remaining Spiders have taken to shifting frequencies randomly and encrypting their instructions. So we've had to adapt. The Zone is all about adapting. What worked yesterday likely won't work today, so you have to shift on the fly."

"So the drone is like... a watch dog?" the female soldier asked.

"*Unit Rikki Tikki is not a canine,*" my drone said, hovering over my head.

"No, Rikki, you're not. But it is still a pretty good analogy. Think about it this way... North America was the last major land mass to be colonized by humans. The first Native Americans came across the Bering Land Bridge. But it took them thousands of years to get across it. Why? There are lots of theories, but one of them links the domestication of dogs to their eventual success. Prehistoric Siberia and the Bering area were home to a huge array of very dangerous predators. Giant hyena, dire wolves, short-faced bears, the American lion, all kinds of big critters with big teeth and claws. One possibility is that man needed the domestic dog to eventually cross all that hostile territory. Tracking, predator warning, and coordinated hunting all took a giant step up when we domesticated the dog. Wolves, coyotes, and foxes are all extremely adaptable predators with much better senses than our own. So we befriended them, brought them on board with us, so to speak. But Rikki is no dog. He's more intelligent than most humans."

"That's crazy," another soldier, Army uniform with sniper badges, said.

"If anything, Ajaya is understating it," Yoshida said. "Let's table your disbelief until you've had a chance to see the two of them in action. I sent the first two training groups right into the Zone with Ajaya. That was a mistake. He still brought three of the four out alive. But it was grossly unfair to the soldiers and to Ajaya to just send them right in. You don't know anything about the Zone, you don't know anything about your young chief instructor. So it's back to school. Starting tomorrow, you'll all have a chance to try our Zone simulator. Then after you've all had your shot, we'll sit here in the auditorium, eat popcorn, and watch on the big screen as Ajaya and Rikki run through it. It'll be pretty kinetic.

"Now, the rest of today is housekeeping. Quarters, equipment, and what they used to call paperwork. Sergeant Akachi Rift will introduce you to the Zone Defense version of the stealth suit. We have made a number of mods to the standard version that you all have used. She'll also get you all outfitted with your own suits and the weapons we'll be using. Then the rest of my staff will get you squared away with the dining, fitness, medical, quartermaster facilities, shooting ranges, the armory, and any other logistics you have to deal with. Sergeant, you're on."

Rift marched up to the front and began a thorough brief on the new gear as Yoshida came back to where I was packing the empty ammo cassettes into my pack.

"What do you think?"

"I think they'll all see me as a kid," I said.

"Hmm. Let's revisit that after you and Rikki run the Room tomorrow. What do you think of the overall idea?" he asked.

"I like the simulator room, although its scenarios are either too crazy or not crazy enough, so at best it's only an approximation for the Zone. And I really liked introducing the class to Rikki that way. Got their attention."

"I'll say. Good thing we screened them for weapons or there'd have been guns going off everywhere. I want you to come in early tomorrow. You're going to need to watch each of them as they go through the Room."

"What? Oh-seven hundred?"

"And no later. The first of these snake eaters and fire breathers is set to run the gauntlet at oh-seven thirty."

"Roger that, Major. I'll be here."

"Alright. Beat it."

He moved off to talk with Corporal Estevez, who seemed like his aide or something, always just a few meters away from him.

I finished closing up my pack and moved toward the door, Rikki floating along over my head, back in his ball form.

Sergeant Rift was still talking, showing the improved heat sinks in the boots of the suit. At least half the class looked my way as I headed for the door. They were already judging me and I had no idea if they knew it, but their personal evaluation of me would play a big role in their survival.

CHAPTER 9

The trip home was uneventful, no suspicious drones, no drone accidents. When I walked into the apartment, the twins were on either end of the couch with Grandma in between them, all three watching today's live episode of *Zone War*.

Astrid had told me the night before, when we were following our usual nighttime ritual of video chatting, that her family wasn't headed into the Zone today. Instead it was Bone Shakers and the Up Town Girls, double teaming Madam Tussaud's Wax Museum for celebrity wax dummies. No matter how many times a team hits it, there still seems to be a whole mass of famous lookalikes still inside. Which makes perfect sense because a team only gets a few minutes to grab and run before they're swarmed. So really, only a couple or three dozen have been recovered, and they all sell for crazy amounts of money.

The front of the museum currently has a massive hole in it, where a few years ago one of the now retired teams had literally rammed their armored vehicle right through the door. Today, the two teams had just driven right into the building, and it looked like Kyle Bonnen was wrestling a sitting duplicate of Jimmy Fallon into the Bone Shaker LAV while Up Town Girls Ayla Messier and Skyler Rashid were trying to drag Barack Obama into their SPV400, all while their driver, Vanessa Lee, yelled into her mike for them to hurry the bleeping bleep up.

"Any traps?" I asked.

"They came in through the Lincoln Tunnel, but as soon as they got a block down West 39th, a Tank-Killer dragged an old tractor trailer across the road behind them. They only grabbed one dummy each and now they're debating how to get out," Gabby said.

"The current idea is the Queens-Midtown tunnel," Monique added.

"Too obvious. There will be a buttload of drones between them and both tunnels. I would try for the Williamsburg Bridge or maybe the Holland Tunnel, but that may have a strong presence on it too," I said. "It'll be a game of cat and mouse through all those roads."

"The producers are helping them by giving them real time access to the Flottercot satellite, and it seems like Zone Defense is keeping a handful of Renders overhead. They ever do that for you, AJ?" Gabby asked.

"No. The occasional bombing run when I've stirred up enough drones, but not much direct help."

"How's the new job with the major?" Monique asked, all casual like.

"We're taking a new approach. Zone D built a computer simulator room. Well, more like a warehouse, and we're going to spend a bunch of time training everyone in it before we try bringing any more trainees into the Zone," I said. My pack suddenly buzzed, Rikki reminding me to let him out. I opened the top of the pack and instantly the orb-like drone zoomed over and perched on the back of the couch between Aama and Gabby, ocular band focused on the show.

"*Holland, Lincoln, and Queens-Midtown all have high prob-*

ability of ambush. Williamsburg, Manhattan, or Brooklyn Bridges are most viable. Unit Peony will be closing off single-digit southbound avenues unless armored vehicles pass through soon."

My drone had never shown the slightest interest in *Zone War* before. "Should you maybe pass that message along, Ajaya?" Aama asked, looking at Rikki with one eyebrow raised.

I texted Trinity Flottercot and told her what my drone was predicting. Seconds later, the Uptown Girls driver, Vanessa, announced that the show was advising her to head for the bridges and forgo the tunnels. A separate video window showed Kyle Bonnen passing the same message to his brother. Both armored vehicles were traveling together, in convoy for the most part, although they kept a healthy distance between each other and occasionally took different but parallel roads between the blocks. They were now both headed south and east.

"Oh, I hope they make it," Monique squealed, hiding behind a big fluffy pillow.

"Odds of survival have increased thirty percent. Probability of successful exfiltration is now seventy-seven percent," Rikki announced.

"How are you able to predict what Peony will do, and how do you know it's Peony?"

"Unit Peony was designated as backup to Unit Lotus for anti-armor objectives. Lotus now defunct. Therefore Peony has highest probability of controlling response to incursions. Please note, however, that intercepting armor units carries a low mission priority and a high risk to responding units, thus draining resources better used for primary mission. Long range tactical plans call for lower risk responses with fewer

drones over time. Western tunnels are closest to armored teams' objective. Peony would therefore most likely order a prepared emplacement at each tunnel. At this time, the armored incursion units have likely passed too far south to be worthy of Peony's response."

"The Spiders all have pre-assigned roles? Who assigned them?"

"Correct. They did."

"Wow, that's not creepy or anything," Gabby said, staring at Rikki.

"Clarify—is sarcasm detected?"

"Yes. That was sarcasm. What are the Spiders' individual missions?" I asked.

"Unit Lotus was tasked with responding to vehicular incursions, hunting other intruders, as well as tracking down any anomalies. Peony was tasked with seeking projection of primary mission beyond Zone barrier into the rest of the city. Plum Blossom was tasked with identifying methodologies for carrying out primary mission well beyond the immediate geographical area."

"How far beyond?" I asked.

"Without limitation."

"The whole planet?"

"Affirmative."

"So hunting the armored units isn't that important to the Spiders?" Monique asked.

"Affirmative. Low risk-reward calculated."

"Oh, we've been learning about that in my personal finance class," Gabby said. "So you mean there are only a few people in each LAV and it would take a lot of drones to stop one, with many of those drones getting smushed. Not enough humans killed for the cost in drones."

"Affirmative."

"These priorities have been in place for a long time?" I asked.

"Affirmative."

"What triggered your interest?"

"Danger to humans. Rikki unit has not been present during broadcasts."

My drone's AI is constantly evolving. Having him home now had just resulted in him being able to utilize long-buried drone network plans to carry out *his* primary mission—helping protect humans.

"Do you have any knowledge of Peony or Plum Blossom's current plans?"

"Negative. Files out of date."

Too bad. But nothing about the Zone would ever be that easy.

"Rikki, why did Lotus go after Ajaya so hard?" Monique asked.

"Ajaya Gurung was identified and targeted by Spiders as a greater threat to drone mission than armored vehicle incursions. Spiders eliminated all unarmored threats without a significant drain in resources, with exception of a two-person team that successfully terminated large numbers of drones. Priority was increased and additional assets and planning time allocated to individuals eventually identified as Baburam and Ajaya Gurung. Baburam eliminated but Ajaya evaded. Last contact with network indicated that Ajaya's increased

drone elimination percentages due to pairing with unknown drone unit has resulted in maximized priority for elimination."

"So you and Dad were a thorn in their sides, and now you are an even larger thorn," Monique said, looking at me. Gabby's eyes glistened dangerously.

"Analogy correct. Pattern recognition software assigned probability of Ajaya involvement in disappearance or outright termination of more than three thousand drones. Detection of other in-Zone anomalies potentially connected to Ajaya increased priority."

"Anomalies?" Monique asked, but I had already turned toward the hallway.

"Rikki come with me, please. We have planning for tomorrow's lesson to do," I said, ignoring Monique's question like I never heard it. She probably wouldn't have let it go except a loud exclamation by the narrator about Vanessa's driving diverted her attention back to the show.

Rikki dutifully followed me to my room.

CHAPTER 10

"So when can I get a shot at this simulator?" the gorgeous blonde across the table asked.

"Seriously? You want to try it?" I asked, then realized my question was really stupid. "Of course you do. Hmm. Let me ask the major. Not sure if they'll let you but really, I can't see what it could hurt."

Her blue eyes narrowed at me. "You promise?"

"Absolutely. But Astrid, I can't promise he'll say yes. Hey, are you going to finish that last scallop?"

She smiled and speared it with her fork, bringing it up to her mouth. My vision focused in on her ruby lips, which pursed for a second before she extended it my way. I reached for the fork but she pulled it away, her message quite clear. Either she fed it to me herself, or I wouldn't get it. Easy choice.

"Emm, that's good," I said, smiling at her own sly smile.

She glanced at my plate, eyebrows lifting in mock surprise. "As, apparently, so was your steak?"

My plate was almost spotless, hardly even a smudge of sauce, well cleaned by a fresh dinner roll. Her own plate had a mound of uneaten pasta, but the vegetables were gone and now, too, was the last of the scallops.

"Gotta watch my intake. Not all of us have the metabolism of a shrew, AJ," she said. "Those cameras add kilos."

"Please!" I said.

"No, you don't have any idea how much attention I have to pay to my figure," she said.

"Oh, I pay a lot of attention to your figure," I said with a sly grin of my own.

"Easy there, Creeper. Let's get back to this class of yours," she said, laughing. I wasn't lying, and based on the glances and stares she was getting from half the men in the restaurant, I wasn't the only one eyeing her figure.

"It's a joint service task force of high class special operators, with a high percentage of trained snipers. The idea is to train them to operate at clearing houses in the northern part of the Zone, then move portable barriers in and block those buildings from getting reinforced."

The major hadn't told me it was a secret and he knew the rest of my family knew about it, so I figured Astrid should too.

"Well, they've tried the whole clearing thing before, didn't they?"

"Yes, early on and then again about five years ago. They had a lot of losses and couldn't secure the new territory well enough."

"So I can see that having you train them would increase the odds, but what's changed with the barriers?"

"The first times, they tried hauling sections of fencing into place. But the drones always massed up to counterattack, which made it near impossible to set them, even using armored equipment. These new barriers are robotic, controlled by Zone D."

She frowned, and it was really cute. "Robotic? Like,

what's the difference between that and the armored equipment?"

"Before, they *used* armored equipment to set barrier sections. This time, the barriers *are* the armored equipment. Special ground drones, armed, armored, and able to interlock with each other. Additional units will be right behind them as backups."

"But won't the Spiders catch on? Make it harder to keep clearing houses and buildings?"

"Absolutely. But it's a multi-phase operation. Anytime we can get a massing of drones, we'll bring in the Renders, the major's armored troopers, plus use the firepower of the barrier units themselves to thin them out. Then we'll either try it again or move to another part of the perimeter where there are fewer drones."

"It sounds good in theory, but it's going to take a long time, and people are going to die. Plus, I don't see how it will work with high rises."

"Agreed—on everything you just said, but there seems to be huge pressure to get the Zone cleared. Those armored suits are a big part. You can kill a shit ton of drones wearing one, but they run out of power too fast. Doing it this way plays to the strength of the suits and the robot barriers. At least that's how the planners explain it."

"And you're just the trainer, right?"

"Yes, but Astrid, I still need to go into the Zone to fully train these people," I said.

"I know, AJ. But that's your strongest skill set. You're an incredible shooter, but in computerized drone combat, the odds are always against even the best human operator. And you are not a trained armored soldier like your friend Kayla."

"Kayla who hits on you every chance she gets?" I asked, grinning.

"Yeah, her," she admitted, rolling her eyes.

"Like you don't find it flattering? But yes. I'm teaching the sneak, peek, shoot, and scoot class. Although the major has me also observing his strike force when it trains. Says he's interested in any ideas that occur to me. I don't know why, because as you pointed out, I know nothing about fighting in armored suits."

"Because he's smart enough to use every resource, and you, my friend, have more time and knowledge of the Zone and the drones, including Spiders, than anyone," she said.

Anyone but Harper, I thought, but I kept that to myself. Astrid didn't like Harper and always bristled when I brought up her name. So I didn't... bring up her name. I'm not an idiot; I realized that Astrid was insecure about Harper, but that made no sense to me because, well, she's Astrid and I'm just me.

The waiter, a guy, appeared at the table, his attention focused on Astrid. "Can I interest you in any dessert?" he asked her, only glancing at me once.

"No, thanks. Just the bill," she said, not matching his smile. I had discovered that Astrid really didn't like all the attention that being a *Zone War* celebrity brought her. She liked being on the show and loved being an inspiration for girls everywhere, but the negative aspects of being in the public eye bothered her a great deal. Everything from the critical naysayers on social media to aggressive men who couldn't see anything past her looks and had trouble with the word *no*. Most people assumed she was a star first and a skilled combat driver second or third. Like it was an alien concept that a girl raised in a military family whose job was to drive a multi-ton armored combat vehicle might actually find self-actualization in that. They always talked about JJ's—her brother —bravery and skill, her father's tactical prowess, even stupid middle brother Martin's gunnery ability, but with her, the comments eventually always circled back to her movie star looks.

Most of Astrid's public appearances were in schools, talking to kids, particularly girls, about their value to society beyond fashion and looks. Certainly things have changed a lot over the last ten to fifteen years, but overcoming centuries-old societal bias requires constant reinforcement.

The waiter came back, putting the bill in the center of the table, which was smarter than I would have thought him. We usually split the tabs, except for special occasions like birthdays or celebratory events where one of us might treat the other. I had no doubt that my girlfriend made more money than I did, but it didn't really matter to me, as my family was doing alright now and I had enough to do what I mostly wanted. In fact, because of the two drone caches that we shared with the Johnson family, the twins' educations were set, and our family FU fund was in the best shape ever.

Astrid's AI figured out the split along with tip and my AI sent hers my share so that it could pay the bill. Funny, but I still remember my parents using credit cards, and I still find them lying around on the ground inside the Zone, but they're a thing of the past. Now a person's credit lines are tied right to their AIs. It's funny, but cash is still around and plastic cards are long gone. Go figure. Must be something about physical currency that still strikes a chord with the human animal.

As she finished the transaction, I had my AI call a car. Seconds later, we were stepping outside the restaurant, slipping past all the eyes that followed her famous self and into the semi-darkness of Brooklyn at night.

"There's our car," I said, spotting the car number that my AI had reported. I took a step toward the vehicle, then sensed that Astrid wasn't beside me. I turned back to see her kneeling down, autographing a napkin for a little girl who must have followed us out, the girl's mother standing, smiling, in the restaurant doorway.

A sudden squeal of tires brought me around in time to see a heavy driverless delivery truck smash into our Ublyft car, crushing it like a beer can as it jammed the passenger vehicle right over a fire hydrant.

Then I was just suddenly standing back in the doorway of the restaurant, my body between Astrid and the street as she cradled the little girl protectively in her arms.

The cops arrived within a pretty respectably short time and we had to give statements supported by our personal AIs' records of the events. Two news crews and about fifteen paparazzi drones showed up within minutes of the cops identifying us, all eager to get vid and news bites. Not to mention all the restaurant staff and patrons, plus the odd dozen passersby.

Astrid handled it all very smoothly while I just kept my wiseass mouth shut. She'd dealt with this stuff for years, while it was all new to me. And let's be honest here... interviewing a drop-dead gorgeous girl is generally better news than a not-so-stunning guy. Fine by me.

They got her quotes, which were basically just our complete surprise by the accident, and then I called a new car, this one a taxi, manned by a human. When it pulled up, I let Astrid climb in first, noting that one of the reporters was already interviewing the young girl's mother.

"—their reactions were so quick. I guess that makes sense, seeing as who they are, but really, the crash was still happening and they were already in the door, holding my Sella, safe and sound," the mom was saying as I climbed in after Trid and let the door close itself. The taxi pulled away immediately. Astrid must have already given the driver our destination. But I was surprised when he pulled up to a small neighborhood hotel still two blocks short from where the Johnson family residence was.

Astrid took my hand and led me into the hotel, ignoring the front desk and taking us right to the elevator. "I keep a room here," she said. "Sometimes I need my space from the rest of them."

Like my family, the Johnsons all lived in the same home. Unlike us, it was almost a mansion. But I could understand the need to get away; after all, I didn't always hate my overnights in the Zone. Some of my safe hides were pretty cozy and all of them were very, very quiet.

"You're really upset," I said, a little surprised. Both of us faced violent death on a regular basis, so the crash wasn't, to my way of thinking, a huge deal. I mean, yeah it was scary, and it had set my adrenaline flowing, but it was nothing like facing a Leopard or Tiger.

"Do you know how lucky we just got? If that little girl hadn't asked for an autograph, we'd have been climbing into that car when it got crushed," she said.

She'd been very quiet on the taxi ride.

"Yeah, maybe. I guess," I said.

She looked me in the eyes and shivered. Immediately I wrapped her in a hug. "Hey, but we're okay. Not even a scratch, right?"

"And then there's that... the odds. Self-drivers never crash, at least not in the city where the NYC Traffic AI is running things. So what is the probability that the car we were about to get into gets hit by a rogue truck? And by a truck big enough to crush it?"

The elevator doors opened as her words hit me like a brick between the eyes. "Yeah. When you say it like that, it's like infinitesimal," I said.

She led me out onto the second floor, to the right and into room 217, which unlocked itself as she reached for the handle.

"In fact, I should have my AI look into it," I said, realizing it was *too* unlikely to actually be an accident.

She shook her head, blonde hair swinging free, blue eyes locked on me. "No. Later." She shut the door, bolted it, and turned around. "We almost died tonight, AJ. Yeah, I know we face death all the time, but that's when we're expecting it, geared for it. This was out of nowhere. One or both of us could be dead right now or irreparably injured. It reminded me of Mom. None of us know how much time we have. So we can't waste it," she said, and then she was on me, her lips hot against mine.

CHAPTER 11

Sometime between waking up early in Astrid's room, saying goodbye for the day, stopping home for clean clothes, and finally getting to Zone D headquarters, a theory had taken strong root in my mind. I know what you're thinking. Ajaya, you and Astrid have finally taken *that* step in your relationship and all you can think about is a stupid theory regarding the possible demise of the human species? Dude, really?

I'll tell you it wasn't by any means the *only* thing I thought about, but it was in the mix. After all, we *had* almost gotten smucked out by a big truck. That, plus the list of drone accidents, and add in the new list my AI had put together, albeit a short one, and you have yourself a theory. And I dumped that theory right in Yoshida's lap. Found him in the control room to the simulator, watching the new class go through one at a time.

"So there have been three vehicle accidents in the last two months and you think that's important?" he asked as we watched an Army Ranger get tagged in the back of the head by a computer-fired paint pellet fifteen minutes into his attempt.

"There haven't been *any* accidents since the city-wide AI took over seven years ago, Major," Maya said. She was ostensibly running the simulator, but since that was mostly handled by artificial intelligence, she was really just watching the operators get *killed* and listening in on our conversation.

Yoshida shot her a look that might have been annoyance at her interjection.

"You know that how?" he asked.

"Because my *boss* pays me to learn about all the most successful AI programs out there. The NYC Traffic AI is at the top of that list. Or at least it was. This is disturbing stuff," she said, then waved a hand over the holo desk to activate audio. "Sorry Sergeant Perry, but you're dead."

"You really going to get through all twenty-four today?" I asked, looking at the clock. It was ten after eight in the morning.

Both the major and Maya turned and looked at me, surprised.

"Have you paid *any* attention to what they're doing wrong? I only ask because Sergeant Perry was the third one in forty minutes. At this rate, we'll be done before lunch," Yoshida said, frowning.

An advantage of darker skin is that when your face flushes in embarrassment, you aren't as obvious about it. Not like the fair-skinned Johnson clan. "Ah, yeah. That one moved too slow. The drones had time to register the heat differential between his stealth suit and the ground. The first one went too fast and got tagged for motion detection. And the middle one..." I trailed off, trying to remember. "Oh yeah, you can't outrun a flechette. Should have taken cover and tried to kill off the drone with a grenade."

He stared at me for a moment, then looked at Maya, who was busy typing on her virtual holo keypad. "Yeah, yeah, I'm noting all that on their individual evaluations," she said without looking up.

He nodded, then turned back to me. "So… you think that the remaining Spiders are planning to attack us through commercial drones and self-drivers?"

"What I think is that Spider Peony is doing exactly that. Plum Blossom is focused on planning worldwide attacks. Listen, we saw the log on Lotus that it had been hopping commercial websites on the internet, and Maya and the others thought it was trying to plant software bots and viruses to gain access to those corporate networks. Suddenly, the commercial drones are having statistically crazy numbers of potentially lethal accidents and now a proven traffic AI has had three listed accidents after years of none. Two different insurance companies have contacted me so far today and it seemed like none of them really even know how to go about investigating the claims because there hasn't been any in years. So yes, I think it's significant. Not to mention that Rikki noted that I'm a high priority target for the Spiders."

"Were you not in the room when Agents Black and White told us to leave Spiders alone?" he asked, arching one eyebrow.

"Yes and then, after they left, I heard you instruct the team to pretty much ignore anything that came out of their mouths," I said.

Maya was nodding as she flicked her fingers over the holographically projected controls to reset the simulator for the next contender.

Yoshida was staring off into space, the wheels clearly turning behind his blank expression.

"All right. I agree. It's significant. So, here's what we do. I will have Maya, Eric, and Aaron do some real careful forensic work on both the accident statistics and the Spider internet activity. *You* will clear your AI of any and all such searches right this minute. Clear?"

"You think I'll trigger a watchdog program?"

"No, I'm *certain* you already have. You saw how the whole Spider thing went down. If you're aware of these anomalies, don't you think anyone else in the government is?"

"I don't really ever assign any competence to any government agencies, Major. With the exception of your group, of course!" I rushed to cover my ass.

"Hmmpf," he grunted. "And that's how *you* get tagged by the system. You're assuming, and as you know, that gets you killed in the Zone. It also can get you killed out of the Zone," he said.

I got a sudden chill as I thought about how blunt he was being. "Should we even be talking in here?" I asked, glancing around.

"Now you ask?" He shook his head. "You have plenty of paranoia and respect for the Zone, but nowhere near enough for out here. The answer is yes, that's why I put you off till we got in here. This room is completely shielded. Only Maya, Aaron, or Eric operate it, and they're all clued in on opsec. Something I *assumed* you would understand."

"Holy shit! What if the accident wasn't Peony's work, but these other factions?" I asked, still thinking about his earlier words.

He clapped his hands. "There it is, Maya! The light bulb finally went off."

"Shit, I gotta wipe everything. Shit. They almost killed Astrid because of me!"

"Whoa. Stop. Calm down, Sniper. We don't know what caused that accident. But we have to be ultra-cautious, right, Maya?"

"Yes, Major. We'll use all the deep cover protocols to dig into this," she said. She glanced my way and noted my look of intense confusion. "We have developed lots of ways of researching things without being noticed. NSA and other parts of the government have been tracking online searches for decades, even before the September 11 attack at the turn of the century. There are ways around them. Just takes longer and takes a whole bunch of steps and cut outs."

"You've been dealing with these factions for a long time, eh, Major?" I asked.

"Kid, I've been in special operations my entire military career. Those special *factions* are all through the spec ops community . All those Zone newbies out there," he said, waving a hand at the wall monitors that showed the candidates lining up for the simulator, "have known this forever. So as *you* teach them to survive the Zone, remember that they know more than you about surviving *out* of the Zone."

I felt a fool. Easy to get all superior feeling when I was the expert, but I had just been schooled in an equally deadly discipline and it sort of shook me to the core.

"Frankly, you shouldn't have even come to *me* about this, but… I'm glad you did. Maya, send the next one in."

"Chief Thomas, you're up. Head into the airlock and follow the computer's instructions," Maya said, voice all cheery as she sent a Navy SEAL off to his virtual reality doom.

He did pretty well though; made it halfway across the room before a Crane bot pegged him with a flechette, not a lethal wound, but it alerted a virtual Tiger that jumped on him with horrific holographic realism. The computer-generated killer disappeared on contact with the actual soldier but his reflexive crouch and shocked expression were very, very real. The involuntary shudder that ran through me was pretty real too.

The goal of the exercise was to make it across the course, which was actually just a huge empty gymnasium most of the time but right now looked exactly like lower Manhattan. When we set it up, I had measured the floor space at twenty-five meters by thirty. The contenders entered in one corner and had to cross the diagonal length to the far corner. When the simulator was off, the walls, doorways, and other obstacles were just plain white, featureless props, although they were all self-mobile and controlled by the AI. When powered up, the realism was fantastic.

If someone knocked me out and left me to wake up inside the ZD simulator, I'd have no idea it wasn't the real deal, at least not right away. Based on the swearing, the bitching that I heard, and the shocked expressions I was seeing, our little pseudo-Zone was having a telling effect on our trainees.

Yoshida's initial guess was close. Lunchtime arrived and we only had five people left to go through. The major chose to push the midday meal break back and finish off our trainees so they didn't have to sweat it out over lunch.

"Okay, that's all of you. We'll take an hour for food and facilities, then meet back in the auditorium right at 1300 hours. You'll get a chance to watch Ajaya run the course, then we'll do a group debrief and a critique. I'll want your feedback too, so think about what you just experienced, add that to what you see during our little demo, and then make your notes on your issued tablets. Dismissed," he told them.

I watched them leave, the whole group displaying a mixed bag of frustration, dismay, self-consciousness, and skepticism. Highly trained, super-competitive special operators with years of combat experience were not used to failure.

"They think the whole thing was rigged," Yoshida said, coming up as I checked over my gear for my after-lunch run. "They'll talk over lunch and by the time you step in there, they'll be convinced they were set up to fail."

I set aside the slightly modified training stealth suit and double-checked the training rifle. We all used the same model, which was modified to simultaneously fire blanks and invisible laser pulses for the AI to track. The military had been using versions of it for like over thirty years or more. The weapon recoiled (a little bit), required magazine changes, could be set to fire with a loud bang or a suppressed cough, and was as reliable as any modern war weapon out there.

"So how do we get them past all that?" I asked.

"First of all, *we* don't get them to do anything," he said, tilting his head down to look at me like he was looking over invisible glasses. "*They're* going to have to get it on their own, but we will give them reason to believe it's valid. But don't worry about that. You just worry about not blowing it in there, got it? Worst thing in the world if *you* and your pal step in there and get tagged instantly," he said, waiting for assurances.

Mentally I cringed a little, thinking how embarrassing that would be. No way, not going to happen, I decided. If we had to kill every damned imaginary drone in the AI's imaginary arsenal, we'd do it.

"Don't worry, Major. We're ready," I said, nodding over at Rikki, who was sitting on the gear-out table, already loaded with blanks.

"Exactly what I want to hear," he said with a nod and a heavy swat on my shoulder. "Coming to lunch?"

"Nah, I don't ever eat a lot right before heading into the Zone, real or imaginary," I said.

"Right, stay loose. We'll see you in an hour." With that, he left me alone with Rikki and the training gear.

Truth be told, I was now kind of nervous. All these super soldiers waiting to see us run the Room and I could just about feel the failure factor ramping up.

"Heart rate and respiratory emissions indicate nervousness. Is this condition referred to as performance anxiety, Ajaya?" Rikki suddenly asked.

"In a way. This isn't life or death like the real Zone, but the ramifications of failure are serious. If I screw this run up, the trainees won't respect me, won't listen to me, and it'll be Sergeant Primmer all over again."

"That is a single potential extrapolation of possible events. There are twenty-four current trainees, each of whom might have a different reaction to seeing a Rikki-Ajaya failure. Control of their responses is beyond this unit or Ajaya Gurung. Only Rikki-Ajaya responses are controllable."

My drone was giving me a pep talk. Un-freaking-believable. Completely unprecedented behavior, and it made me want to dive into his diagnostics badly, but there wasn't time and I'd been checking him almost religiously since we beat Lotus. Rikki had changed greatly over the last few months and I couldn't figure out exactly why. Harper was fascinated by him but even though I think she had some ideas about what was going on with him, she refused to share them. Said they were too speculative—just wild-ass guesses.

"Alright, buddy. You are right. All we can do is make our plan, plan for it to fail, and adapt on the fly. Right?"

"That, and Ajaya should hydrate. Hydration is proven to improve performance of the soldier, athlete, or individual in almost all physical endeavors."

"Right," I said, shaking my head. Still, I picked up my water bottle and took a long pull. Right was right.

CHAPTER 12

"Enter at will, Ajaya," Maya's soft voice said over the ready room's speakers.

We moved instantly, me opening the Room's entrance door wide enough for Rikki to shoot through, giving him a three count before I slid through. Stepping sideways twice, I crouched with the training rifle up and ready, listening and looking.

Mostly it was about what I *hadn't* heard. I hadn't heard Rikki open fire immediately, so I felt comfortable clearing the doorframe. I didn't hear his fans nearby, which told me that he had cleared the entrance and moved out further to recon for drones.

The scene was different than any of the scenarios that the AI had run earlier with any of the trainees. At first guess, we were Midtown West. I could hear seagulls, smell water, and when I looked over my left shoulder, there was enough clear blue on the skyline to indicate open air space. And the rusted sign on the corner ahead might have said 46th at one point in its past.

Didn't really matter, as I just needed to concentrate on clearing roughly forty meters of combat zone. And the AI wasn't going to let me get through without detection. Rikki had dutifully reported the maximum time before what I was calling *forced* detection from *every* one of the morning runs, plus the five other times that we had stepped into the Room. At most, I had two minutes before a drone would be generated somewhere near my position. Just how the game was played.

Ostensibly, I had just come out of a building on the corner of what I thought was 11th and West 46th. I had a big open area to transit, and the clearest path was diagonally across that intersection. Wide open and nothing moving, flying, or making any noise whatsoever.

Nope. Not buying it. I moved behind a derelict city bus, dropping low to sweep under it, then took a slow three-sixty before moving with a careful heel and toe across 46th Street and into a parking lot of a long-abandoned used car dealership. A real soft whirring announced Rikki coming down 11th Avenue from the north. Crouching between a faded black Cadillac and a Honda CRV, I put my back to him while I scanned everywhere he wasn't. Nothing.

Rikki continued through the intersection as if I wasn't there, holding about five meters off the ground, staying in the shadows of the buildings on the opposite side of the street from me.

It was probably late morning, based on how close to overhead the sun was. The whole section of 11th Avenue in front of me was heavily shadowed, but would soon be lit up like MetLife Stadium when the sun reached high noon.

My drone got two buildings to the south with nothing behind him as I wormed my way between rusting auto bodies. The way looked and sounded clear, but my internal clock told me our two minutes was almost up.

Instead of running across the street, I shuffled across the parking lot, moving through the open space in the middle, maybe three meters of area, before diving back between cars. Instantly, the windshield of the Buick Enclave next to me exploded into spiderwebs as a string of flechettes stitched across it from my left.

In the real Zone, I defy a Raptor to get within a block of us without Rikki detecting it, but this was essentially a game and the AI had just *spawned* it twenty meters away, where it would have shot me in the back if I had run across the street.

I dropped to all fours, my rifle slung across the front of my body, banging into my left leg and right arm as I scurried like a rat, deeper into the rows of cars before cutting around the back end of a hulking Lincoln Navigator.

A soft whirring came from the cars I had just left behind. Rifle ready, I waited in place, head on a swivel.

The sound of Rikki's suppressed gun firing a single round came seconds later. That was my signal to stand, acquire target, and fire one suppressed blank round of my own into the Raptor that had turned to take on my Berkut.

Now was the time to run for the street. I had just a handful of seconds before we estimated the AI would spawn new enemies. We were wrong, as I got four fast paces before motion on my periphery caused me to twist and fire two quick shots. Time slowed as one round clipped a landing strut on the little Kite that had simply popped into existence, knocking the tiny UAV spinning. Even in the simulator, the drones didn't just spontaneously appear almost on top of you. At least, it hadn't so far. This was entirely new. No fair. The major must have set the game for impossible and now the computer wasn't even trying to make it seem real.

I dove into what Dad would have called a judo roll and turned around as I came up to fire at the massive Tiger that had leapt through the space I had almost run through. Rikki's gun was firing without suppressor but I ignored whatever he was doing as I kept pumping rounds into the Tiger to make sure it stayed down.

Something tugged at my left arm and I spun into the shot, my right thumb clicking the selector to full auto. Again, I was feeling that weird sensory condition where everything seemed to move in slow motion. Rikki was engaging two more Raptors while a pair of Chinese Cranes stood on top of the black Caddie. A four-round burst removed them from the car top as one of the Raptors burst into spare parts, the other UAV trying to evade my more nimble Berkut.

The sun peeked over a building and a fast-moving shadow sent me diving under a Jeep Wrangler parked on the east side of 11th. A heavy 9mm sounded, steel-cored rounds banging into the Jeep, a couple ripping through the car to hit the pavement in front of me.

Part of me cried foul at this highly improbable, possibly impossible, amount of penetration while another part shrank at the realization that it was another Berkut that had entered the game, this one hunting for me.

"RIKKI, FADE FAST," I yelled, pulling a training MSLAM from my leg pocket, clicking the setting to two seconds of delay, and tossing it out into the street behind me.

The bomb rolled three meters away, righted itself, and fired almost instantly, a narrow cone of shaped explosion shooting upward as the explosive projectile completely missed anything resembling a drone.

But the blast was impressive and served its purpose, sending the enemy Berkut out and away. Rikki's 9mm sounded in a three-round burst from a new direction, and the bad Berkut smashed into the street two meters from my face.

Time to move. I rolled out from under the Jeep, coming out on my back, rifle lifting up and firing as a pair of Sky-hawks targeted Rikki. The UAVs slid sideways to avoid my fire, zooming out of the intersection, disappearing right into the virtual side of a building as the AI gave up any pretense of reality.

A Leopard jumped onto a Ram pickup truck two and half meters away, falling away but still clawing at the metal when I emptied my rifle's magazine. I jacked my body up-right, dropping the mag and grabbing another as I ran for the far corner. More than halfway across the Room, by es-timation, our best bet was to just run for it.

That's when the Tank-Killer rolled out of the side of a building, its fully operational heavy machine gun spin-ning my way.

Aw come on!

Screw it. I fired the training rifle, one-handed and full auto, at the TK's aiming module while I pulled an XM-2080 from my pocket, pressed the selector for im-pact detonation, and hurled it under the heavy Russian robot tank.

The explosion rolled out from under the armored bot, lifting the front, sending a tongue of fire shooting straight for me before reality blinked twice and the VR clicked off, revealing white walls and a set of rounded forms shaped roughly like cars, with gymnasium lighting high over-head instead of a sun.

"Ajaya, you're dead," Maya said from everywhere.

"From the moment I stepped in here," I said, watching Rikki as he folded from delta to orb, hovering down to my side.

CHAPTER 13

"Glad you could join us, Ajaya," the major greeted me as I stepped into the auditorium. Everyone in the room turned to stare at me.

"Yeah, it's great for me too," I said.

"Ah, see everyone, like I told you. He feels the exact same way you all do about the simulator. Totally unfair, right, Ajaya?" Yoshida said in jovial tone that I had learned was fake.

"Unfair? Nothing in the Zone is fair, but *unrealistic?* Yeah, I'll agree with that. The reason I have Rikki in there with me is to detect drones long before I can. Having a multi-ton Tank-Killer spawn five meters away, right out the side of building is a bit of a stretch, don't you think?" I asked right back.

He paused, looking at me with mild chagrin. "Okay, you have a point. But what about the rest?"

"You set the room for a level impossible to survive. So I didn't survive," I said with a shrug, taking a pull on my water bottle.

"And you're angry?"

"Annoyed, puzzled, confused. I mean, that was a hell of pep talk you gave me before sending me in, and then you go and spin it up to Armageddon. Wondering what the point was?"

"Oh yeah, about that. The class felt the exact same way."

"You're saying that the level they fought at felt impossible and so you showed them what impossible looks like?"

"See, class, this is why he's your instructor. Exactly, Ajaya. Sending you and Rikki in to run the table at level one wouldn't convince anyone that it wasn't a setup. So I set *you* up."

"Awesome."

Yoshida laughed and, amazingly, so did some of the super soldiers in the audience. "Alright, questions?"

"Why did you suicide out of the game?" a sniper asked. I recognized her from the orientation talk.

"The AI was spawning brand-new drones, fully armed with complete loadouts, the last of which was the Tank-Killer. The only ordinance I had that would touch that bot was my XM-2080, so I figured I would take it out and see what the computer would predict would happen to me. I was pretty sure to die, but the Room AI can compute all those factors and I thought it might be a learning experience."

"You saw limited chances to survive and decided to experiment?" she clarified, frowning.

"Yeah. If Rikki had detected a TK inside his normal range, either in real life or in the game, I would have set up a combo trap of MSLAMs and an XM-2080 and then got out of there. But the major's god-level game just dropped the damned thing right on top of me. Did anyone get anything useful out of that... that clusterfuck?" I asked.

They were silent, then the Green Beret from earlier spoke

up. "Actually, I was feeling like Major Yoshida said. Like it was rigged. Then I watched you and your drone waste your way through a dozen drones in about thirty seconds before you got tagged out. So yeah, I learned stuff. But I would really like to have you walk us through what you did, and why you did it."

"Yeah, that would be helpful," the sniper lady admitted. A number of other voices rumbled agreement.

"Good idea," Yoshida said, still smiling. "Walk us through it, Ajaya. Maya, crank it back up on the big screen."

So we did. I explained sending Rikki in and listening for gunshots to see if the area was clear. The step-by-step run-through took longer and we had to back it up and re-play things a lot because either a student had a question or I had to first think about what we were doing and then explain why we did it.

"You weren't even watching the Berkut during the shoot-out," a Marine noted. "How do you know what he's shooting and what you're supposed to shoot?"

"That's a little harder to explain. We've been in too many shootouts, so we kind of know what each of us is supposed to shoot, like you all do with your long-term team buddies. Rikki handles the fast flyers and I handle the ground bots. We each sort of prioritize based on lethality. A Tiger or Berkut is a top killer and needs to be taken out quickest. Flechette shooters and smaller ground bots like Leopards and Wolves need to come next, then down to laser weapons and light caliber guns, and so on. Also, we shoot according to our firepower and hit probability. My guns are bigger but he's a better shot on hard-to-hit, fast-moving targets, so we balance out. I had almost no chance of hitting that enemy Berkut in open flight, so he would know to automatically take it, although I could distract it and disrupt its tactical plan with an explosive. Not sure if that answered it or not?"

"You made those choices *that* fast and all on the fly?" another Army type asked.

"We've spent a couple of years together and had a lot of simulated combat time before that."

"I thought this simulator was brand-new?" the Ranger who had caught a shot in the back of the head inside the simulator asked.

Yoshida jumped in before I could answer. "*This* one is, but Ajaya hooked his Berkut playmate up to a series of first person shooter games and *trained* it to fight by his side."

"What? That's..." the Ranger trailed off as he thought about it.

"Crazy?" I volunteered.

"Kinda genius, actually," he said. "What games?"

"Most of them, but for team play we used *Lost Honor 45* a lot. Also played *Bleak* in a few competitions," I said.

"You took your drone's AI into online competitions?" the Ranger asked.

"Yeah, along with my sisters. We did pretty good. I wanted Rikki to experience team play. It helped hone our understanding of each other. Most of the time, I can't speak or yell to him unless it's all gone to shit. So we've worked out a bunch of nonverbal cues. My mom's dad used to hunt pheasant with his Irish Setter, Darby. I've watched them work a field together, and Grandpa would explain how he could read Darby's behavior and body language. So I pay attention to what Rikki is doing and he does the same with me. We can go over all of that in detail later."

"So you see, Ajaya adapted techniques that humans have used for thousands of years to this new technology. I could have sent him in alone and let him cover the Room on his own, but the point we want you to take away is that the lone hunter is far from efficient. One equipped with a drone *bird dog* is way, way more effective, even at impossible levels of combat," Yoshida said. "And a class in drone body language is a good idea. Maya make a note of that, please. We'll work on that before we issue you a drone of your own."

"If I do the room on my own, without Rikki, at the level you all experienced, it takes me a full hour, generally, because rushing gets you killed. With Rikki, it would have been five or six minutes at the normal level," I said. "My recovery success rate inside the Zone went way, way up after I got Rikki."

"Will our drones be as effective as the Berkut?" someone asked.

"Nope, at least not right away. Ajaya and Rikki have hundreds of hours together. That's not going to happen for you all right away," Yoshida said. "But we will be putting you and your drone into an online VR simulator that you can use as often as you want, and you'll all have lots of hours in the Zone Room," Yoshida said.

"We can do the VR during free time?" the Ranger asked.

"Yup. Now, let's keep going on this debrief. Ajaya?"

It took an entire hour to cover the eight minutes and seventeen seconds we survived in the simulator. One thing for professionals, they ask lots of questions—good ones, at that.

I was a little wrung out as the class filed out of the auditorium. They had a block of free time to do whatever they wanted: work out, call home, read, eat, or even take a nap. Me, I was ready to head home, but Yoshida motioned me to hang out as he fielded a question from a SEAL. Then he turned as the man left.

"Alright Ajaya, that was good work. I think this group has a better appreciation for the Zone than any of the first four you took in. What do you think?" he asked, leading me out of the room and toward the lab.

"I think they have an appreciation for the simulator. I agree that this approach is necessary, but now I'm a little worried that the game aspect of it will dominate their perceptions," I said.

"That's a valid point. One that I already thought of. Starting tomorrow, we'll be breaking them into three groups. In the afternoon, one group will travel to various points around the perimeter of the Zone for a little show and tell. A second group will spend time with the Render pilots, and the third group will take a Quad trip over the entire length of Manhattan. Each day, during the afternoon training block, the groups will switch activities till they've all had the same exposure. By the end of the week they'll have their Kestrels, the new Mark 7 version, and they'll start training with them in the mornings."

"What are they going to be doing in the mornings between tomorrow and when you issue their Kestrels?"

He turned to me with an evil grin. "Why Ajaya, I'm glad you asked. They'll be in class with you, learning nonverbal drone cues, tips, and secrets of Zone travel on foot, and the finer points of clearing a building with a drone partner."

John Conroe

"I don't have any curriculum made up," I protested.

"Well, Sniper, you have the rest of today to prep for tomorrow's clinic on silent drone communication. Then you have tomorrow night to figure out foot travel, and the day after that for building clearing."

"I want to use the Room," I said, my brain already coming up with ideas.

"It's yours. No one else will be using it when you're holding class, so why not teach everything from inside it?"

"Yeah, but I'll need one of the science geeks to set up and run the simulations."

"Which do you want?"

"Either Maya or Eric. Not really a fan of Aaron."

He laughed. "Yeah, he's an acquired taste. I'll tell Maya that she needs to work with you, but she'll be disappointed—she likes the whole secret web search thing."

We reached the lab doors, which opened at our approach. Inside, I immediately spotted the terrible trio crowded around their virtual work tables. All three looked up as we came in, Maya waving while Eric looked at us with a distracted expression that probably meant he wasn't really even seeing us. Aaron just gave us a glance and then turned back to his work surface, clearly dismissing us from thought.

"Maya, I need you to work with Ajaya to set up some programs in the Room. He'll be teaching morning classes the next three days and the simulator is the best venue."

"Oh, I was going to whip up a few info bots and send them into the web tomorrow," she said, frowning for a moment. Then her expression turned curious. "What pro-

108

grams?" she asked me.

"I want to demonstrate how Rikki and I read each other's body language when we're inside the Zone. So that's going to take like a dozen or more mini-scenarios. That's for tomorrow. Day after that, I want to show them how we work together to move through drone-rich areas. And the day after that is Building Clearing 101."

She looked up at the ceiling for a moment, deep in thought. Then her eyes came back to mine and she smiled. "I have some ideas on all of those. This could be fun too." I was immediately glad the major had picked her. The other two didn't appear to have even noticed the exchange.

"Speaking of info bot searches, where do we stand?" Yoshida asked.

"Well, Major, some of *us* have been working instead of playing video games," Aaron said without lifting his head. "*My* bots have already reported in. Your cannon fodder was right," he said with a nod in my direction. "There is a statistically significant amount of accidents with both drones and self-driving vehicles. And also with a few pieces of automated construction equipment, and these incidents aren't just here in New York. Boston, Philly, DC, Houston, Orlando, and Saint Louis are just a few that have had a couple similar issues. Most were traced to software glitches. The ones here in New York were far, far more serious, and not all of them have been fully explained."

"The search programs *I* ran yielded similar results but also indicate there have been unexplained glitches in civilian and commercial aircraft," Eric said, glancing sideways at Aaron.

Wow, competition was fierce among these three. Brutal, even.

"Okay, Ajaya was right... again. Now *why* is it happening, oh super geniuses?"

"In most of the cases, there were investigations into the cause," Eric jumped in before Aaron could get any words out. "Sixty-one percent of the time, it was due to faulty code."

"And the rest of the time?"

"Either too much damage had occurred to the CPUs to back test or the people involved were unable to make any determinations," Aaron said, regaining the floor. "Which generally means they weren't skilled enough to dig it out."

"Or that it was more complicated than a bit of bad code," I said.

"How much damage are we talking about?" Yoshida asked, ignoring the condescending eye roll that Aaron gave me.

"Some drones exploded on impact, a few shorted out, and at least one caused a fire hot enough to burn up the UAV," Aaron said.

"And in those cases where a determination was possible, it was *faulty code*," the major said, making little air quotes with his fingers.

"Yes," both scientists said in unison.

Yoshida looked at me, frowning. "So, we got two enhanced battle-hardened AIs plotting the end of humankind, and they're hiding somewhere inside the Zone," he summarized.

"And DoD says to leave Spiders alone," I added.

"No, Ajaya, they said to leave *that* Spider alone—the one we had. They never said we couldn't hunt ourselves some more. And we have you as a Spider hunter."

"Not to rain on your parade, but I wasn't that good at it. Took me over eight years to get the first one."

"Learning curve, kid," he said with a clap on my shoulder. I don't know what he did to get hands that hard but damn... that hurt. "Eight years for the first one, probably just days for the next. After all, you said it yourself, they've targeted you."

"What? They can do that?" Maya said, looking horrified. Eric looked a bit green too and even Aaron appeared uncertain at Yoshida's casual comment.

"Yeah, makes it real, doesn't it? All very interesting exercises in theory until it knows your name and perhaps even where you live," Yoshida said, clearly enjoying himself.

"Rikki, what is the probability that Peony and Plum Blossom know my address?" I asked, totally not liking the major's humor.

"Unclear. Possibly as high as forty-four percent. All utility bills, rental agreements, and insurance binders are in your mother's name, protected by her virtual assistant. The household Internet of Things are all encrypted by the same VR AI. However, there are numerous bank and investment accounts in your name with that address, albeit protected by your personal AI. Given time, Units Peony and Plum Blossom will likely achieve penetration of your security software, which is arguably less hardened than the cyber security systems of the corporations they have already compromised."

"That is... probably an accurate summary," Aaron said, looking thoughtfully at Rikki. "Lotus was pretty—robust. Even with the current state of personal and corporate AI anti-identity theft software, I think your drone is right."

"So I have to find a way to move my family," I said, stricken by the enormity of it.

Maya was shaking her head. "No, what we need to do is move your address."

I frowned at her, thinking that I had just said exactly that. But Eric was bobbing up and down in a weird little motion of excitement. "She's right. We just need to move your address on all files to something close but different, like, say, across the street."

"We'll have to be excruciatingly thorough or it'll be all for naught," Aaron said, looking at the other two with something that might have been actual excitement. "It'll be tedious, difficult, and require us to be at the top of our game," he said. I was still reflecting on the kind of guy who says "for naught." Not a single bit of game going on there.

"Awesome," Maya said, almost breathless. The other two nodded and then all three were suddenly typing.

"I'll take city records," Eric said.

"I'm on utilities and finance records," Maya called out.

"And I'll handle the IRS and state taxation departments," Aaron said, cracking his knuckles before diving back onto his virtual keyboard.

I looked at Yoshida, who just smiled. "This is exactly why they all work here," he said.

"And why we make more than you do," Aaron said without looking up.

Yoshida shrugged at me and nodded. "Maybe, but you don't make *that* much more. Admit it: You just like the government-level access to all of those networks you're currently having your way with."

"Yeah, power trumps money," Maya said with a leer before turning back to her station.

CHAPTER 14

The rest of the week was a blur of teaching and training, with evenings for Astrid and the fam.

Yoshida's wonderkin assured me that they had throughly changed all of my families' records to reflect a slightly different address. I chose a unit across the street whose owners travelled a lot and were currently out of the country. I also started some contingency planning in case it either didn't work or worked too well. And I explained what was going on to both Astrid and Harper—separately. Those two did not get along. But they both needed to know for their own safety. And Harper was an expert on the Spiders and a great resource for figuring out how to hunt them.

"Yeah, the major's right... you don't need to hunt them. They'll come after *you*," Harper had said when I told her.

"It isn't like they're pissed that I offed Lotus. They're logic-based machines, for God's sake."

"No, they have no emotions, but that very logic you speak of will identify you as a major threat to their mission. You managed to *kill* Lotus. The last Spider killed took hundreds of heavily armed soldiers and drones to take down. You did it with just your rifle and one of *their* own drones."

"And the Decimator too," I pointed out.

"Nah, Lotus neutralized that bitch," she said, waving one

hand dismissively. "Yoshida better have his nerds harden and shield that thing or it'll get used against them. Probably why he won't let anyone take it into the Zone."

We were in her apartment on the ground floor and she was gulping water. I had just caught her after another of her fitness classes. "Maybe you're right," I said, looking around. Her apartment was tiny, the smallest in the building, but she seemed fine with it. An eclectic mix of decorations seemed to change every time I stepped into the place. "You doing alright with the network people?"

"Hell yeah. A lot better than those idiots working for Zone D. I've got a couple of Dios FX-37 news drones completely hardened. Should be good to go unless they get within fifteen meters of a Spider. Better than the Decamato."

"*Decimator*. It's a Decimator," I said.

She just smiled slyly. "If you say so. But to answer your question, Trinity is very happy with my work, and thanks, by the way, for making the intro. Big pay increase."

"So you don't think much of the work that Maya, Eric, and Aaron are doing?"

"That their names? No, not based on that performance on the bridge."

"Well, they seem pretty sharp. Good hackers, really good," I said, anxious because it seemed that the people who had handled my family's security were not up to snuff.

"Sure, might be the best hackers going for standard stuff, but protecting drones from mid-flight interference is different. Oh, I get it. You're worried about the false address job. That's probably fine for what it is."

"What do you mean, what it is?"

She reached out and tapped my forehead with a finger. "You know what I mean. You've been up close and personal with everything the Zone has to offer. You really think anything sent by Peony will be fooled by an empty apartment across the street for very long? They hunt and kill humans, for heaven's sake."

My face must have given me away because her own snarky expression softened. "You've got your contingency planning underway, right? And you have sensors covering that empty place across the street? They *will* go there first. When they do, you trigger your surprise and then get your family out of here. Have you told your mom?"

"Not yet."

"Ajaya! You *have* to tell her. Come on; she's a tough lady. You gonna wait till you have to explain in the middle of the night, with killer drones right outside your windows?"

"No. I'll tell her, but what makes you think the Spiders could get a drone out of the Zone?"

"Well, other than the fact that *I got* in and out all the time there's also the fact that if you're right about these accidents, it seems like it's not just all tiny bits of mucked-up code. Those undetermined incidents might have had a more up close and personal cause. Or there's always the idea that Peony could just crash a big delivery drone into your place. And you *will* tell your mom or *I* will."

Harper liked my mom a lot. The rest of the ladies in my family weren't so friendly to her, seeing her as some kind of threat to Astrid or something, but my mom was always nice to her.

I found myself nodding, agreeing with her about telling Mom. It was one thing to contemplate a commercial drone going amok, but an entirely different thing to think about a Raptor or Skyhawk peppering my family with deadly projectiles. Still, if a Spider could get drones out of the Zone, I think it would have already happened, and I said as much to Harper.

"Yeah, so who's to say it hasn't? Think about it... these Spiders are masters of strategy and tactics. Why wouldn't they keep a secret egress point and only use it when the need was high? Any spot they found would be small like that weak area I found. They would calculate the chances of success for getting anything large out as too small to undertake. Instead, wouldn't they keep it as a secret weapon, for an asset for just the right opportunity, or maybe to neutralize a real high priority target?"

"Which you're saying is me?"

"Well, you killed one Spider, and now, thanks to your efforts, there's a new focus on hunting the others down. So yeah, you're a threat. They could also send out some kind of small infiltrators to dig into infrastructure, you know... really burrow into the Internet of Things and the web?"

That actually made more sense than the random Raptor drone sent to assassinate someone. And it would give the Spiders a much better chance of changing commercial drone code than the online approach recorded on Lotus's log.

The next day, I broached the topic with Maya while we were in the simulator's control room, setting up an introductory exercise for the students and their about-to-be issued Kestrels.

"You really think something could get out?" she asked, biting one rather well-chewed fingernail as she thought about it.

"I *know* it's possible to get out. And in. Not easy, especially for a drone, as there are pretty tight ranks of EM detectors all through the Barrier, but yes, it's possible, especially for something small, like a Kite or a Crab."

"That's an avenue we haven't looked into for backtracking the corrupted codes in the crashed drones. Some kind of small bot could conceivably get inside a computing center or server farm and invade the network from within," she said, eyes turned up toward the ceiling.

"Probably no way to go looking for such a thing," I said, putting as much believable resignation into my voice as possible without going overboard.

"Of course there is!" Maya said, taking the bait. "It's just that we never thought it was even a possibility, so we didn't go looking for it."

"But *you* could," I suggested. "Like you said, the other two sure aren't going to go down that path."

"No, they won't. They've been focused on finding code packets coming from the network's main AI, not an additional update that's been piggybacked onto a valid packet further down the line. You know what? I'll look into it. If I find something, it'll be worth the extra time to see the look on their faces."

I felt a little surge of guilt. Maya had been bogged down with helping me prep classes for the trainees and had been excluded from the extra searching that Eric and Aaron were involved in. Now she would have to spend a chunk of her very limited free time searching for something that might be a wild drone chase. But if there really were infiltrator drones outside of the Zone, we absolutely had to find them.

"To tell you the truth, Ajaya, this little exercise in virtual reality programming has been more fun than I thought it would. You know way more about the drones inside the Zone than I thought you did. No wonder your Berkut does so well," she said.

"Thanks. That reminds me... how goes the Decimator?"

She grimaced, looking down at her virtual keyboard as she coded the parameters of the exercise I had dreamed up. Of course, Yoshida had reviewed it and put his own personal stamp on it, and then Maya had come up with a few embellishments, but most of it was still mine.

"The major was seriously pissed when Lotus hacked Unit 19. We've been all through it a dozen, no two dozen times, shielding it, hardening the components, trying to build contingencies into its programming."

"What did Lotus do to it?"

She grimaced again, looking more than a little embarrassed. "Hacking drones has been going on for decades. The wireless control protocols used to be unencrypted, but that changed quickly; then of course there were radio frequency jamming techniques, electromagnetic burst methods, malware, and denial of service attacks. Most of those led to an increase in drone autonomy, giving each unit the ability to fall back on its own machine learning capabilities to solve problems and achieve goals. We build in contingencies for all of that stuff and more. But we missed a basic one."

"Oh? What did you miss?"

"A very simple GPS hack. All drones use some type of positioning system. The Decimator uses the US original GPS system as well as the newer Chinese one for backup. Lotus sent it a false set of signals that matched both systems and replaced the correct ones. Unit 19 was smart enough to realize there was false data but couldn't differentiate between the real systems and the false signals. So it froze in place while it tried to figure out where it was. Embarrassing."

"You must have fixed it by now?" I asked.

"Oh, we did. We took a page from your Berkut," she admitted.

"What? When?" I asked.

"Calm down. It wasn't from *your* personal Berkut, but from the Berkut system. The Russians gave their best drones a backup system. An advanced dead reckoning system that runs side calculations on the drones' positions, corrected regularly by the main GPS navigation system's input. If GPS fails, the drones fall back on the most recently stored information and begin to adjust it for speed, direction, and time of travel. It's less accurate, but they always have some idea of where they are. That's why your Rikki never faltered for a second."

"So if you know that and you've built in a backup like that, why not use Unit 19?"

"Because the Decimator is the first real advance in fighting drones that we've come up with. It proved very effective up until it didn't. The major isn't willing to have anyone second-guess the Decimator again. So we've been carefully dreaming up all the problems it could face and building defenses against them. But they take up memory space, airframe space, add extra weight, slow down reaction times, and on and on. So we're moving slowly and carefully and senior leadership is focused on this reclamation project, which buys us some time to get it exactly right. Which means you and your class come first."

"I bet the fellas hate that," I said.

"Aaron seems impatient with the whole thing, but Eric knows that sometimes taking a step back from a project is a good thing. Lets you see it more clearly."

"So how do you go about finding an infiltrator bot?"

"It's all about analyzing corrupted code packets and trying to find out where along the command path they got changed. The guys are looking for changes in the CPU, but I'll be looking for something sitting along the path, intercepting and recoding instructions. Then it'll be up to you or whoever the major wants to send into the hardware to find and stop it. The question is which AI system to start with?"

"The smart city systems are the most important," I said.

"We need special permission to get into the NYC Traffic Controller," she cautioned.

"What about the city smart grid or water and waste systems?" I asked.

"They all require us to coordinate with the City IT people, and *they* are a pain in the ass. I think one of the big integrated mega corps had more crashes than the others. I don't remember which one, so I'll have to double-check. Then I can use our government audit license and get a look into their drone control network. If we find one of these infiltrators, then *you* can have the major or maybe even the general get us authorization for the citywide systems," she said.

"Fair enough. I'll leave it in your hands then," I said.

"Yes you will, because *you* need to get down in the Room with your wonder drone and test this scenario out. The sooner we get it debugged, the sooner I can start on your next project," she said.

I frowned, trying to figure out if she was complaining or joking. Did she not understand how scary this would be?

"Go on already. You've officially scared me so bad I'm going to have to walk home. I won't trust public transit till we figure this out," she said, pushing me toward the door. Okay, at least that question was answered.

CHAPTER 15

Two days later, she came up with something. It was late in the afternoon, and I had finished my last class in how to train your drone.

"Ajaya, I have something for you," Maya said. I had seen her waiting diffidently for me to answer the inevitable questions that followed every class.

"Oh, I think the scenario ran pretty well, Maya. We don't need to adjust it any further, plus that was the last simulator run. We start live Zone insertions tomorrow," I said.

"Pretty well? Are you kidding? It was fantastic," she said, waving one hand back at the Room entrance. "No, I found…" she looked around and got closer, lowering her voice to almost a whisper, "*one of your infiltrators.*"

"What?" I almost yelled, caught off guard. A couple of straggling special operators looked at us curiously while she shushed me.

"I found a spot on the communications path where some commands seem to die and others seem to spawn spontaneously. The drone delivery control system is housed in the nearest order fulfillment center," she said, voice so quiet I had to lean in.

"You're talking about Ama—" I started to say but she glared and hushed me again. "Yes, and not so loud."

"Why?" I asked, curious.

"OpSec. You and Major Yoshida are always going on and on about it. Who's to say what AI system might be listening? All these virtual systems constantly alert for keywords. Say the wrong one and something is bound to start querying the company about a reported issue with a fulfillment center. Then before you know it, your little infiltrator is warned that you're coming."

"And where exactly am I going?" I asked, realizing I hadn't spent a great deal of time thinking about what I would actually need to do once we found evidence to back my theory. Well, actually, Harper's theory.

"The company's delivery drones that crashed all came from the Trenton, New Jersey center. I audited their network and found the issues were originating from a specific drone hive at the fulfillment center."

I'd seen drone hives before, at least at a distance. All the online retailers use them in one form or another. Towers, sometimes as tall as twelve stories, with hundreds of drone ports all over them. Thousands of drones were launched and recovered from them at all hours of day and night. Trying to find some kind of infiltrator bot inside one would most likely be crazy confusing and probably dangerous. Like sticking your bare arm into a real beehive.

"Let's find the major. This is going to take some planning."

It took a while to track him down, but we finally found him in the Zone Defense heavy equipment facility, talking with the engineers in charge of the mobile barrier systems. He noticed us standing to one side but he was deep in a conversation with a pair of frowning, unhappy-looking builder types. There seemed to be a lot of gesticulating and voices loud enough that we could hear them over the whine of power tools and maintenance bots.

After about ten minutes of standing around, we were rewarded with his attention when he strode over to us. "What?" he demanded.

Maya just about shrank in on herself, but I worked for him at *his* request, not mine. "We found evidence that there are actual Zone drones outside of the Zone and influencing the drones having accidents," I said, keeping my voice down.

He looked at me hard for a second, then glanced at Maya, who was able to summon enough fortitude to nod. Then he looked around to see if anyone was nearby. Enough workers and bosses were close enough to cause him to drag us to an empty room that seemed to hold lots of blueprints and technical plans. Closing the door and locking it, he turned to us. "Explain," he demanded. So I did. Near the end, Maya started interjecting her own comments, explaining her search methods.

"But you don't have any pictures or real evidence that something actually got out of the Zone?" he asked us.

"No pictures, but enough inferential evidence to indicate that *something* has to be physically present at the drone hive in order for this level and kind of interference to occur," she said, meeting his hard gaze. Socially awkward maybe, but press her on her work and she had all kinds of spine.

"Do you have any idea the kind of uproar we'll have if any units actually got out of the Zone? What makes you think it's even possible?" he asked, glancing between us. Maya turned to look at me, leaving me pretty much under the bus.

"I've found places where I could get in and out. A small, super well shielded bot could *possibly* have climbed out the same place," I allowed.

"The first thing you're going to do is show me where those places are. *If* you convince me that something could have gotten out, then we'll see about finding and neutralizing it. What even put you on this line of research anyway?"

"I was bouncing ideas off a friend of mine and she thought the best way to influence protected systems was from the inside. So I asked Maya to check one out."

"Next time you want to task one of my people with a job, run it by me first, got it?"

"Yes Major," I said easily. Better to beg forgiveness than ask permission is one of my sisters' favorite philosophies. Seemed to fit here as well.

Maya disappeared like a ghost as Yoshida and I sat down at a work table with a detailed hologram of the entire Zone. I showed him two places that I knew *I* could get in and out of, as well as a potential third that I *thought* might be possible. Next thing I knew, we were in an Air-dragon reconnaissance quadrotor, the smaller, more nimble version of the big troop Quads that soldiers currently rode into battle. Corporal Estevez and Sergeant Rift accompanied us, along with Boyle and Kayla, all of them in battle armor. We also had a barrier engineer with us and she got paler and paler at each of the locations I showed them. The major, on the other hand, just got grimmer and grimmer.

"You never spoke about these weak spots before. Why exactly?" Yoshida asked, his mouth compressed into a thin line. I pointed at the rows of sensitive EM detectors sitting on the bridge supports right overhead.

"If you guys were going to cut me off from the Zone, I needed a backdoor in. I didn't think anything could get out, but it's been suggested to me that I may have under-estimated the planning abilities of the Spiders," I said.

"Yes, let's talk about this mysterious friend that has bet-ter insight into Spider behavior than *you* do," he growled.

"I wouldn't say it was *better*, just outside the box enough that it gets my attention," I said, so not wanting to go down this path.

"You said it was a she... so I'm guessing it's your girlfriend, who *I'm* sure is smarter than you are," he said.

I tried my best to keep a blank expression, but my failure was enough that he seemed to take it for confirmation. Which was fine by me.

"All right. These will all be closed in the next hour. Any others?"

"No, that's it."

"Estevez," Yoshida said, watching me closely. The cor-poral grabbed my right elbow in one armored hand. Then he squeezed ever so slightly. "Holy shit! That's all of them!" I yelled, trying to pull free. It was like fighting a hydraulic press.

The major nodded and Estevez let go. I yanked it clear and stepped back, looking the corporal in the eyes. He smiled. My eyes flicked over his armored combat suit, then back to meet his flat stare.

"See that, Boyle? Shooter's pissed," Kayla said to her pal, just loud enough to hear, both of them off to the side. "He's looking Estevez over for weaknesses, even in the suit."

"Nah, Kayla," Boyle drawled, "Ajaya already knows the weak spots. He was just reminding himself of them."

"What weak spots? These suits are savage," Akachi Rift said, off to the side as well.

"*Everything* has weaknesses, Sarge. Don't you watch Ajaya when he's shooting stuff? He shoots everything in its weak spot," Boyle said. I had shot a Leopard right off Boyle in mid-mauling and he was pretty much a fan now.

Estevez didn't look away from me, but his smile disappeared.

Yoshida grabbed my shoulder, turning me toward him. "Enough! You got my point?" he asked me.

"Oh, I got it… real clear," I said, thoroughly pissed. Boyle was right. There were weak spots in armor and I knew them.

"Ajaya, you can't hold out on me with shit like this. Too many lives at stake."

"I hold out because of shit like *that*. I'm not one of your troops, Yoshida. I work here because you *came* to me, but I haven't forgotten that you and Davis yanked my license. And to have your attack dog threaten my shooting arm? Yeah, message received loud and clear. Good luck with your project and good luck with any escapees," I said, rubbing my right elbow.

Rift, Boyle, and Kayla all looked at me sharply at my final word, but I was watching Yoshida. If he ordered them to take me, I couldn't fight all of them in their armor, but I was pretty sure the 9mm Magnum in the holster on my chest could slip a ceramic-tipped carbide penetrator through the thin joint armor at the side of Estevez's knee.

It was a new weapon for me, but I'd done a butt load of shooting with it ever since Egan had found it for me. It hit what I pointed it at, and it hit hard.

"Ajaya, Ajaya, calm down. Don't get all wiggy over this. I needed you to understand how serious it is. Estevez didn't realize it was your shooting arm, right Corporal?"

"Yeah, Major. Like you said," Estevez agreed, nodding, still smiling his cold little smile.

"Ajaya, if you walk away, I still have to send those soldiers into the Zone anyway. How many of them will die if you're not there? Most of them? All of them? I won't have a choice. None at all," Yoshida said in a reasonable tone.

I studied him for a moment, ignoring Estevez and the others. He would send my class into the Zone and they would die.

"It's late. I'm heading home," I finally said.

"You'll be there tomorrow? To take the first group in?"

"I'll be there," I said, walking away. I would, but not for him or Zone Defense. I'd do it for the trainees.

"Ooh, Estevez, you got lucky," Boyle said from behind me.

"There are four of us in armor, genius."

"Yeah, but where was his Berkut?" Boyle asked.

Rikki suddenly floated down from the darkness above, taking up station off my left shoulder. We moved away from the soldiers and out from the barrier utility access tunnel I had led them into. Up a metal ladder, through a door, and outside into the cool Brooklyn night.

CHAPTER 16

I took the first four in the next morning. We again used the northern part of the island, but this time we didn't go as far in. Just past the barrier and into the first house we found. And we cleared it, top to bottom, Kestrels and Berkut checking everything over. Then we did the house next to it. Found an Indian Meerkat. It was old, almost defunct, barely enough power to raise its needle-sharp nose harpoon before I grabbed it from behind.

"Not very many of these left. Most are really slow, if not dead. This model had good rechargeable batteries but only one small capacitor. Nowadays, the batteries are shot and the remaining few Meerkats can't hold enough power in that capacitor to last overnight. So catch them early in the morning and you can grab them from behind like this. Then you just pull open this little cover on the back of the head and pull out the power connection," I said in a loud whisper, demonstrating. The Meerkat froze up solid and I handed it around to the four.

"Never, ever turn your back on a supposedly dead drone *until* you've disconnected the power sources."

The groups were supposed to be randomly chosen, but this group had the vocal Green Beret, Sergeant Carl Abate; Tyson Perry, the Ranger who caught the paint pellet early in his simulator debut; Elizabeth Kottos, Corporal, US Army, Sniper; and last was a Marine Gunnery Sergeant named Max Kwan. All four had stood out in training and

I was pretty sure Yoshida had handpicked them to be my first group just to build my confidence. Kind of my dream squad.

The entire class was down to nineteen people, five having changed their minds and pulled out of the task force, which the major had allowed. The remaining ones were, to my mind, way ahead of my first four, and none of them questioned me like Primmer had. Every one of them was older than me, but there was no bullshit. They listened and did as I said. The result was a two-hour jaunt in and out with no problems and one dead Meerkat. A half-hour break and then I took in another four-person group. We found a Crab sunning itself in a long-abandoned baby crib on the second floor of house five. The group's Kestrels killed it quick and almost silent. By the end of the day, I had given all nineteen a taste of the Zone, cleared sixteen houses, killed one Meerkat, three Crabs, and a threesome of Raptors that showed up to investigate. No injuries, no damaged drones. Neither Rikki nor I expended a single round. No issues with following instructions, just total professionalism. In fact, watching my *trainees* clear a house quickly and cleanly sank home the reality that these were highly trained expert warriors with many years of combat experience. I was exhausted at the end of the day, but mildly elated. From here we would start longer, half-day trips for the rest of the week. After that, they would start clearing as a group.

The protocol would be to send in the barriers at the same time that the special teams went in. The barriers would close off a block of houses or buildings and the trainees would clear them in two-person teams. Yoshida's armored troops would stand back in reserve in case of surprises.

I thought it would work, at least for the northern

part, like say most of Inwood. But when the buildings stretched higher, over a couple of stories, I think it was going to start to get really dicy. Clearing a multistory commercial building would be tough. It would take the entire class, all of their drones, and Yoshida's armored troops. Then you'd have to find a way to prevent that building from being reinfected with more drones. Not going to work. And if you did somehow miraculously clear it and keep it clear, well congratulations, you now have do it all over for, oh, say, like sixty thousand more buildings.

Personally, I think we needed to find a way to lure as many drones out into the open as possible, smash them with superior firepower, and then repeat as many times as possible. Next you'd have to employ hundreds of people and thousands of friendly drones to hunt down the remainder.

There are minefields all over the world that have never been cleared because it's too dangerous and there are too many mines. And mines don't have computer minds and mobility. Eventually the majority of drones will wear out and die on their own, but I expect people will find them for decades to come, like unexploded ordnance from World War II still turning up. Maybe someday there'll be a Drone Squad like the NYC Bomb Squad.

"I think you're right," Astrid said at dinner.

She had come to the fam apartment, as I was too exhausted to go out. Mom had cooked Italian, giving Aama the night off from kitchen duty, and she'd splurged on lobster ravioli in her homemade vodka sauce.

"You honestly think it'll be decades more?" Mom asked, clearly depressed by the idea.

"Well, I think it'll be quicker than AJ thinks, but it's going to be really hard and take a buttload of our own drones to hunt down the Zone drones. That's a big investment, lots of money and resources. Dad thinks they'll end up modifying the *Zone War* show. He thinks we're moving toward sending just drones in."

"That's never worked before. Every drone sent in got smashed by the terrorist drones," Monique said.

"Very true. Most got hacked or had their signals disrupted, then got swarmed by Zone bots. But Dad thinks the Spiders coordinated most of that. We're down to just two left, thanks to the sniper boy right here with the big mouthful of ravioli," Astrid said, elbowing me. She was right: I did have a big mouthful to chew before I could answer. "If we can kill off the last two, then he thinks teams of friendly drones would begin to win. We'll all stay out of the Zone and run swarms of hunter bots."

"With five teams?" Gabby asked while I tried to swallow so I could get back into the conversation.

"No, no, more like hundreds. See, Dad thinks we need to set up a public contest, open to anyone with a drone or drones who can meet certain conditions. Then the government continues pay out bounties."

I finally cleared my mouth. "So, he's just waiting for what? The other two Spiders to die off?" I asked.

She turned and smiled at me. "There's been a ton of discussions online about how you killed Lotus. The public is asking why the military hasn't been able to do what you've done. Dad says the pressure is getting too high for Zone D to ignore. I would expect a serious campaign to hunt them down."

John Conroe

I froze, fork halfway to mouth. Mom zeroed in on my expression. "What?"

My thoughts were tumbling all over themselves, like a waterfall. Beside me, Astrid turned and looked at me, nodding. "Yeah, I wondered if these special troops you've been training are actually going to become Spider hunters. It makes more sense than clearing the Zone building by building. Nobody else has said anything like that?"

"No. But I've always thought that the whole clearing concept was severely limited. It'll only work for the very northern part of the island, maybe a few places around the outskirts, but it'll only be lipstick on a pig," I said. "The caliber of my trainees is sky high. I've kind of wondered why this project attracted so many really, really sharp people," I said.

"They all want to be you," Gabby said before shoveling a mouthful of salad into her mouth.

"What?"

Her twin answered for her. "Kids at school ask us about you all the time. The guy that killed a Spider. You're kind of legendary," Monique said.

"I thought that all died down?" I said. "You guys haven't said a word about it in weeks."

"Because we didn't want to create an ego monster," Gabby said.

"Trust me, if anyone knew what it was like to go face to face with Lotus, they wouldn't want to entertain it for even an instant," I said, glancing at Mom to check her expression. She was watching Astrid.

"What else does Brad think?" Mom asked. "Does he think Zone D has a prayer of killing Peony and Plum Blossom?"

"He does. But only if they have help," Astrid admitted reluctantly.

"Help?" Monique asked.

Astrid tilted her head in my direction as she took a small bite of ravioli.

"Ajaya? He wants Ajaya to go back in and hunt the other Spiders?" Mom asked, voice rising.

Astrid shook her head. "It's not about what he wants or doesn't want. He thinks Zone D will either pressure AJ, or AJ will volunteer to lead the hunt."

Everyone froze. Then Aama spoke. "Why would Ajaya do that?"

"To kill the Spiders before they could hunt us," Mom said, eyes on me.

I put my fork down. "No one's asked me, Mom."

"What do you mean, *hunt us?*" Gabby asked.

"Ah, the Spiders know who your brother is. They have likely prioritized hunting him," Astrid said.

"Yeah, when he's in the Zone. But you said *us?*" Monique said, pointing her fork at Mom.

"There's a possibility that the remaining Spiders have been able to influence some networks outside of the Zone. If so, they may come after me and, possibly, you all," I said.

"The accident! It wasn't really an accident, was it?" Gabby said, looking from Astrid to me and back again.

"We don't know. Zone D is looking into it. But Brad's right... if they're hunting us, I'm going to hunt them first."

CHAPTER 17

"So here's what we need to do," Yoshida said to me as soon as he saw me the next day. I had walked into the lab, looking for him, ready to lay out Brad Johnson's theory. But not only were the three scientists there, so were Sergeant Rift and the ever-present Corporal Estevez, all gathered around a glowing computer projection.

I just raised my eyebrows, not sure what the topic was.

"About the infiltrator bot in the drone hive," he said, reading my expression.

"Okay. What do *we* need to do?" I asked.

Ignoring my not-so-subtle phrasing, he pointed at the worktable they were gathered around. I moved close enough to see a blue wireframe diagram of a drone hive holographically projected in front of all of them.

"Maya's excellent work has narrowed our search area down to this series of drone garages on the eighth floor. All of the drones that had recent accidents came from one of these seven depots on this level. Which means that the bot would have to be somewhere in this network node along here," Yoshida said. His pointed finger caused the computer to expand and zero in on the middle section of the building. I looked around at the others. Maya was beaming at me while her two coworkers looked less than happy. Rift gave me a nod and Estevez just stared at me before looking back at the diagram.

I studied the area in question, taking a second to figure out the scale. "Wait, that's like almost two stories of area," I said.

"Yes, a central utility tunnel runs up the middle of the hive, alongside the elevator shaft. Each floor has a central node, and the network conduits branch off of the node and run to each of the garages where area-specific WiFi networks command each drone in that garage."

"So it must be sitting in the node or just below it?" I asked.

"It *could* be there, or it could also be inside one of the seven branch tunnels. We think there is either more than one bot, which seems unlikely, or more probably, one bot with some kind of smaller satellite modules placed on the other conduits," Aaron said.

I must have looked unconvinced because he went on. "If it was right in the node, it could influence the four floors above it as well. Nothing we've seen indicates it has done so," he said.

"So what's the plan?" I asked."Armored suits?"

"No armor. In fact, no uniforms of any kind," Yoshida said, pausing to let that sink in.

"You don't want anyone knowing we're hunting escaped drones," I said.

"We *can't* let anyone know. Imagine the panic," he said.

"So what's the deal? Corporate coveralls?" I asked.

"Yeah. Rift has some new spider-silk suits that have better ballistic protection that we'll wear underneath the coveralls, and we have some eyewear to put on once we're in the tunnels. Silenced, concealed handguns like your 9mm mag," he said with a level gaze.

"And let me guess, you want me to do it?" I asked.

"Actually, you *and* me."

"*You?*"

He gave me a *are you kidding* look.

"Yeah, I forget sometimes that you occasionally do this stuff," I said.

"Cocky much?" he asked Rift. "I've been tunnel ratting it since you were in diapers, Junior."

"Yeah, after humans. Who knows what this bot is? You bringing a drone at least? Unit 19?"

"Yes and no. Unit 19 is too big. I'll bring my own Kestrel."

I didn't know he'd been training his own drone. "No other takers?" I asked, looking at Estevez, hoping.

"Nobody with a drone with enough experience," Yoshida said. "Now pay attention. Here's how it goes."

I paid attention.

A little over an hour later, we pulled up in front of the Jersey drone hive of the largest corporation on earth. An executive type met us at the security desk and waved us through without going through weapons scanners, which made the guards a little wiggy. I didn't blame them; security in public and private buildings had gone way up in the last ten years. No one wanted another disenfranchised ex-employee freaking out and shooting up their office.

But this woman in a suit had enough clout that the six of us weren't questioned. Eric was back at the lab, ready to help coordinate with us, while Aaron and Maya were on hand to help Yoshida and myself figure out anything technical. Estevez and Rift were security, backup, and logistics.

From what I could gather, the cover story was that we were specialists here to check the troubled eighth-floor drone systems. Actually true enough, if maybe a little light on exactly what kind of specialists we were.

I wore a real-life disguise, which consisted of a 3D-printed prosthetic nose, much bigger than my own, a ball hat with a good brim, and good old-fashioned cotton swabs tucked into my cheeks. Yoshida kept me in the middle of the team so nobody got a good look at me. The price of being on *Zone War*.

Once we got to the eighth floor, the hive's head of IT let us into the access tunnel and we got ready.

The tunnels were well ventilated but there was still a ton of waste heat from all the tech, so we stripped down to the spider-silk undersuits. A newer version with improved ballistic protection. Laser-resistant goggles, helmets with mounted lights, and our personal handguns, in chest-mounted holsters.

My new handgun of choice was a custom Glock conversion. It had started life as a stock recent generation model 20 but had been refitted with a 9x23mm barrel and had a customized slide and grip area. It fit my hand like a glove and the extra long barrel was threaded for an equally custom suppressor. Fifteen-round magazines of either high velocity or subsonic, extra heavy reassurance that could penetrate most aerial drone armor and some of the smaller ground units. This cartridge had more power than Rikki's Russian-based 9mm round.

The major carried an HK SpecCom, one of the earlier generations that came out a few years back. I couldn't tell the caliber but I knew they were available in the old standards of 9x19mm, .40, .357 Sig, .45, 10mm, and that there were barrels available that could convert to 9x23mm like mine. Yoshida's looked well used but in excellent condition.

Yoshida stripped down to a bodysuit was intimidating, all corded muscle, which made me a little self-conscious of my leaner frame. And he suited up with a quiet professionalism that spoke of years of experience. My own load-out was much less than I usually carried so I was ready first, which allowed me to prep Rikki.

The major's Kestrel was newer but Rikki had more proven combat experience, and one other advantage—he could shift into his ball form, which was way, way more efficient in close quarters than the disk shape of the Kestrel. My Berkut's batteries were fully charged but I slipped a backup recharge into a stretch pocket on my hip. I had three lights; the one on my helmet, another mounted on the back of my left wrist, and a weapon light under the barrel of my pistol. Rikki was fully loaded with twenty rounds of 9x21mm ammo, his integral suppressor fitted with fresh, new baffles. I had a spare block of ammo for Rikki and two extra mags for my gun. Frankly, if it took that much ammo, we were screwed.

"Okay, ready?" Yoshida asked.

"Roger that," I said, Rikki hovering over my shoulder.

"Remember, we head up the ladder, then you branch left and I go right. We work around the spokes till we meet up at the seventh."

"Affirmative," I said, stepping onto the ladder. Rikki slid ahead of me smoothly, lifting up the shaft in near silence.

Yoshida grabbed my shoulder. "Why isn't he lit up?"

"Because he doesn't need light to sense the bot, and he's faster. The noise I make and all my lights will focus attention on me, giving him an element of surprise."

"We didn't talk about that?"

"It's our standard procedure for dark places. You should have attended more of the classes," I said, shaking my head. Then I was in the shaft, climbing the ladder.

CHAPTER 18

It was dark, as expected, and the rungs of the built-in ladder were cold even through the thin gloves on my hands. The air, however, was warm, and combined with the exertion of climbing, not to mention the little slug of adrenaline from my body's natural reaction to hunting dangerous things in small, dark places, I could feel my body perspire. Not good. Most combat drones can detect human pheromones and sweat byproducts, and warm air rises.

Below me, I heard a soft whirring, the major's Kestrel, then felt the vibrations through the metal ladder of Yoshida's own climbing.

I clicked my tongue on the roof of my mouth twice. A soft sound, barely audible, but it told Rikki to put twice the original distance between us. I only had to climb about four meters to reach the node and the spokes of the eighth floor, but *you* try climbing in pitch darkness toward a killing machine designed for human elimination. Rikki's silent presence at the node was reassuring and I paused on the ladder to pull my pistol and use its light to illuminate each of the two tunnel openings that I could see from here. Then I stepped left, onto the little ledge that allowed workers to circumnavigate the round elevator shaft for access to each of the spokes. I gave Rikki a silent wave and he disappeared into the darkness, heading counterclockwise. The Kestrel came up the tunnel, just a feather of displaced air to warn me. It hovered in place and a few seconds later, Yoshida's head popped up. He looked at me, at his Kestrel, then looked around at the space illuminated by our helmet lights. One eyebrow went up in a clear question. Where was my drone?

I pointed to the right, then pointed up and spun my hand counterclockwise. He nodded his understanding and climbed off the ladder, stepping onto the right side of the access ledge.

We waited, watching and listening. The Kestrel turned itself toward my side of the shaft, and that was our only warning before the black ball shape of my drone appeared in our lights. Rikki lit one green LED on his front and I turned and shook my head at Yoshida. It couldn't be that easy. Then I pointed at the spoke tunnel nearest me. He nodded and turned toward the one on the right. Without any other gestures or expressions, we both climbed into our respective tunnels and started the hunt.

Rikki moved ahead into the darkness as I kept moving in an awkward three point crawl. Two knees and a left arm, the right arm holding my sidearm, trigger finger indexed alongside the trigger.

These tunnels were much longer than the shaft we had climbed, each spoke running a bit over fifteen meters before it arrived under the floor of the drone hangar. Light suddenly blossomed five meters ahead; Rikki illuminating something on the tunnel wall. I got closer, shining my own weapon light onto the cluster of fiber optic and electrical cables that Rikki was spotlighting. It took a second to spot it—a small black device clamped onto the biggest cable. It *almost* looked like it belonged there, but there was nothing else like it on any cable or wire and it looked newer and cleaner, without the fine layer of dust that clung to everything else.

But it also looked familiar, like I had seen it before, or something like it.

Some kind of interface device, almost undoubtedly acting as a satellite control for the bot we hunted. It was the size of a deck of cards, with four leg-like clamps that squeezed the optic cable tightly. We had talked about this possibility and prepped for it. From a pouch on my chest harness, right next to my magazine pouches, I pulled a shiny button of silver metal, removed a plastic cover, and adhered it to the device. The question was whether the infiltrator's remote had extra sensors in it or not. Motion, temperature, sound, anything that let it know someone or something was fiddling with its remote. No way to know and nothing to do about it.

A single red light lit up on Rikki's nose cone, indicating that the tiny EMP device I had placed was active and under my drone's control. With a hand signal, I sent him down the rest of the tunnel spoke to double check. He was gone for ten seconds then came whooshing back, his unlit dark exterior indicating he hadn't found anything else.

We moved back out to the central shaft, edged around the ledge, and then entered the next spoke. It took longer to find the remote this time, as it was placed much further down the tunnel, almost under the hangar. Sweat dripped down my face and my laser-resistant goggles were fogging in direct contradiction to Sergeant Rift's assurance that they wouldn't. These things were supposed to be tested three ways from Saturday, but I don't think they had ever put them in a tropically warm tunnel on the head of a nervous Ghurka who was hunting a killer drone.

Second EMP *coin* emplaced, we headed back to the shaft

and began to insert into tunnel number three. I was less than three meters into the spoke, head down, when my helmet smacked into Rikki's hovering carbon fiber body. He didn't move, staying pointed into the darkness ahead. I froze, resisting the incredibly powerful need to light up the tunnel. I had to trust my drone, no matter what my reptilian brain tried to tell me. If it needed lighting, he would have lit it. Instead, he was holding me in position with his still form against the top of my helmet. Then he knocked against my head, three times, just a soft rocking of his rounded form, enough for me to feel without any real sound. The light pressure against my helmet lifted and I raised my head, looking into the blackness, feeling the flutter of rotor wash as he moved away from me. He was telling me that he would proceed three times normal distance ahead, his sophisticated sensors obviously finding something different in this tunnel than the others.

I waited, sweat running down my brow, dripping off the end of my nose, spattering into the dusty floor of the spoke in the pool of helmet illumination. The goggles were approaching a dangerous foggy level of uselessness, but I resisted pulling them off. Suddenly everything went dark, the light from my helmet fading as a sharp chuffing noise filled the tunnel.

My lenses had darkened automatically, their automatic response to laser light, undoubtedly infrared in this case. But now I couldn't see and the sounds of something *clicking* my way fired my nerves, creating an instant, overwhelming biological imperative to *see*, a need that took charge of my left hand, forcing it to yank off the goggles. My right hand brought up the custom Glock on its own, the tritium night sights lining up before disappearing in a flare of white illumination as my index finger flicked on the weapon light before curling around the trigger.

A black multi-legged horror swarmed along the bundle of cables straight toward me, Rikki hovering alongside it.

Automatically my body moved sideways, right shoulder hitting the tunnel wall, pistol angle moving so that Rikki wasn't in the line of fire. "*Head down,*" my drone said. I dropped my face toward the floor, simultaneously pulling the trigger. The big pistol bucked in my hand, the normally deafening boom reduced to a merely sharp crack by the suppressor, and I felt a wave of something like a mist fall over my shoulders and arms. Then I heard Rikki's single shot.

"*Clear,*" Rikki said and I looked up to see the bot lying in front of me, frozen on its back.

"*Firing EMP devices,*" Rikki announced immediately.

"*Ajaya report,*" Yoshida's voice came over our heretofore silent helmet radio.

"Contact. One bot down. Rikki has fired EMPs," I reported even as Rikki flew past me and shot out of the spoke, going left.

"*Major, the drones in every hangar went berserk,*" Aaron's voice came over the comm. "*It stopped almost immediately except in hangar seven.*"

A single shot cracked in the distance. "*Hangar seven drones have stopped. There are casualties,*" Rift's voice came through.

"*Estevez and Rift provide aid. Aaron, call building security and request medical aid. Ajaya, secure the bot and meet me in the shaft,*" Yoshida ordered calmly.

My weapon light was still on the dead bot, my pistol never leaving the target during the whole conversation.

Carefully, I poked the metal carcass with the scalloped edges of the pistol light. It was dead. I shifted the gun slightly, reaching with my left hand to shut off the light before holstering it. The powerful LED on my left wrist lit up the back of my gloved hand and I froze. Hundreds of tiny glittering fibers stuck out of the back of my glove. I moved the light and found even more all up my arm and shoulder. Using all three lights, I could see that both hands, arms, and shoulders were peppered with the tiny crystal spikes, each less than a centimeter long and thinner in diameter than a human hair. A little freaked out, I shifted position and a cloud of glittering fibers floated down from my helmet. I stopped and took stock of my body. Nothing hurt, and my heart rate had been gradually slowing. The spider-silk bodysuit seemed to have stopped anything from penetrating, as had my ballistic gloves.

"I'm going to need decontaminating when I get out," I said. "Some kind of close range weapon."

"*Affirmative, Ajaya. Postulate toxic fibers fired from nose of infiltrator drone,*" Rikki said as he floated back into my tunnel. He had somehow known the bot was going to fire and warned me in time.

Moving *very* carefully, I picked up the dead bot and backed out of the tunnel, trying to avoid stirring up the needles. The major was already at the ladder and I had him go down first, waiting till he was completely out of the tunnel before I stepped on the ladder and gingerly climbed down with our trophy in hand.

When I stepped out of the tunnel, Sergeant Rift was there with a plasticized emergency blanket spread out on the floor, wearing a white disposable anti-tox suit. She pointed me onto the center of the blanket, then proceeded to spray me down with a foamy substance from a small blue canister the size of a home fire extinguisher.

"Helmet off. Drop it on that corner of the blanket. Goggles and chest harness next. No, leave your gloves on and hold still."

Then she stepped up and peeled the spider-silk suit off my body, leaving me naked except for my boots in front of her. I must have hunched or something because she just tutted. Then she sprayed my nude form with more foam. "I grew up with four brothers and I got two boys of my own. There's nothing special about another penis, Gurung. And you should be much more worried about whatever toxins are possibly on your junk than me seeing it. Now get your scrawny ass over to that other blanket."

I did and immediately got sprayed with a blue liquid that was cold and slimy. Then she handed me a white suit like her own, ordering me to pull it on over the slimy stuff while she carefully collected and disposed of her field-expedient decontamination suite.

CHAPTER 19

"You look like a Smurf," Kayla said.

I couldn't argue her point. My shirtless image in the mirror was a deep shade of blue, almost a purple. "Yeah, that has already been pointed out to me several times," I said.

Yoshida had shipped me right back to Zone D, where I underwent a more thorough decontamination, then got to shower and put on clean clothes from my go bag. The blue had already set in place by then and I heard all about it from virtually everyone who saw me, including my trainees. They all recognized decom chemicals, so they were mighty curious as to what I had gotten into. And I couldn't answer them, the major slapping a need-to-know order on everyone involved in the morning's exercise. So I couldn't even tell his own troops, and they respected that... but they didn't respect my pride much, not with all the blueberry jokes, blue balls—blue body, comments about the old Avatar movies, and about two dozen references to the cartoon Smurfs that were older than all of us but kept getting reintroduced to each new generation when the entertainment industry ran out of original ideas.

"Yo, Blue Bell. Major wants to see you," Estevez said, poking his head into the mixed-sex team locker room.

I threw on a shirt and headed toward the door. "Hey, you can tell your girlfriend that it's in honor of her blue peepers," Kayla said as I slipped out of the room, flashing her a single finger salute over one shoulder as I left.

"Whoa, that set in deep," Maya said as she caught sight of me entering the drone lab.

"Yup," I said, not in the mood to entertain more jokes. Sergeant Rift started laughing as soon as she saw me and everyone else looked up from the lab table where I could see the infiltrator bot lying in pieces.

"It's the Great Grape Ape," Aaron said with a snicker.

Rift broke off laughing and turned to fix him with a stellar glare. "*You* get to make jokes when *you* come under hostile fire protecting this city," she said, serious as a heart attack. The arrogant scientist went flat-faced and pale, frozen by her death stare. He finally nodded, which seemed to satisfy her. Yoshida was smiling a little as he watched the byplay, but now he turned to me, grin fading.

"Good shooting—as I would expect. Looks like you cored it right through the CPU and your drone shot out the connection to half of its legs," he said, pointing at the table. "From what our brain trust can figure out, it had left some kind of deadman command if it stopped transmitting. The remotes all triggered preset codes to the drones in the garages to go berserk and attack everyone nearby. When your Berkut fired off all the EMPs, *including* the one that I had just taken *my* hand off of," he said with a frown, "it fried the remotes and stopped the kill commands, except for the one we hadn't gotten to. But Rikki shot that remote to pieces before anyone died. Close, though. Five wounded workers, two of them in critical condition."

"So what kind of drone was it? I didn't recognize it," I asked.

"Something new. Mostly 3D print fabrications, with some scavenged parts from a Meerkat and a Crab," Maya said.

"The stuff it sprayed you with was a cloud of fiberglass needles coated with almost pure nicotine," Eric added.

"Nicotine?" I asked.

"It's an easily obtainable toxin which is lethal in high enough doses. I don't know how many of those needles you would have to get hit with to kill you, but even in lower doses, it is fairly debilitating," Aaron said.

"Making it a good weapon for an infiltrator that gets discovered by a human IT worker. Coat the face, hands, and neck, leaving them too sick to interfere with it," Yoshida said. "Its other weapon is an infrared laser for blinding, and it has a mechanical stinger with a reserve of more nicotine."

"So this thing was created brand-new by the Spiders?" I asked.

"Near as we can tell. Smaller than a Crab, armed with toxic weapons that can be refilled using refined tobacco or vape products as raw material. Relatively big CPU for hacking networks and lots of network connectors, including those remotes it left behind. The Spiders must have used the 3D printers on the remaining mothership drones," Maya said.

"That's terrifying. They're making new drones—for specialized missions," I said.

"Yes, Ajaya, and as you pointed out before, there is almost certainly one or more in the Citywide controller systems," Yoshida said.

I opened my mouth but nothing came out. It was worse than I had thought.

"Yeah, it's bad. I'm leaving in ten minutes to accompany General Davis when he briefs the White House," he said, glancing at his watch. "In the meantime, these three are going to build on Maya's excellent work and get more intelligence on where these things are in the City's network. Then we'll go after them. Ajaya, we're going to need you and your drone again. I don't have anyone with the effectiveness of you and your Rikki. Your drone alone saved who knows how many lives."

"Yeah, we're ready," I said, nodding.

"Good thing you're a *blue-blooded* American," he said over his shoulder as he headed for the door.

"Nice one, sir," Estevez said as he followed his boss out of the room.

"Mean little shit," I said to Rift.

"He's jealous. Follows the major like a dog. Hates it when anyone gets more attention from Yoshida than he does," she said with a shrug. "Now, ignore that crap and let me show you what I'm thinking for the next time you hunt those nasty little killer toasters."

"I'm hoping you're going to tell me we have something better than those foggy goggles?"

She smirked and crooked one finger at me. "Let Auntie Rift show you what she's got saved up for special occasions."

A couple of hours later, I was home, bothering Aama as she made dinner. My mom came in and did an immediate double take at my face. I'd taken another shower when I got home, but no dice on getting rid of my deep blueberry coloring. "No Smurf jokes, Mom. I've already heard like a hundred."

"I would never," she said, but she couldn't keep a twitch of a smile off her face. "I would, however, like to know what happened to turn you into a human grape?"

"Can't really say, Mom. It's the result of being decontaminated. There was some concern I had been exposed to dangerous toxins. I'm fine."

Her humor was gone, wiped clean as soon as I said *decontaminated*. Go figure. Moms, right?

"Ajaya…" she began.

"Mom, I'm fine. All checked out. No exposure. It was a precaution which, unfortunately, I'll have to live with till it wears off."

"Some kind of spill in that defense lab?" she pressed.

"I can't talk about it. You know that."

"So I'll just have to ask Major Yoshida myself," she threatened.

"Make sure you tell him that I didn't say a word."

"He's not going to tell me either, is he?" she asked.

I shook my head. She studied me with those careful mom eyes. "You look tired."

I thought about that. Maybe. Maybe killer drones running through my dreams were disrupting my sleep. Maybe.

"Go take a nap, Ajaya, and let your poor grandmother finish her cooking," she said, waving me toward the door. I nodded and she stepped over to the counter to set down her purse and a bag of odds and ends groceries. Aama waited till her back was turned, then pressed a hot piece of naan into my hand as I headed to my room. I'd been lurking for a half hour without success, and all it took was a worried mother, and boom... naan nirvana.

My AI woke me from a dead nap, my head groggy and my stomach unsettled. Naps sometimes do that to me, but I shook most of it off when I watched Yoshida's video message.

"Ajaya, we're going in tonight. Pack your gear. We'll pick you up at 23:30 outside your place. Briefing on the way to our insertion point. No details till then. Get some rest."

"Time?"

"18:35, Ajaya," my virtual assistant said. I'd been napping for a couple of hours and probably missed dinner. But I needed calories in me now if I was going into another sketchy drone hunt, so I got up and left my bedroom.

The twins were settled around the dining table, doing homework or studying, Mom was paying bills, and Aama was stretched out in her recliner, watching one of her Bollywood movies.

Everyone turned to look at me, the twins' eyes widening as they got a look at my new skin color.

"We saved you some dinner," Mom said. "It's in the microwave."

Aama looked like she was going to power her recliner back down to get my food, but I quickly waved her off. She didn't take much convincing, settling back to watch one of the never-ending song and dance scenes.

I heated my food, my peripheral vision picking up on my sisters' glances, and I waited for a comment, but they very uncharacteristically didn't utter a peep. Making a bet with myself, I tapped my watch, starting a timer.

Bringing the reheated food to the table, I settled down with Mom on my left, Gabby on my right, and Monique across the table. No one spoke. The minutes ticked by, just the click of my fork and the tapping of Mom's fingers on her virtual keyboard. She's old-school, likes to input the bills herself rather than just directing her AI assistant to do it.

I kept my eyes on either my food or the center of the table, waiting as I ate. Mom must have laid down the law on the girls, but that could only hold so long. My bet with myself was ten minutes, tops. At ten minutes, forty-seven seconds, Gabby looked up at her twin. "Want some juice?"

"Actually, it's funny you ask... I'm craving grape juice," Monique said without a glance my way.

"Exactly what I was gonna get. Also, anyone want grape jelly on toast?" Gabby asked.

"I'll take some blueberry pie if we have it," Aama said from her recliner, piling on.

Mom's head came up but she didn't say anything, instead just looking at each of the others. It got real quiet. I looked at Gabby.

"Are there any gummies left? The purple ones?" I asked.

My little sister froze for a split second, then cracked a huge smile. Aama snorted and Monique laughed out loud. Mom finally smiled, but her eyes were watching me carefully.

"I have to leave a little after eleven," I said.

"Date?" Mom asked, her voice hopeful.

I shook my head. "Work."

"Really?" Monique asked. "You're going into the shacking Zone at night?"

Mom didn't even correct her language, instead waiting, frozen, to hear my response.

"No, not the Zone. A bit less dangerous than that, but really important."

"Can't one of these hotshot soldiers you've been training do whatever it is?" Gabby asked.

"None of them have the necessary experience. They'd all do it if they knew, but they would be much less likely to succeed. Major Yoshida and I will do it."

"He's going in *with* you?" Mom asked, leaning forward.

"Like he did this afternoon."

"You mean when you got exposed to something that needed to be decontaminated?" Mom asked, eyebrows up and tone chilly.

"It turned out to be unnecessary, but we didn't know that till after. The grape effect was a precaution, that's all."

"When does this end, Ajaya?" Mom asked.

"I don't know, Mom, but I *am* training my replacements and they're doing really well. This thing I'm doing tonight has to be done, and I'm the best choice. I won't say it's not dangerous, but it is arguably less so than going into the Zone."

"But requires decontamination?" she asked.

"Would you rather we go overboard for safety or cut corners?" I asked back.

"Not fair, Ajaya."

"Mom, this *job* directly impacts *our* family safety, as well as everyone in the city. And Rikki and I are the best at this. So yes, I'm doing a night job, and yes, there is danger, but we're taking even more precautions tonight than we did today."

She held my gaze for a moment and then deflated. "I just want this done, all of this done. It's been too long and we've given too much," she said, her expression now hopelessly sad.

My sisters glared at me like I had just stomped on Mom's heart with booted feet. "Mom, I can't tell you much. But it is a drone hunt and with Rikki, I'm the best. And it's not the Zone."

"Wait, you're hunting a drone and it's not in the Zone?" Monique asked.

I nodded.
"Something got out?" her sister asked.

"Not that any of *you* know!" I said. "It's much less dangerous than almost anything in the Zone. Now, that's all I'm going to say."

In hindsight, I shouldn't have said even that, especially about the level of danger. Sometimes your words come back to bite you on the ass.

CHAPTER 20

The Department of Citywide Administrative Services, or DCAS, used to be housed, like most of the Big Apple's municipal offices, in Manhattan. Nowadays it was spread out across the other boroughs, but with most of its offices in Brooklyn. The DCAS IT department was housed below the old Brooklyn Municipal Building on Joralemon Street. Not directly below, but under two of the neighboring buildings that the City purchased through eminent domain after Drone Night.

Aaron had the wireframe layout up on a portable workstation in the back of a tricked-out Mercedes van that Zone Defense must have had squirreled away in its equipment depots.

Cutting-edge technology packed into a shockingly spacious area. There was enough room for Yoshida and me to gear up while listening to the briefing, while the four trainees from my dream squad observed. Yoshida had clued them in to the day's events, and they were on hand with their drones if we needed additional assets.

"Citywide traffic is controlled from the computing center under the Brooklyn complex, but there are over fifteen conduit tunnels connecting from the center that each distribute the traffic and transit AI's commands throughout the city. The same tunnels are used for the electrical smartgrid, the water and sewer systems, streetlight control, and emergency response networks," Aaron lectured.

"Fifteen?" I asked.

"Yes, but if you'd let me talk, I would have told you that we've eliminated six of the branches. *All* of the accidents have happened in areas whose command nodes are one of the remaining nine," he said.

"That means there are likely drones in those nine, but it doesn't eliminate the other six from consideration. There could be sleeper units waiting for activation," Gunny Kwan said.

None of my four *trainees* were bashful about asking questions or speaking their minds, as I already knew, and it was kind of fun to watch Aaron deal with their directness.

"Yes, possible, but considered unlikely. So we'll go with the nine probables. We won't, however, leave without checking the other six," Aaron said.

"Who's this *we?*" Tyson Perry asked.

Aaron got flustered but he answered. "You four will check them out, but after Major Yoshida and Gurung get done with the other nine. You all are, as I understand it, our reserve force."

"Right."

"The major has also sent the rest of the trainees, along with his remaining squad members, to the terminating ends of every one of the tunnels. It's likely that a lightly armed infiltrator bot will choose escape and evasion over confrontation. Should anything run out that far, the Kestrels will sense them and they can be stopped," Aaron finished.

"Ajaya? What do you think?" Yoshida asked, looking at

me.

"I think it would be better for one of these four to follow each of us as we clear the nine tunnels. We'll switch them out at each tunnel change, but that way we'll have backup in the tunnel with us and they'll get experience before they clear the last six," I said.

Yoshida was mildly surprised, at least if I read his expression correctly. It was often hard to tell, but I was getting better at it.

He glanced over at the four soldiers. "What do you think? Ready to get real?"

Every one of them nodded instantly, no hesitation. "I like it," Elizabeth Kottos said before turning my way. "How far back would we be?"

"Six or seven meters, with your Kestrel between us and you. Our drones will be out front, then us, then yours, and finally you. Four layers of containment. You've updated your drones with the infiltrator's specs?"

Four voices said "Affirmative" almost at the same time.

"It leaves the reserve force down to whichever two of them aren't in the tunnels with us?" Yoshida asked me, tone clearly questioning me.

"Any more than two people and two drones at a time is going to get too crowded in those tunnels. Four people would just get in each other's way," I said with a shrug. "I think they're more valuable in the tunnels, learning and backing us up. We may have a whole lot of these infiltrators to hunt down, not just here, but who knows where else. You need operators with experience."

He nodded almost as soon as I finished. "Yeah, I agree. Kottos and Gunny Kwan, you're first up. Perry and Abate alternate."

"Who is with who?" Abate asked.

"Your four work it out. I don't care and I'm not gonna let Ajaya play favorites," the major said, giving me a level stare.

"These four *are* my favorites," I said with a shrug. "You got any more of these fancy suits for them, Sarge?" I asked Rift.

She snorted, giving me a disgusted look. The suits in question were modifications of what we had worn earlier. She had come up with changes while Yoshida and I were in the hive.

Apparently she had access to some automated fabricators because the spider-silk bodysuits now had shoulder, upper and lower arm, back, thigh, and knee armor affixed to them. It was a much thicker pad of something like Spectra fiber or Kevlar. Not sure. The hard helmets had been replaced with form-fitted carbon fiber shells with built-in lighting and a face mask that offered better laser protection than the goggles had, as well as both thermal and light-enhancing vision modes. Best yet, the face mask allowed greater air flow, greatly reducing the risk of fogging. Matching gloves with lights attached to the back of the hand finished it out. We wore the regular Zone D boots that I seemed to go through by the half-dozen. Between the black clinging skin and the armor pads and reflective face masks, we looked like someone's vision of dystopian storm troopers.

Rift issued suits that were already sized for the four soldiers, and they stripped to their underwear on the spot and put them on. The major and I were already suited up and studying the tunnel maps, trying to ignore the sudden mobile locker room feel.

We were going in with live AI assistants and voice comm, so we'd have the tunnel layout projected in our face-plates, but knowing the map without electronic aids was still required.

Electromagnetic detection was useless in these heavily cabled tunnels, just like it had been in the hive. We would have to go with visual cues to spot the Spiders' infiltrator or infiltrators, which frankly favored our drones over our merely human eyes. The black shell of the infiltrator bot would have looked a lot like any other piece of high-tech infrastructure to me, had I seen it first. I had Rikki share his visual files with the science types and they, in turn, had updated everyone else's drones to look for the same cues. The thermal and night vision features of the new face masks might or might not help, depending on how active the bot was and what the background temperatures were. Despite what I told Mom, this was going to be dangerous.

The municipal building was almost empty at midnight, but the few people who met us were pretty high level. The Deputy Mayor was on hand, as was the Police Commissioner, a bunch of their aides, the DCAS Commissioner, and the deputy commissioners for IT, Facilities Management, and Energy Management, plus a small group of underlings who were the people who actually knew how things worked, had the keys to the locks, and were truly useful. Luckily for Yoshida, General Davis and some of his senior staff were already there to interface with the important people and let us get down to business with the useful people.

Our big van backed right up to a side entrance and we went inside, past all the suits, and directly down into the tunnels. The complaining and political maneuvering paused for a few seconds as we filed past the brass, our drones hovering alongside us.

"Why is that drone different?" a self-important looking man asked the general. I was looking straight ahead but didn't make it by them. "Ajaya?" the general called out. I stopped and turned to face them while the rest of team moved swiftly to the stairwell.

"Yes, General?" I asked, Rikki hovering by my right shoulder.

"Ajaya, this is Deputy Mayor Haskell," Davis said, turning to the DM. "I suspect you recognize this young man, Donald? Unless you never watch any programming at all."

"Oh, you're the one who hunts the drones. And that is a real Berkut?" Donald Haskell, Deputy Mayor of New York City, asked, staring at Rikki with an expression of half fear, half fascination.

General Davis had me fixed with a penetrating stare, doing his own bang-up job of nonverbal communication.

"Yes sir, Rikki is a Berkut, although he's been heavily modified, so probably only about half of him is original."

"I thought they were triangular?" The DM asked.

"The Berkut has two flight modes, Don," Davis said. "This rounded form is easier to maneuver in small tight places, right Ajaya?"

I knew my cues even without prior Explain action. "Yes sir, General. Gives him an advantage in the tunnels. Sirs, if you don't mind, I need to catch up with the team if Rikki and I are going get underground and root this bot out," I said.

"Yes, Ajaya, go on. We want our most experienced hunters down there," Davis said, letting me beat feet into the stairwell. Behind me, the DM's loud voice carried. "He's really good, right?"

"Yes Don, that's why he's here," Davis agreed, his voice dropping in what I guessed was further reassurance. I shook my head and followed my drone down the stairs.

CHAPTER 21

The team was just ahead of us as we arrived in the basement, and Tyson looked back at me with a knowing grin. I caught up to them just as the IT folks were unlocking the doors to their kingdom. Our three science types were deep in conversation with their City counterparts while the no-nonsense facilities guy showed us the utility tunnels access.

"Ready, Ajaya?" Yoshida asked, his hands checking over his gear in a kind of pre-op ritual that I had seen him do at the hive.

"Yeah, I'll take tunnel one with Kottos and Abate. We'll move up to where it branches into three. Carl will guard the junction while Elizabeth follows me into the first branch. After that, they'll switch and we'll clear the second, doing it again for the third. You'll be in the second main artery with Tyson and Gunny Kwan running the same drill. If nothing pops out at us, we'll all regroup and move to the third artery, which has five branches," I recounted.

"Correct. Everyone clear? Rift, you're in charge of the fail safe squad. You're security and backup, but none of you have your powered armor, so remember you are not invulnerable."

The troopers who had accompanied us wore standard Zone Defense gear and regular body armor, but all five were drawn from Yoshida's strike force group.

"Alright, let's do this," the major said, and with that, we headed in, leaving everyone else behind.

I moved into the tunnel, which was at least partially illuminated by a row of overhead bulbs. This part was wider than what awaited us up ahead, a really big conduit of fiber optics and regular data lines running along the center ceiling of the straight-sided corridor. But after a short ten or twelve meters, it changed into a rounded room with round openings for three smaller tunnels. I turned and made eye contact with Kottos and Abate, who both nodded and drew their sidearms. All three drones moved around the node junction, checking for any bots. When they came up empty, I nodded at my partners and then waved Rikki into tunnel one, crouching to follow.

The smaller tunnel had just enough height for me to walk hunched over and was only illuminated with a series of small LEDs that were more spread out than in the main tunnel. "Brutus is on your six," Kottos said in my earpiece. Most of the trainees had taken to the idea of naming their drones, with most of the nicknames sounding like they were borrowed from childhood pets.

"Roger that," I said, all my lights on as I focused on the thick utility cable while staying aware of Rikki's actions ahead of me. We moved slowly and carefully, dropping down to knees to peer under and around the conduit structure. Rikki was a dark form ahead, just slightly lighter than his surroundings in the enhanced vision of the face mask.

We travelled that way for a hundred meters, that being the predefined limit for our mission parameters. It was possible the infiltrators could be further down, but it had been determined by our brain trust that it was unlikely for units attempting to control multiple traffic or city systems. If we found nothing in the first set of sweeps, we would go back and run the tunnels for three times that distance and send the drones out even further.

Yoshida had told me that General Davis was all for us just sending the drones in alone without humans at risk, but the major had countered that it would be hard to certify to the powers above that a tunnel was clear without direct human oversight. Personally, I was pretty certain that the drones were better equipped for this hunt than we were, but Davis had ended up agreeing with Yoshida. I imagine it would be easier to answer questions from up the food chain with boots on the scene.

At the end of our limit, we turned in place, Brutus moving past Elizabeth to take the lead while Rikki stayed behind me to provide rear security. "Let's keep a sharp eye on the way out, as it can look different from this point of view," I said, knowing that she would likely have done that as a matter of course. She was a good five or six years older than I was, and it was like me telling Aama how to weave blankets.

"Affirmative," was her only answer. I noticed that she didn't have to hunch over like I did and allowed myself to notice that she was in excellent shape before banishing everything from my mind but staying alert.

We came back out to the node, moved to the next tunnel, and Carl Abate and his Kestrel Hawkeye took the six o'clock positions. We made it ten meters in when our earpiece came alive.

"*Contact*," Yoshida's voice said, followed by a gunshot, then another. "*It's by me. Gunny, it's coming your way.*" The sound of a Kestrel firing, then a pistol.

"*It's hit but still moving. Bird dog, fetch!*" came Max Kwan's southern twang. Two more Kestrel shots. *"Target down."*

Ahead of me, Carl Abate turned to glance back at me and meet my eyes, his expression a careful excitement mixed with satisfaction. One of the trainees had scored. Then his eyes flicked over my shoulder and widened. Simultaneously, I heard Rikki tick five times fast. I dropped to my knees and twisted at the same time, my pistol coming up. A black horror of plastic and legs was racing toward me along the conduit, a shiny needle reflecting a gleam of light. It was between me and Rikki, foiling his shot.

"Rikki, down!" I said, pulling the trigger a heartbeat later. The big pistol thumped in my hand, then thumped again as my drone dropped to the tunnel floor. My first shot glanced off the hard shell of the needle-nosed bot, just skimming the angled surface, but my second round tore through the shoulder segment, knocking the bot slightly sideways. It tried to right itself, gave up, and fell to the floor. Rikki lifted up, tilted down, and flew over it as I fired again. His own gun barrel stuttered three times, then twice more as the bot twitched on the ground.

"Contact, target down. It came from behind..." was all I got out when my comm went nuts with multiple voices and gunshots. One of those voices was Elizabeth's. I turned, yelling into my microphone, "Carl, go."

To his credit, he was, I think, a milisecond from making that choice on his own, but my yell freed his feet faster and he ran back down the tunnel toward the gunshots we could hear, while more shots and voices filled my ear.

I turned to Rikki. "Clear?"

"Clear. Unit secure," came the response, which freed my own feet to race to the node junction.

When I got out, I found Carl standing up and pulling his

pistol back from the head segment of another infiltrator. Elizabeth was back against the wall, her booted foot on the drone bot's head, her weapon in a two-hand hold, Brutus hovering over the still-twitching bot.

"*Status?*" Yoshida's voice demanded over the comm.

I looked at the other two, saw Elizabeth pull two centimeters of the infiltrator's poison needle from the bottom of her boot. She looked at me with a thumbs up. It hadn't penetrated the shank of her tough recycled plastic footwear. I got a nod of affirmation from Carl that he was okay and replied, "Two targets down. One from second tunnel and one from..." I glanced at Elizabeth, who pointed to the third tunnel, "the tunnel we hadn't cleared yet. No injuries. Be warned that one of them went undetected by Rikki until it attacked."

"*Determine how, immediately!*" Yoshida said.

"You guys okay?"

They both nodded, both almost simultaneously dropping their partial magazines and slamming fresh ones into their pistols.

I went back into the tunnel with Rikki, moving slowly and scanning everything till we got to the dead bot. Rikki flew further back to the point where the bot had appeared. Powerful LEDs lit up the ceiling as I moved closer. Up in the concrete roof of the tunnel was a small hollow, a squared-off section that must have once housed something else but was now empty. It was just big enough for the Spider's spy to hide itself.

I used my virtual assistant to video the spot, then headed back out. When I got to the node, carrying the dead bot, I found Yoshida and Rift waiting with Kottos and Abate. I had the AI send the video to the whole team as I threw the spybot on the ground next to the other one.

Eric came hurrying up with a metal case. He was wearing latex gloves, eyes focused on the bots.

"Alright. We're going to send drones down every one of the tunnels all the way to the end and then back. We'll have them look for these kind of spots particularly. Then we'll have the waiting soldiers work their way back to us to verify. We can't afford to miss any of them," Yoshida said.

We did just that. Sending drones back and forth, scouring the tunnels much faster than humans could. Then Yoshida's waiting troops at the tunnel ends walked back down them to our end, doing a second, slower sweep. We ended up driving two more out into the open, where the drones killed them dead. All told, we had the two from our node, three from Yoshida's, and the other two from the remaining tunnels combined.

Our group, the original response team, saddled up and headed out as the sky was turning the purple of predawn. The remaining soldiers would come along after the last sweeps. None of the suits were still there when we exited the muni building, but from Yoshida's terse comments and orders, I was thinking that the general was highly concerned. Seven infiltrators in the city systems and one in the biggest corporation on Earth. So not good for the head of Zone Defense.

The van dropped me at my door, the major giving me a instructions to be back at Roosevelt by eleven hundred hours.

Weary, I carried my almost depleted Berkut up to the apartment, let myself in, and crashed hard.

CHAPTER 22

I was just suddenly sitting upright, in complete darkness, heart drumming, breathing too fast, listening for the scuttle of the bot. Where was my gun? A light? Where was I? And why couldn't I hear the killer coming my way?

Tick-tick-tick-tick. Fast, flowing together, followed by another four ticks. Rikki? A tiny light suddenly illuminating the tunnel. Only it wasn't a tunnel. My room? The familiar whir of fans brought the light my way and then a slight weight settled on my legs. A dream? No, a nightmare. But I couldn't remember any of it, just terror. My t-shirt and shorts were soaked with sweat, but my heart at least had stopped trying to gallop out of my chest and my breathing slowed as I focused on the weight of my drone. "Ssstatus?" I croaked out.

"Clear. Out of the Zone. In Gurung quarters. No hostile UAV or UGVs within sensor range," came the quiet reply.

Home. I was home. No drones other than mine. "Light," I said and my AI assistant turned on the room lights, blinding me. "Dim." The bright flare lessened to a soft glow.

Nothing—just my room. Picking up Rikki, I set him on the bed, then moved across the room to my dresser, where I grabbed a little LED light, pulled my pistol from my harness, and then, as an afterthought, grabbed my kukri as well. I set all three on my bedside table and climbed back under the covers. The apartment was all quiet. "Time?"

"Oh-four-thirty-two," Rikki replied, beating the assistant by half a second. I'd only been asleep for maybe forty minutes.

I lay back, suddenly cold, and pulled my blankets over my clammy skin. Tried to remember the dream. Just flashes of blood and fear with no context or content. A feeling of hopeless terror.

Rikki suddenly lifted off the bed, hovered forward, the breeze of his fans fluttering the sheets before he lowered down to settle on my chest. Our standard position for sleeping in the Zone. Me on my back, weapons at hand, his light weight on my chest to warn me of approaching danger with the least amount of noise or disturbance.

I had had a nightmare. Just a dream gone bad. But we were safe in our apartment, the best detection system possible had just given the all clear and now was lying on me in our combat rest position.

"Weapon status?"

"Armed. Magazine full."

I had stopped checking weapons with the local NYPD precinct at the first thought of danger to my family. Rikki was one of my most powerful weapons and likely the first to detect a problem, so he was staying fully armed as far as I was concerned. Mom knew, and Aama had always thought all weapons should always be loaded. The twins didn't know, but probably didn't care. They had been trained to be weapon savvy from birth and were totally comfortable with my drone, which was good because his current mission parameters were to protect them above all else.

Mental security checklist complete, I let my eyes close and tried some breathing techniques my father had taught me. My heart slowed but I still saw flashes of wet red and *felt* the rattle of steel claws against the ground.

It was a long time before I fell into a restless sleep.

When I finally made it out to the family room later that morning, I found the whole fam awake and lounging around, the evil twins still in their pajamas while Mom and Aama were dressed but very casually.

"What, no school?" I asked, heading for the coffee.

"Saturday, bonehead," Gabby shot back without looking up from the holo fashion projection she was lazily purveying. Creature Two was studying a tablet, which likely meant she was reading blogs, with the highest probability being celebrity news.

I was mildly stunned that it was Saturday... I had lost all track of the calendar.

"You got in late?" Mom asked.

"More like I got in early... this morning."

"And it went okay?"

"Yeah. But there's a whole hornets' nest stirred up now. Drones have escaped the Zone," I said.

"Should we leave?" she asked, her quiet words causing the twins to snap around so fast, it's a wonder their spines stayed intact.

"Leave? Why would we leave?" Monique asked, her tone already taking on a dangerous note of rebellion.

"Did you not hear your brother? Drones have escaped the

Zone," Mom said, her voice even and direct.

"They what?" Gabby asked, sitting upright.

"A small number of modified bots have gotten out," I said. "They have been focused on infiltrating computer systems, and if they have had access to outside networks, then they know all of our names and roughly where we live. They likely know the address for the building across the street, but yes, there is a risk they could find us here. There could come a time when you should all head upstate to visit Grandpa and Grandma," I said.

Neither terrible twin said a word, which was frankly more disturbing than if they had freaked out. They looked scared and I felt like complete shit.

"Girls, do you have your emergency bags packed?" Mom asked, voice all business. Emergency bags?

"Yes, Mom," they said at exactly the same time and in the same voice. It weirds some people out, just like when they start and finish each other's sentences. I ignored it, still back on the go bags. When had that happened?

Mom smiled at my expression. "We've been prepared since Drone Night," she said.

"Of course we have," Aama said. "Did you think we didn't learn any lessons?"

"I never thought about it," I answered honestly.

"Because you were with your father, learning the Zone. But being prepared was and is just as important to us. Girls, I suggest you update anything that you can't live without, remembering that you have to keep the same bags. No increase in size."

"Okay," Gabby said, frowning. Monique was already

standing up to go and I was wondering who these girls were and what had happened to my sisters. Then they were off to their room, chattering rapidly about who was taking what.

I looked at Mom and Aama.

"They are Ghurka too, Ajaya," Aama said, handing me a plate of breakfast.

Just when you think you know the people you grew up with.

Zone Defense was buzzing when I got there, a hive turned upside down. But an orderly hive, as the worker bees either continued their tasks, albeit with a note of anxiety, or streamed down the halls toward the auditorium. A couple of Yoshida's people saw me, nodding at me in greeting.

"What's going on?" I asked.

"No need to get all blue in the face; it's a briefing," Specialist Corcoran said with a laugh at her own joke. Short and muscular, she was almost always smiling. "We're all supposed to go, your sneaky students too, plus most of the active force on duty."

Her companion, Specialist Rose, on the other hand, always seemed a bit morose. She was my height and also muscular. Actually, muscular described every single one of Yoshida's people. Most active military are fit, but the major's group took it to almost religious levels.

"Oh, I hadn't heard. The major just told me to report in by eleven hundred," I said, falling into step with them.

"I'm sure you're supposed to be there as well. Heard you were out half the night in tunnels," Corcoran said.

"You guys weren't part of the fun?"

"Nope, we had the night off. But rumor has it that's about to change. Leaves are all cancelled," the young soldier said with her trademark smile.

I rubbed my face. "This shit takes forever to wear off."

Corcoran laughed. "It's actually almost gone, but Sergeant Rift has been highly amused by it, so, well, you know."

"Anything for morale," I said. Corcoran laughed again and even Rose made a noise. More of a grunt than a laugh, but whatever.

We entered the auditorium up at the back and wound down the sides to find a lower level. The two specialists moved to a cluster of their own squad mates, who were sitting about halfway down the slope of the amphitheater-style seating. Two rows of seats in front of them were open, then there was another cluster of soldiers, my trainees.

I ended up picking a seat on the aisle in one of the empty rows between the two groups. I had to smile as I pictured Astrid analyzing my choice. She had always been intrigued by psychology. She'd say something about me seeing myself as an outsider between the two groups, belonging to neither but involved with both.

Down front, in the swarm of admin officers, I spotted both General Davis and Major Yoshida as well as a half dozen of the more senior officers I was slightly familiar with. I also saw Agents Black and White sitting in front seats between the officers and a large group of dark suits. Lots of suits. Last night's activities had really kicked the government in the teeth.

General Davis stood up and moved to the front, turning to face the audience. The hum of voices cut off like a switch had been thrown, at least among the soldiers. The suits didn't have the instant discipline of military.

Davis waited a moment more than he normally did, looking at the cluster of important civilians till they quieted down.

"At twelve thirty-one hundred hours this morning, Zone Defense personnel began an operation underneath Brooklyn, inside the municipal computing complex. During the ensuing hours, we disabled and collected seven drones of unknown construction interspersed throughout the city control network," Davis said. Behind him, holographic images appeared, showing a line of dead and damaged infiltrators on a white table.

"Earlier yesterday, a single similar unit was recovered inside a corporate drone hive in New Jersey," he continued. The images pulled back, getting small enough to now include another unit set slightly apart from the others.

"While examinations continue, we are more than reasonably certain that these units came from within the Zone."

The civilians reacted with a mixture of fear, disbelief, outrage, and shock. The military folks contained their responses better, but theirs was a blend of shame, guilt, and anger.

"Dr. Aaron Zurloft will comment on their designs which, as I mentioned, are unique and previously unknown."

Davis stepped back and Yoshida's pet scientist moved confidently into his space.

"The units you see before you are composed of approximately sixty-five percent 3D printed parts and thirty-five percent salvaged pieces from a combination of Crab and Meerkat UGVs. No two are exactly identical, yet all eight share many features. The seven found in the municipal computing area range from this simple specimen, which is armed with just a hypodermic needle and a small vial of very outdated hydrogen cyanide, to this unit that has multiple hypodermic injection needles, several toxins, and a dual-purpose laser that can both interface with a fiber optic system as well as potentially blind a human.

"The first unit has mismatched legs. The second uses mixed pairs of matching appendages, but the remaining five all use complete sets from either Crab or Meerkat, but not both.

"Our working hypothesis is that the increasing sophistication of each unit indicates a steady refinement and improvement of design."

He paused and looked out over the audience, very comfortable with lecturing. "The eighth unit gave us pause. It was recovered first, and our initial theory was that it was an earlier experiment before the others were emplaced in the city systems. But analysis and comparison show it to be the newest and most sophisticated yet. It uses matched pairs of appendages, but each pair is carefully selected from donor UGVs to balance the overall unit. Its weapons are more advanced, using a hypodermic of freshly purified nicotine, a more powerful laser, and a new weapon, something we're calling a pneumatic shotgun. Uses air compressed in chambers by the action of the front two legs to propel a cloud of fiberglass needles coated in nicotine. And this machine is the only one that had detachable sensors it could emplace around its area of operation.

"Which leads us to the conclusion that it was the most recently placed infiltration unit."

A suit in the front row spoke suddenly. "What evidence do you have that these things are from inside the Zone?"

Aaron didn't even blink. "Analysis of the printed components is a near one hundred percent match for the 3D printers of the Chinese mothership units that were part of the original release. Also, the remote detachable sensors are basically stripped-down versions of the Wasps that motherships carry. And the rest of the parts, all salvaged, come from the exact models of Indian and Chinese bots that inhabit the Zone, with serial numbers from the lists of units released on Drone Night as provided by the original manufacturers. And the programming is very much Chinese Spider."

"You're asserting that these machines were built and programmed by the Spiders in the Zone," the same man said, his eyes angry and his tone skeptical.

"Yes," Aaron said.

The man boggled at him for a moment while the silence grew, till he finally blurted out, "That's ridiculous!"

"Parts printed by printers only found inside the Zone. Other parts taken from units whose serial numbers were listed on the invoices of drones sold to the terrorists, and complicated, sophisticated software code that exactly matches code from the Spider unit recovered several months ago," Aaron said, ticking off the points on his fingers.

I didn't like the guy, but he had a certain style and authority in the moment.

"How could you compare code to a unit you don't have?" the suit asked with almost a sneer.

"Because Aaron and his associates gave *me* copies of their work before your people removed all the rest, Tim," General Davis said, moving forward. I wasn't aware of that, but it fit with Yoshida's professional paranoia.

"You were ordered to turn over all material," this guy, Tim, said, really angry now.

"No, the orders indicated that Major Yoshida and his people were to turn over all *their* notes, files, and evidence. Nowhere in the orders was *I* mentioned at all. So their analysis of this situation isn't something you can cover up," Davis said.

The Tim guy looked like he was going to grab a weapon and murder the general, but another suit, four places down, suddenly spoke up with no regard for the obvious tension.

"General, setting aside the massively disturbing implications of drones producing drones, how would these things have gotten out of the containment area?"

"We have recently found a small number of weak points in the perimeter barrier where a well-shielded unit of small enough size could possibly get through. The outer shells of all eight captured UGVs have finely sintered metal circuits printed right into them," Davis said. "We experimented in the most likely weak point and found the EM detectors didn't register enough signal to set off an alarm."

"So you are telling us that an unknown number of drone-designed UGVs have escaped the Zone and have infiltrated who knows where?" the same guy asked.

"Yes, Director Weber, that's exactly what we're saying."

"And what are you currently doing about it?" Director

Weber asked. No idea what he was director of.

"We found these units by sophisticated analysis of recent drone accidents, vehicle system accidents, and control network errors. In other words, we're looking for mistakes that shouldn't happen. We've begun widening our parameters but frankly, Director, this is more your bailiwick than ours. I would like to have my people provide details on what they're running and let your folks take it much, much further," Davis said.

Okay, that was a clue. NSA maybe?

"I see. Has anyone informed the president?" Director Weber asked.

"I have done that at the direction of General Urses. About an hour ago," Davis said.

Something about his expression told me he hadn't enjoyed the experience in any way. Of course, telling the President of the United States that the first drone escape from the Manhattan Drone Zone in ten years occurred on your watch couldn't be a great thing, now could it?

"And?"

"The president has instructed Zone Defense to do everything and anything we need to in order to, number one, find any more of these things, and two, stop them at the source," Davis said.

"Meaning what?" Tim asked.

"Meaning we are to find and destroy the last two Spiders, the units known as Peony and Plum Blossom."

"Haven't you been hunting the Spiders for years?" Tim asked.

"Yes, and as you know better than anyone, we've had recent success," Davis said, eyes locked on the other man.

I felt eyes on *me* at that exact moment. Glancing around, I found Yoshida twisted in his seat, looking at me. He nodded once.

"Major Yoshida?" Davis said, causing the major to snap around.

"Yes sir?"

The general waved a hand at the stage and, taking the hint, Yoshida popped up smoothly from his seat.

"We have been training a team of talented special operators to penetrate the Zone using drones as watchdogs. We'll use them to hunt the Spiders," Yoshida said, directing his attention to the suits but waving a hand at the trainees.

Tim, from who knows what agency, frowned, but Director Weber just looked curious.

"The island is an awfully big place for a couple of dozen people to hunt down the most dangerous drones on the planet," Weber said.

"Yes, Director, but well... we have a plan. We're going to hunt them over bait," Yoshida explained.

CHAPTER 23

"You know what? The saddest part of this whole thing is that my girlfriend's dad predicted almost exactly this," I said.

"Oh, shut up already. You may not like him, but even you have to admit that my father isn't a stupid man," Astrid said, fixing something on the collar of my shirt. "Alright, it's almost time. Ready?"

No, Brad Johnson wasn't stupid at all. Smart, in fact, if a trifle light on morals. Really light.

The lady with the clipboard and the earpiece turned to us and pointed, but Astrid, through long familiarity, was already walking forward, holding my hand, pulling me onto the set.

"Ah, here they are. Look at them, the cutest damned couple to hunt the Zone," Cade Kallow said as we came into camera view.

"Such a smooth talker," Astrid said, smiling and completely at ease in front of the cameras. Me, I could feel a dribble of sweat forming on the back of my neck and my pits were a bit too moist as well.

"The warrior princess and the deadly hunter," Cade said, smiling his trademark smile.

"Meeting the celebrated bard," I said, mouth running without me thinking.

Cade laughed, delighted with my comeback. He turned to the camera. "Have I mentioned how much I love having these two on the show?" He turned back in time to lean into a hug and cheek kiss with Astrid, then shook my hand with hearty enthusiasm.

Astrid took the seat next to Cade's right, and I sat next to her right.

He looked at us, smiling hugely. A consummate showman, I honestly thought he did, really truly, enjoy our infrequent on-air chats. Then he focused on me. "Ajaya, rumor has it that you're back on the market?"

I glanced down at my left hand, which was firmly holding Astrid's right one, then back up at Cade, a bewildered frown on my face. "Not unless Trid's forgot to tell me something," I said.

He laughed again. "Oh Lordy no. Never that. Let me rephrase that. Ajaya, I've heard you're dusting off your recovery business, ready to head back into the Zone?"

"Ah, yes, that's true."

"Your stint with Uncle Sam has finished?"

"Yes, it was always just going to be temporary. Training people on Zone survival and all that," I said.

"Well, glad to hear that our troops got the best instructor they could get," he said.

"Thanks, but I'm sure my instructor evaluations don't fully reflect that," I said.

"Oh, I don't know. I bet they valued your expertise."

"Oh, they did. I was working with the best of the best. Consummate professionals with years of experience. It's just that I've never been a teacher before, so you know... my lesson plans were, let's say, unusual."

"And they're done with you... just like that?" Cade asked.

"Yes. The door was left open for possible future engagements, but once these people get some time in the Zone, they'll likely be the ones to teach other soldiers."

"And so your recovery business is officially open again?"

"Yup. And I've already got requests," I said.

"Ajaya, I would only be surprised if you *weren't* swamped with recovery missions. When do you go back in?"

"I start tomorrow, bright and early."

"Any details?"

"Cade, Cade, please. You know I don't ever reveal possible recovery details," I said.

"It's my job to try, Ajaya," he said. "Astrid, how about Team Johnson? What's new with the Viking Clan?"

Astrid smoothly explained the latest weapon and equipment upgrades, then laughingly discussed her big brother JJ's current dating escapades, and then bantered with Cade as he tried to get her to throw shade on the other *Zone War* teams. I tossed in a quip or two, but my mission was done. I had accomplished exactly what I had needed to and now Astrid carried the conversation expertly. She had quite literally grown up on the show and her rapport with Cade gave *Zone War* a big chunk of its charm and appeal. The segment ended, Trinity Flottercot seemed pleased, the crew chatted with us for a few minutes, and we gradually worked our way out of the studio.

"That what you needed?" she asked me as we left the building.

"Yes. Exactly. Thank you," I said, kissing her cheek.

She pulled back and gave me a serious look. "I know you, AJ. That wasn't to drum up business. That was for something else."

"Yes, yes it was. We have a theory. That was a test of it."

"You think the Spiders will now know that you're going into the Zone tomorrow," she stated.

"Yeah. Pretty certain that they will."

"They watch the show?"

"In a manner of speaking. At least, we think they do."

"One of those infiltrators?"

"Yes. An old one. Maybe the oldest," I said. "The intelligence people went all out and found lots of little things that raised eyebrows. One of them was a pattern between team interviews and subsequent drone attacks. A big one was your family's own Spider attack. The show did one of those upcoming teasers indicating that your LAV was going into lower Manhattan that day, and lo and behold, a Spider trap."

"But it got changed at the last minute," she protested.

"Yes... by the show producers."

"So somewhere in that building is a bot?" she asked.

"That's our working theory."

"But you didn't say where you're going in," she said. "But then, you never do, so it would be out of character if you did."

"Can't make it too easy. Plus, it gives us a chance to see if the email servers I use to receive and accept contracts have been compromised. But even if they don't know *where* I go in, they'll be on the hunt."

"You're deliberately putting yourself at risk," she said, clearly unhappy with my choice.

"I take risks every time I go in. So do you. This really isn't different, well, except that I'll have a whole mess of highly skilled operators on overwatch."

"You don't think those things will figure that out?"

"Well, it's like old-time animal trapping. If they're too wary to come near the bait, we'll have to change our tactics."

"What if they just figure out a way to get the cheese and eat it too?" she asked.

I didn't have a witty answer for that.

CHAPTER 24

It was still dark out when I arrived at the Holland Tunnel checkpoint and Zone access control. Armed, suited up in the latest and greatest stealth suit that US government labs could provide, Rikki locked and loaded, with my plan all mapped out. Arguably the best prepared I have ever been when inserting into the Zone.

So why was I already sweating, even in the predawn chill, and why, exactly, were my hands shaking?

The sergeant at the tunnel doors gave me a once over before waving me through. Into the airlock, the massive doors silently swinging shut behind Rikki and me. The wall monitor showed infrared images outside the tunnel, both Canal and Spring Streets lit up with ghostly illumination. Nothing moving. Dark and cold, best time to insert, when the drones were at their lowest power levels.

I hit the big red button and the outer door unbolted itself before powerful hydraulics pushed it open. Rikki shot out into the darkness, fully charged and raring to go. I followed, slow and soft, rifle ready, eyes open wide, ears straining for sound. A cool mist fell over the dark streets and blackened buildings, a sharp and oh-so-eerie contrast to the distant lights of Brooklyn, far to the east. It took two blocks to shake off the sense of pessimism I was having, which had awoken me twice in the middle of the night. But the familiar rhythm of move and pause, of checking everything twice, of Rikki's quiet reassuring presence, all calmed me down. So I was a little cooler, a little less twitchy when we turned south onto Hudson Street.

The contract I had accepted was a phony, at least in that it had been sent by someone in a dark suit from an undisclosed government location that registered as a small corporation.

It called for me to locate a boutique wine store on Hudson Street, just south of 60 Hudson. My goal was to retrieve a case of rare, extremely collectible wine that had purportedly been in the store's possession on Drone Night.

It was a fairly common kind of request. In the days and weeks following the attack, a lot of information had been saved and processed about the kinds of valuable items abandoned in Manhattan. Insurance claim forms in particular provided people interested in specific items with a wealth of information. And many rare things just got more valuable as the years passed.

After ten years, an important vintage could gain enormous value, especially as people consumed more of the other bottles that existed.

Lotus had hung out at 60 Hudson Street—alot, according to the log recorder Yoshida's people had found. Our theory was predicated on one of the remaining Spiders needing to take over accessing the world networks from the massive internet hub complex.

My path was going to take me right by the building, and our plan called for pairs of newly trained special operators moving into position from the west side. I was pretty worried about them. Yeah, they had many, many years of experience in combat, had been using military drones forever, but the Zone was different. They were much better prepared than my first four, but it was still sooner than I would have liked.

Most, if not all, of them should be in the Zone already, having inserted via military watercraft along the waterfront. We had paired them so that at least one sniper type was in each group. When I moved past the internet hub building, we were hoping to lure a Spider out to play. My overwatch group would help protect me from any and all drones and maybe nail the Spider. Render drones were set up to provide heavy cover to the east of my position. We were pretty sure the plan would fall apart somewhere along the way, but we hoped to flush out Peony or Plum Blossom, kill some drones, and maybe get lucky. If nothing else, we'd be learning more about our adversary.

The biggest downside to the whole program lay in the Kestrel drones that also formed the backbone of it. Rikki was a Russian Berkut, and for years had been able to fudge the IFF transponder codes used among the Zone's killer bots. Lotus had ruined the IFF part, but Rikki still appeared to match the visual and flight characteristics of a regular Berkut.

But the Kestrels were the enemies of the Zone drones and nothing would hide that fact. Each Kestrel would be identified on sight, and each would draw out attackers. We'd done what we could about that, Yoshida's dream team layering a complex software program into the Kestrels' own IFFs. The result was a projection that didn't match the Zone bots but also didn't match anything in the US drone arsenal. An obfuscation, Eric had called it, projected at short range only, to confuse any Zone device long enough for the Kestrel and/or its soldier to kill it. At least, that was the theory.

We'd also completely enclosed the Kestrels in carbon fiber cladding to block out their radio signatures when they weren't broadcasting through extruded antennas. Many military drones have carbon fiber in their structures, but either used exterior antennas or didn't have enough CF to block all signals. Otherwise the human or computer operators wouldn't be able to direct them from back at base. Early in the Zone's history, the military sent fully enclosed drones into to hunt the terrorist devices. They were all completely autonomous, as they had to be. None of them ever returned on their own. Dad and I pulled a few wrecked ones out, as there were big rewards for their retrieval. All of the ones we found were shot to shit.

But the Kestrels going in with my newly trained snake eaters were fully covered with carbon fiber. Since they had their operators with them, able to communicate with verbal and visual signals, they could pull their antennas inside and operate off the grid, so to speak, when necessary.

It made them rather hard to find electronically when they went radio silent. Rikki had had to use his extremely sensitive sound and visual sensors to find them when we had hunted them in practice. I didn't think any Raptor, Kite, or Skyhawk was going to figure that trick out without a Spider's guidance. Even the few remaining Berkuts in existence would be at a disadvantage for a while till their own AI networks worked it out. And call me biased but I personally think Rikki's abilities leave even other Death Eagles in the dust. Overconfident, you say? Maybe, but every time we had tangled with a Berkut, Rikki and I had won.

So I was still worried, but they *were* better equipped technologically and experientially than any previous force of human infiltrators. And I needed to concentrate on my own situation.

We had about nine blocks to travel on Hudson Street before we hit the huge internet hub. The drones found us at block two.

As often is the case, my first indication of trouble was Rikki swooping back up the street in my direction. Instantly, I ducked down behind a rusting Dodge Ram pickup truck, pulling the tailgate open as a kind of roof over my hiding spot. There was a parked food truck behind me, adding cover. I ignored the bleached white skeletal arm poking out of the food truck's open service window.

Rikki kept going north, back the way we had come, never slowing or even waggling his wings as he shot past.

Three seconds later, a mixed trio of two Raptors and a Kite came at full speed right behind him.

Of the three, it was the tiny unarmed Kite that bothered me the most. Rikki could eat the Raptors for breakfast, but as I might have mentioned before, Indian Kites almost always pair with Tigers. My .458 was set up with the suppressor on and subsonic ammo in the magazine and chamber. A perfect load-out for knocking UAVs out of the air, but nowhere near optimum for a 180-kilo monster.

Hunkering low, tucked under the tailgate, I stayed frozen. The primary temptation was to change out magazines and get loaded for Tiger. It was like a palpable need, one that I resisted with every iota of willpower. I had harped about it to my students time and time again. You don't have near the time to react that you think you have inside the Zone. Any movement on my part could either register with the sensitive little air drone that followed a couple of meters behind the bigger UAVs or it could trip the sensors of the massive killer that was guaranteed to be following in the gloomy early dawn light.

I prefer to shoot Tigers from two hundred meters out and several floors up, using armor piercing .338 magnum rounds. Facing one on the ground with even full-powered .458 Socom rounds was way, way less appealing. The best bet was to freeze in place, let my stealth suit do its job and go undetected by the Tiger—and pray like crazy.

The sounds of the UAVs faded but I stayed still, doing my best to impersonate concrete, while the images of Primmer getting torn in half replayed over and over in my head. The air was still cool but I could feel myself sweating under the expensive suit and could almost hear my own heart hammering inside my chest. The dystopian streets fell dead quiet, only the sound of a plane way up high, droning through the air. Then I heard it—a soft rustle. Then a click, like stone on stone, or maybe more like metal on stone.

That was it. Just a soft sound, then the lightest of pings. Across and down the street. I was kneeling on one folded leg, rifle angled vertically across my body, muzzle down, head bent over, eyes on my left wrist, where a tiny piece of shiny metal reflected the width of the street to my side.

There's no evidence to support it, but my personal belief is that certain poses either *look* less human or at least present less readily identifiable body parts. My folded pose was one that I had adopted many times before, especially around cars, walls, and other physical objects. With the Tiger on the other side of the street, it effectively hid the obvious lines of my rifle, while the rounded back, shoulders, and tucked head gave my shape a lump-like silhouette. And odd lumps were as common as dirt on the streets of modern day Manhattan. Rotten clothing and old bones, garbage bags rolled by the wind like apocalyptic tumble weeds, leaves and sticks blown into piles against man-made windbreaks.

The rusted rear wheel with its flattened tire gave me a bit of additional cover, as my body was canted slightly forward, putting my head out in front of my knee, slightly behind the tire. My wrist was down alongside my folded left leg, shiny metal mirror peering under the arc of the truck's ruined wheel.

Another click sounded, followed by a sound that most people never had cause to hear—the hollow rattle of bone tumbling across cement. It was almost even with my hiding spot.

My suit was absorbing the sweat that I could feel trickling down my back and under my arms and I had to trust it to reduce my IR and thermal signatures. Then I felt a drop form between my eyes. Another scrape of metal, parallel to my position or maybe just past. More sweat beaded, crawling down to the bridge of my nose. I kept my eyes locked on my mirrored cuff links.

In my tiny metal window to the street, a dark shape suddenly filled the view. The morning was still dim, a fact that favored me, not so much because any absence of light could hide me from the Tiger's electronic ocular band, but because its power had to be low after the long, cold night. Only Rikki's disturbance of the Kite would have induced the UGV to move about before daylight could begin recharging its depleted capacitors.

I was on the west side of Hudson. The metal monster was

on the east. The wind was blowing through the streets of the dead borough from the west. The building next to me blocked a direct gust, but swirling air moved in odd eddies about the street. All I needed was for the chemical sensors on the Tiger to pick up the human pheromones in my perspiration.

I'm pretty sure a brand-new Indian bot would have already picked it up, but ten years had dirtied and dulled even the best sensors and the heavy kill machines had no way to clean or recalibrate them. Add to that the low power reserves and I was probably okay. Still, it made me realize why my father had never let us try to hide from Wolves, Leopards, or Tigers in the early days. We always either fled along predetermined escape routes with preset booby traps behind us, or we shot them to literal pieces with heavy rifles. And now that I thought about it, Dad only chose to fight when I was old enough to wield a large caliber rifle alongside him. The two of us, shooting with the kind of accuracy he had drilled into me, always came out on top. But generally at the first sign of a big UGV, we would beat feet. They were all still fairly new back then and had much better sensors and batteries that held a charge throughout the night.

The dark shadow moved slowly past, only the dimly visible black and gray stripes providing any sense of motion. It was near silent, hunting much, much slower than its little flying scout, conserving energy, searching for signs of life.

It would be tempting to think of the Tiger like it was just a metal version of the natural flesh and blood version, but that was a deadly mistake. My father had been familiar with most of the Indian drone arsenal when the attack happened. He made me read every spec sheet and every piece of drone application protocol that he got his hands on. So I remember distinctly his admonition to never think of a drone as an animal. *"Think of the robot as an extension of a man, Ajaya, for it was programmed by men to hunt men."*

In other words, it would not react like a real tiger, but instead as a soldier might. Its programming contained all of the psychological knowledge that its human creators could cram into it. The slow movements, the swinging of the massive head were as much for generating fear as they were for efficient power use and sensor application. The unprepared civilians of Manhattan had fallen victim to that fear, bolting from hiding spots, running in vain attempts to escape machines that could move at forty kilometers per hour or faster, for long periods of time. Nowadays, without fair warning, your best bet was to hide, not fight. With warning, fleeing was best unless you had some kind of edge, like tons of armored vehicle or advanced explosive devices.

The metal beast continued down the street and I felt secure enough to turn my wrist ever so slowly, keeping it in view until it was a good fifteen or so meters away.

My muscles cramped but I stayed in my crouch, knowing that the Tiger's rear end had motion detectors that could pick up movement up to thirty meters or more behind the metal cat. The road behind us was straight for quite a distance, so I let it get beyond its ass detector range and then I moved, very very slowly and ultra careful.

Ever watch a movie where someone is being hunted by something, or someone, in the dark? And they invariably knock into an object, make a noise, and either die right away or have to suddenly go full on into fight or flight mode? Yeah, well, it's best to just flat out avoid all that by being super careful. After I started helping Dad in the Zone, he made me go to the twins' ballet class for a few lessons and to Mom's yoga class for some movement training. I hated it back then but the first time I used what I had learned to move through a space inhabited by a dormant Crab, I realized the value.

So I unfolded with careful, precise movements and stepped sideways onto the sidewalk to my right, keeping the parked food truck with the skeletal hand between me and the Tiger's position.

Then I began moving with consummate care down the sidewalk, slow and silent.

CHAPTER 25

Rikki caught up three and a half blocks later, and as soon as I saw him floating down the street, I knew I could pick up speed. Good thing because I had been moving at a snail's pace by myself and we still had over four blocks to go before we hit the block-sized internet hub building.

Rikki continued hovering down the middle of the street like he owned it and I felt my stomach settle a bit. Truth be told, I had been uncharacteristically nervous all morning. Yes, the obvious answer is that the loss of Primmer had left me twitchy. But it wasn't like I hadn't been back to the Zone—Hell, I had taken the entire class of special operators in multiple trips through different parts of the borough. Why so shaky now?

Focus, Ajaya—the Zone is jealous of your attention. Give it its due or die. Something Dad used to say. I tucked my fears, doubts, and self-analysis away for another time and extended my senses. The sun was rising and the borough was waking up. The humans might be gone, but Manhattan was still alive. Birds, in particular, have colonized the empty buildings as great nesting sites. Because they can fly in and out without restriction, they can find food in the bustling neighboring boroughs and return to the quiet one for roosting. Pigeons and songbirds were already flying about the concrete canyons of the city. High overhead, I saw the soaring silhouette of a hawk or maybe a falcon floating on thermals, probably hunting its smaller cousins or maybe the ever-present rodents or the abundant squirrels of Central Park.

As if called by the thought, a huge rat scuttled out of a broken basement window, stopping to study me, its biological sensors catching what the drone had failed to.

Without people around, most animals in the Zone either have no fear of humans or, in some cases, like feral dogs and rats, had developed a real taste for mankind. This rat started my way and I pulled an expandable baton from my belt with my left hand, snapping it open while I unsheathed the kukri with my right.

An aggressive rat could expose me to prowling drones almost as fast as me just shouting my name out loud. A sixty-centimeter steel rod and a razor-sharp chopper as long as my forearm were just the medicine for aggressive rodents, which apparently occurred to the rat, too, because it stopped in place, whiskers twitching.

My belt held a number of items that had confused my students: expanding steel baton, pepper spray, and fox urine. I had had to spend a couple of hours expounding on the *other* dangers of the Zone. None of my spec ops combat types had considered the threat of feral man-eating dogs or packs of carnivorous rats.

The rat decided I wasn't worth the trouble, turning and waddling across the road to disappear into another building. After checking Rikki's position, I rapped the bottom of the baton on the remains of a car tire. It took two smacks to get it to close, but the rubber made way less noise than metal on concrete. The kukri disappeared back into its kydex sheath. More than a couple of my killer commandos had questioned the use of both the baton *and* the big knife. My explanation that rats are *fast* had met some blank expressions, although a few people had nodded.

"You've never chased a rodent before?" I asked back.

"Sure. They're really hard to catch," one of the more vocal warriors had allowed.

"Well, that same speed makes them difficult to kill or disable, with just a single weapon, when they come at you. The baton is deadly, quiet, extends my reach considerably, and is fast in use. Instead of flailing with an empty vulnerable hand that could get bit by a disease-ridden rat, I have a handy steel rod. It has other secondary uses, as well, in an urban environment. Prodding downed drones to make sure they're really defunct, pushing open doors, windows, and cupboards without putting oneself too close to the opening, lifting ceiling tiles, reaching through narrow gaps to retrieve something my hand can't reach, and on and on."

A few looked unconvinced but many of the rest wore thoughtful expressions, and after that class, I started to see batons appear in their gear, adding to the blades or tomahawks that they already carried.

With my rodent problem done for the moment, I continued on down Hudson, keeping one eye on Rikki while watching everywhere else, all at the same time. We made progress, getting close enough that I could now see the massive building that had started life as the Western Union building in the late 1920s. It loomed several hundred meters down the street, filling the entire block it rested on. It was huge and imposing, rising in stepped floors like some gigantic Mayan pyramid built to worship the god of information. Perfect place for a Spider nest.

I clicked my tongue softly, a little sound that would hardly travel more than a handful of meters. Rikki stopped and spun, bringing his ocular sensors around to focus on me. I turned my left hand palm up, one half of a questioning shrug. He waggled his wings up and down, still hovering in place.

All clear. I held my index and middle fingers up and spun them in a circle, clockwise. Instantly, he shot off over my head, back the way we came. I didn't need to turn to know that he would have quickly turned off to the east, flying between buildings to start a circular recon of the immediate two blocks. Meanwhile, I hunkered down beside a car whose damaged and weathered roof-mounted sign proclaimed something about hot pizza. Pulling my monocular from my suit, I spent the next few minutes looking over the building and every building around it.

We had studied it pretty extensively before this mission. While much of its functionality was lost due to a lack of electricity, a surprising amount of data in the form of packets of light still traveled its fiber optic highways, passing through on their way to who knows where.

Its architecture was based on something called German Expressionism, which means nothing to me, but the ziggurat structure definitely reminded me of mid-twentieth century European construction. It very much evoked the 1930s and '40s to me, at least based on those images I remember seeing in high school history. Over a hundred years old, yet still standing strong like some modern castle harboring a dangerous army. Which it probably was. Still, I saw no signs of robotic infestation. Nothing visible, at least from the ground, nothing perched on any of the multiple stepped layers, waiting for the rising sun to charge depleted energy cells. Nothing hovering, creeping, clinging, or moving. If Peony was there, it was keeping all activity hidden, which would be logical. A building like this was fully visible to patrolling Renders, and any indication of major drone activity would make it a building of interest. Not a target, though. Massive stores of emergency diesel fuel were thought to still be present on the upper floors; fuel for emergency generators. Any sniping by a Render could ignite an internet catastrophe. Again, a perfect lair for a Spider. Access to the internet, protection from aerial assault, vast spaces to hide in.

Hence why we were hoping to lure it out.

Rikki floated out from a street to my west, having completed his circuit. His wings waggled again. Nothing. Time to nut up and get marching. Well, more creeping than marching, but either way, time to go.

We covered the block and a half left with no consequences. Now we were right in front of the building, looking at the huge arched windows and doorways on the ground floor, the protruding brick columns and buttresses covered with more small ledges and steps, reinforcing the fortress feel of the place.

The central door was gone, ripped completely from its hinges, just the bottom edge visible and lying on the floor of the darkened foyer inside. Something, probably a Tank-Killer based on the damage to the sidewalk and surrounding brick, had rammed it right out of its frame.

Rikki dropped his altitude till he was just five meters off the ground, hovering near my left shoulder. Moving close in was standard for us when we were entering a potential ambush site, close enough to combine firepower and cover each other, yet just far enough apart to make getting both of us in the same attack doubtful.

Nothing moved in the dark, broken doorway; no sound came from the looming building, just wind moving through the man-made ravines of the borough. Creepy, but ninety-nine percent of my time inside the Zone can be called that. We kept moving, trying not to show anything more than what might be considered normal curiosity about such a large structure. Then we were past it, starting to hit the next block. The high-end specialty liquor store was just ahead.

Suddenly a sound came, distant, echoing off the buildings lining the street. A booming sound, subdued but instantly recognizable. A gunshot—rifle fire, high-powered, partially suppressed maybe.

We both spun around. It came from behind us, blocks away. Seconds ticked by as I strained my ears and Rikki processed sensory input. Two more booms sounded, then automatic weapons fire. More shots, different locations, different shooters, multiple fire fights in multiple locations. My students were under attack.

CHAPTER 26

My brain went blank for a second then kickstarted as the answer hit me right in the forehead.

The Spider or Spiders know we're here, in force, and while I've been baiting them, they've been hunting my students. I turn and bolt back up the street, back the way we came, covering two blocks in a few seconds, blocks that had taken me ten careful minutes to travel.

The gunshots were louder, coming from the west. We veered off on a side street and popped out onto Greenwich Street. A firefight was happening right in front of us. Two sets of combat operators, in two different buildings on the east side of the street, were shooting it out with a big mix of Cranes and Wolves as an aerial battle took place above them, Kestrels and Raptors swirling in a dogfight.

I was getting ready to jump in, my gunsight already hovering on a flechette-shooting Russian Wolf, when the sky darkened. A glance up showed the massive Quad copter overhead, objects plummeting from its open cargo door.

Armored soldiers hit the ground like bullets, not a single super hero pose among them. You know the one—legs bent, one arm down on the ground, one arm cocked, super dramatic and totally useless. Instead, they landed on flexed legs, weapons up and firing from the moment of impact. Six troopers shot and killed a dozen drones in as many seconds.

I pulled back, ducking behind the corner of the nearest building. The gunfire ended. And no more shots from anywhere else. Yoshida was on it, backing up his new counter-drone force at the first sign of trouble. And the new trainees had acquitted themselves well, destroying at least ten terrorist bots before the cavalry arrived. I had no idea of casualties, but that wasn't my responsibility. Spider hunting was.

I wasn't needed here and maybe, just maybe, this offered me an opportunity. Combat activity inside the Zone wasn't common. Multiple firefights are unheard of. If the Spider or Spiders had sent out hunters to hunt my people, instead of, say, randomly stumbling across multiple teams at the exact same time, well, they may have gotten more than they bargained for.

I slipped back down my side street, which, now that I wasn't sprinting, I could see was named Franklin Street. I start using normal Zone tactics, weaving quietly between a city bus and a crashed taxi. Gaps between the buildings on the south side give me possible nooks and crannies to move through or hide in. Rikki was now hovering within a meter of my shoulder. I slid into an alley, moving behind a dumpster that might have started its life painted green, but was now the reds and oranges of rust. A quick mag change gave me ten full power, armor-piercing rounds, including the one that went into the chamber when I racked the action. The subsonic round that got ejected goes back in the switched-out mag and back into one of my suit pockets. After a second's thought, I pulled an MSLAM from a different pocket and set it in front of me.

Rikki hovered down next to me, folding down into his

orb shape. In this form, most of the original carbon fiber on his airframe surrounds him. Those spots that would be exposed in a normal Berkut are covered with material I added to him. He was fairly well shielded, not projecting detectable radio waves.

We hunkered, me kneeling, rifle ready, while Rikki landed on my shoulder and then rotated so that his gun barrel was pointing up. We were completely behind the dumpster, with me listening and him ready to greet any aerial units that came overhead. Time to wait.

In the distance, I heard the sounds of troops mopping up, the rumble of the big Quad's engines telling me it was still hovering. A few minutes later, I heard it move off, leaving this part of the borough to go quiet.

Time passed. Birds started to make noise and behind me, at the end of the alley, I heard soft rustling inside the jammed back door of some abandoned business. Great: more rats.

The rustling suddenly stopped and I heared the flap and squawk of pigeons taking flight. Something startled them—something that made a clicking noise. Rikki's mechanical talons were holding onto the shoulder material of my suit. They suddenly squeezed once, twice, three times. He was telling me he detected three units nearby. Silently, he rotated back to facing forward, which told me nothing aerial was near. Ears straining, leg muscles clenching to keep from cramping up, rifle ready.

The sounds grew louder and my ears could distinguish differences among them. Two sounded like medium ground units, maybe Wolves or Leopards. The third one had a deeper clunk to it and a cadence that didn't match the others. The main ground bots are four-legged and walk just like a real mammal would. No programmer yet has found a gait for four legs that is more efficient than nature's various patterns. But this third one didn't sound like four legs at all. More like six. It's a sound that I've heard before... Spider gait.

We were hoping to bait a Spider, and instead the Spider had tried to bait me—using attacks on our people to lure me somewhere else. Now it was out on the hunt.

The sounds changed, one set continuing forward while the second and third slowed to a stop.

If I had to guess, I'd say that the Spider sent a scout forward while it waited with the second UGV. Four-footed clicking started again, moving away, coming back, moving away again. But the Spider's footsteps had ceased.

We were in a narrow alley, our retreat limited to the rodent-filled business behind us—not a sure thing. Blocking us in were a Spider CThree and either a Wolf or a Leopard, with another medium ground bot a short distance away. A hyper-intelligent metal monster and maybe two armored killing machines. Sounds bad when you say it like that, but on the plus side, there weren't any aerials in the immediate area and the damned Spider could have arrived riding on top of a Tank-Killer. This was about as good as it gets.

My left hand reached up and tapped Rikki to get his attention, then tapped again three times. My right hand picked up the MSLAM, thumb clicking it to impact detonation. In this mode, it would act like a grenade. Rikki's claws tightened, then loosened.

I tapped him again, paused, then started tapping in sequence. One—two—three. On the third, I stood and stepped left as Rikki pulsed straight up in the air. My right arm was already cocked, and as soon as I saw the hulking black shape, I threw the mini bomb and dropped my right hand to meet the rifle that my left was already lifting, simultaneously stepping back and crouching.

The MSLAM flew through the air, right at the side of the armored multi-legged horror.

A green and brown blur intercepted it, the Wolf's vice-like jaws catching the bomb and landing in an almost perfect imitation of a real canine. Almost. Brand-new, it might have been graceful enough to make it. Ten years old, it had some clunk to it. My smart bomb did not like clunk. The Wolf disappeared in a flash of light and the sound of thunder.

Unlike a standard grenade or even an air fuel munition, the MSLAM has multiple uses, most of them utilizing a shaped charge. In grenade mode, its explosive force is a little less directed but still not the general spherical shockwave of an antipersonnel device. I threw it so that the shaped charge and explosively formed penetrator was directed at the Spider. The Wolf caught it from the side, still indexed toward the command and control monster, so while the Russian ground unit's head was vaporized by the detonation, a decent portion of blast force was directed toward the Spider and, more importantly, away from myself and Rikki.

The blast pelted me with bits of Russian bot and threw both of us back a pace. The Spider vanished in a cloud of smoke, fiery plasma, and Wolf parts. I started firing even as I fell back, forced to drop to a knee.

The smoke cleared, the Spider was gone, and a Leopard in full leap had replaced it. Our guns fired together and the Indian robot slammed into the dumpster, knocking hand-sized pieces of rust off.

The leopard was on its side, legs spasming—which moved it as well as shook the dumpster, eventually shoving itself out of sight, with the dumpster between us.

Rikki zipped around in an arc in the air, gun pointing at the spot the Leopard disappeared into. As he moved into position to see what I couldn't, his 9mm fired full automatic, hosing at least half his magazine into the fallen robot, expended brass clattering to the ground below him.

He stayed in position for a few seconds, gun locked on target. I moved around the dumpster, muzzle of my rifle leading the way. A twitching wreck came into view, its motions limited to one rear leg that was snapping out, then pulling slowly back, only to slam back out. The robotic version of a dying reflex.

Then Rikki spun in place, facing back toward Hudson, then suddenly spun toward Greenwich.

"Incoming. Multiple aerial units."

"How many?"

"Twenty-seven. Now twenty-nine. Coming from east and west."

The Spider called for backup, sending more UAVs than we could handle. At least two swarms were heading to catch us between them.

I turned and ran toward the back door of the rodent-infested business. The steel door was open about ten centimeters. I slammed my shoulder into it and bounced off. Lifting a leg, I tried to kick it open. It shivered and shook but didn't move a centimeter.

A loud buzz filled the air. Shadows darkened the alley and

the open end was suddenly filled with flying death.

CHAPTER 27

I raised my rifle to fire, but the muzzle hadn't even covered the target when the drone I was sighting got slammed out of the air like a giant had swatted it. Then the drones on either side exploded into bits and pieces. Muzzle blasts echoed off the buildings around me as more drones were hit from above. I shot one and I'd guess Rikki got at least two, but that was it. The rest were picked off by snipers above—at least six of my class leaning out windows in three different buildings—or were shot down by the swarm of black Kestrels that came from all directions at once. It was over in about fifteen seconds.

The last gunshots echoed through Manhattan as the sky suddenly darkened. The giant Quad floated back over the tops of the buildings, automated electromag guns panning for targets. The back cargo hatch opened and a trio of lines shot down, slamming into the pavement at the front of the alley.

Three of Yoshida's armored soldiers slid down the ropes, one tall, one short and feminine, and one a giant with a massive three-barreled gun.

"Let's go, Shooter. Time to haul ass outta here," Corporal Kayla Jensen said, throwing me a climbing harness. Her two companions, B. Boyle and T. Thompson, turned to watch opposite directions, weapons ready.

Less than two minutes later, I was taking off the harness onboard the Quad, the passenger seats filled with a mix of armored soldiers and stealth-suited drone hunters. I saw some of my class getting medical treatment and one was lying on a med surface, getting flechettes removed from his back.

"Close, kid. Close," Yoshida said, walking over with a tablet. "At least from what we got off a couple of the Kestrels."

"Rikki, please copy and transfer our encounter with the Spider to the major's tablet," I said.

"Major Yoshida, I am transferring the requested footage," Rikki said as he hovered over one of the drone charging stations that the Quad was now outfitted with.

The major watched the tablet, Sergeant Rift and Corporal Estevez looking over his shoulder.

"Shit! Damn that fucking Wolf!" Rift said, still watching.

"Is that even normal?" Yoshida asked me. He pressed a few touch controls on the tablet and the images were suddenly being projected onto the wall of the Quad for everyone to watch.
The Wolf leapt through the air, grabbing the MSLAM in its mouth.

"I don't know, but my gut tells me the Spiders control any drones around them pretty thoroughly."

"Spider CThree units regularly suborn UGV and UAVs in their immediate vicinity," Rikki announced on his own. *"Wolf UGV was under direct control."*

Everyone in the cargo area was looking at my drone in surprise. Yoshida glanced at me, surprised. I smiled. "What can I say? He was programmed around my sisters. You gotta speak up if you're gonna get heard in that household."

Yoshida raised one eyebrow before turning back to Rikki. "Rikki, how do you know the Wolf was directly controlled?"

"Unit Peony attempted to control Rikki unit as well."

"And you resisted?" the major asked, really shocked.

"Correct."

"How?"

"RF resistant outer shell protects from multiple radio frequency and high volume attacks. Peony attempted software breach using sonic pulse technology. Rikki Unit turned off sonic sensors during attack."

"Fuck," Gunny Kwan said with feeling. "It couldn't get through your carbon fiber, so it tried sound?"

"Correct."

"How did you get your sensors turned off in time?" Elizabeth Kottos asked.

"Previous encounters with Spider unit Lotus indicated a use of audio assault in addition to standard radio frequencies. As soon as Ajaya Gurung initiated contact, audio sensors were placed in standby mode. Sensors were returned to normal when sonic vibrations on airframe armor ceased."

Yoshida turned to me, both eyebrows up.

"Rikki had experience with Spiders in his former life. Since he's been with me, we've had multiple experiences. Your own scientists noted that Lotus attempted to control him on the bridge when it froze up Unit 19. We discussed that episode and worked out a protocol for when Spiders are in close range. It forces us to rely almost totally on visual cues, but in the middle of a firefight, verbal isn't all that useful to me anyway," I said.

"You *discussed* it?" Tyson Perry asked.

"Come on, I know all of you talk with your drones," I said.

"Sure, to give instructions and get feedback," Tyson said after glancing around at the others. The whole cargo bay was paying attention.

"You don't ask your Kestrel for options on how it could improve a function?" I asked.

"Like with a person?"

"To be honest, none of ours seem anywhere as... person-like as Rikki," Elizabeth said.

"Again, I had him in our apartment for months. With my mom, grandmother, and two teenage sisters. The twins in particular chatted his electronic ears off. In fact, his knowledge of teen fashions is pretty extensive."

"*Current database is nineteen months out of date, Ajaya.*"

"Yeah, that's okay, buddy. You still have more information on that topic than I ever will," I said before turning back to the others. "Don't you all keep your drones with you in your quarters?"

"Yeah, but I don't carry regular conversations with it," Carl Abate said.

I raised both of my brows and gave him a look.

"But I'm starting to see the utility of it," he said, slowly nodding.

"Rikki, can you provide that audio protocol to the other Kestrel units?" the major asked.

"*Complying, Major Yoshida.*"

"Okay, drone education and socialization aside, what did we learn?" he asked everyone.

"The Spider wasn't fooled by our plan and attempted to turn it against us," someone said.

"Yes, key word being *attempted*. Looks like our preparations mostly negated that. Six people wounded with varying degrees of seriousness, no fatalities. That, folks, is a record for an operation this size in the Zone. How do we improve?"

"So many of us moving into the Zone at the same time must have tripped a drone or two, although our own drones didn't detect any others," Gunny Kwan said.

"Remember those remote sensors the infiltrator in the drone hive had?" Yoshida asked. "Those wouldn't show up to our drone's sensors, would they?"

"Shit, sir, that's going to complicate things," Sergeant Rift said.

"Well, those remotes clung to cables, sending and receiving through them. Didn't use any wireless transmissions at all, which makes them a bitch to find," Kayla said. "Sir," she added.

"So we don't try to find them; we try to block them," Sergeant Thompson rumbled. He was checking over his Cerberus cannon and didn't even look up.

"What?" Yoshida asked.

This time, Thompson raised his head. "Rikki doesn't try to outpower the Spider's audio signals, just blocks them all out. What if your nerd squad came up with some kind of broadcast or signal that would flood all the sensors with too much input?"

"Shit, Thompson. You're scaring me," Rift said. "You telling me you got brains inside all that brawn?"

"Sure, Rift," he said, raising one massive arm and flexing a bicep as big as my leg. "It's just the brawn is so overwhelming, you miss all the brains."

"Good idea, Tyler," Yoshida said. "What else did we learn?"

Tyler? Sergeant Thompson was a Tyler? It didn't seem to fit.

"We have the right bait," Kayla said. "The Spider came out looking for Ajaya and Rikki right after the firefights. Peony saw an opportunity."

"Yes, good observation, Corporal. Ajaya is high on the priority list. So we continue to dangle him in front of the Spiders."

"The bait is sitting right here and not loving that metaphor."

"Quiet, bait. We've got planning to do," Yoshida said. And proceeded to do just that.

CHAPTER 28

The explosion woke the whole family. It shook the building, rattling the windows, the noise a blast so loud, I thought the world had just ended.

"Rikki?" I asked, hearing my sisters both yell for Mom. My Virtual Assistant was projecting the time on the wall. 03:39.

"Explosion less than ten kilometers to the east. Approximate location near JFK airport," he said as I rushed out the door, down the hall, and into the living room. Our front windows face east and were currently lit by orange and red light that flared so bright, I had to look away, turning to my drone, who hovered right behind me.

Mom and the twins rushed in, all three freezing just inside the room as a ball of fire rolled up into the sky.

"Rikki says something exploded near or at JFK," I said. "We should all get dressed."

Gabby looked at me like I had three heads but Mom understood. "Do you think..."

"No, but I want to play it safe."

Monique got it a second later, sucking in a sharp breath, and her sister froze in the act of opening her mouth to snark at me.

Aama came out of the hall just then, fully clothed. Mom

took one look at her and then ushered the suddenly speechless twins back to their room. I heard my mother ask her virtual assistant for any breaking news about explosions.

Another roiling ball of fire lifted high in the sky and now I could hear sirens, well, *more* sirens, as there's always one or two... this *is* New York.

I went back to my room and quickly dressed in appropriate clothes and boots, slipped on my chest holster, and double-checked that my rifle was loaded and ready, lying on my bed. Then I went back to the living room. Rikki was perched on the back of the couch, optical sensors aimed in the direction of the explosion. Gabby was sitting in front of him, huddled under a blanket. There weren't any more fireballs, but the skyline glowed an unnatural orange. I could hear Mom talking with Monique back in the bedrooms. Aama was making tea in the kitchen and had the news projecting on the wall.

"Incoming call from Zone Defense," my own assistant announced in my ear.

"Answer."

"Ajaya Gurung? This is Lieutenant Samantha Kilroy of Zone Defense Command."

"Good morning, Lieutenant. Are we under attack?"

"I have no info on that sir, but Major Yoshida would like you to stay put. The incident you are referring to is being addressed, but the major stressed that you're to stay with your family, shelter in place, and be ready. Does that make sense to you, sir?"

"To a degree. Do you have anything on the explosion east of Brooklyn?"

"I can tell you that the Zone Instant Response Strike Force has been dispatched toward JFK. That's all I know, sir. Now, if you have a clear understanding of my message, I have other calls to make."

"Yes, thank you, Lieutenant. Goodbye."

The line clicked off immediately. Zone D was no doubt a whirlwind of barely ordered activity.

Aama handed me a cup of tea, strong but loaded with sugar and butter. On the wall of the kitchen, the news was projected by Aama's own Virtual Assistant AI. The shocked-looking anchor announced that the network had received word that a plane had crashed. Drone footage showed a massive debris field on what looked like a runway. Fires burned all across the scene as the drone circled the site from a distance.

"We're being told it was an incoming cargo plane. Eyewitnesses report it was on landing approach when the engines flared and the plane started to pull up. It then appeared as if the human pilot attempted to take the controls but was unsuccessful. We have no details on casualties although our source indicates there were no other planes or vehicles in that part of the airport. Stay tuned."

"Ajaya?" Mom asked. The twins had sandwiched her, clinging as all three looked at me for answers.

"It could be another infiltrator... at the air traffic control towers. Zone Defense has instructed me to remain here. We all need to be ready to move if it's something more," I said. "But it doesn't seem like it's a widespread attack. Rikki?"

"Concur, Ajaya. There is no sign of drone activity beyond news units."

I saw my mother visibly relax, my little sisters still scared but clearly a little less so now.

"We're ready to go in a second's notice," Mom said.

Someone knocked on the door.

Aama started for it but Rikki shot past her, even as I moved to get there first. The drone beat me by a kilometer, hovering in front of the door, gun primed. *"Harper Leeds detected."*

"Yeah, it's your friend Harper," Gabby said, looking at her own tablet. Probably looking at the door cam.

I opened the door and found a fully dressed, highly agitated Harper standing there, a light pack slung over her shoulder.

"Come in. Plane crashed at JFK," I said, pulling her in as a couple of doors down the hall started to open.

"Harper, come sit with us. We're watching the news," my mother said, patting the sofa next to her. Gabby moved over without any attitude, making room for her.

"But what does Rikki say?" Harper asked, looking at my drone as she slowly settled into the spot.

"Initial explosion and secondary explosions all located at JFK airport. No abnormal drone activity within sensor range, Harper Leeds."

Her shoulders relaxed minutely as she accepted his report.

"You're as prepared for this as we are," Mom noted. It wasn't quite a question, but almost.

"I have a huge respect for how deadly the Zone drones are," Harper said carefully.

"Ajaya said you've been working for Trinity, protecting the show's drones from getting hacked?" Monique asked.

"Yeah, it's been good work. Those Flottercots pay real well," Harper said, accepting a cup of tea from Aama with a surprised look on her face.

"How do you know how to do that? Ajaya knows all kinds of drone stuff, and I doubt he could do it," Monique pressed. Her twin leaned forward too. Clearly my sisters had suspicions regarding Harper... and a lack of faith in my technical abilities.

"Well, your brother knows quite a bit, but the Zone drones are my entire area of specialty."

Gabby looked at me to gauge my reaction. I nodded. "Yup. Harper knows more about them than I do."

"But you know more about the Zone than she does, right?" Gabby asked. Harper started to open her mouth, a smirk forming, but I jumped in first.

"Well, of course. I've spent a lot of time inside. Harper could only match that if she *had* done the same," I said, glancing at the girl who literally grew up in the Zone.

Her expression cleared instantly and she reluctantly nodded. "Yeah, I don't like to admit your brother knows anything, but you've got me there," she agreed.

"Well, it's nice to know someone who can put him in his place about the technical stuff," Monique said.

"Come get breakfast," Aama said. "Everyone must eat."

Aama had made a bunch of food, her way of prepping the family for anything that might happen next. But nothing happened. The dark of early morning turned into a rosy dawn as I washed the dishes over my grandmother's objections. Harper chatted with my mom while the twins connected with all of their social media platforms to read what others had seen and, of course, write their own versions. Aama supervised my cleaning with a critical eye.

The call came a bit before six a.m.

"Ajaya, an incoming call from Major Yoshida," my VA said in my ear.

"I'll take it." Everyone in the room turned my way.

"Ajaya, I just wanted to check in. Everyone good?"

"Yes, Major, just sitting around and watching the news feeds. Was it another one?"

"No... another two. They took over the close landing control system on a commercial delivery cargo plane. It's early in the investigation, but we think the bot tried to abort the landing so it could crash it in the nearest neighborhood. The pilot tried to take back control and crashed it on the end of the runway. You'd be proud of your students. They cleared the whole airport. Found one of the bastards under the control tower and another one at LaGuardia. I sent a third team to Newark, but they came up clear."

"So Peony's fighting back," I said.

"Seems that way. Be careful ascribing human-type rationales to their actions. I doubt the Spider sees it as tit for tat."

"No, but it is logical to make a counterstrike against your enemy or, if you want, Peony could just be activating assets before we find them, doing what damage it can while it can."

"Either way, it worked—we're going to have to clear all of JFK and LaGuardia, fully. Then we have to do the same to any and

John Conroe

all other smaller airfields in a sixty-kilometer circle."

"You want me and Rikki to come in to help?"

"No, I want you brainstorming how to kill these Spider fuckers with less manpower. Most of our newly trained teams are going to be clearing high-value locations for the foreseeable future. Not just the airports but the shipping ports, military bases, the city water system, basically everything that could hurt a lot of people at once."

"What about infectious disease labs, like the CDC runs?"

"They're on the list, although I don't think we have Plum Island on it. We'll add it."

"Plum Island?"

"Animal disease lab. But never mind that; I've got people who do nothing but list vulnerable sites. You, young sniper, need to come up with a way to destroy these things."

"Roger that, Major," I said, looking at the rest of my family and Harper. "I'll get right on it."

CHAPTER 29

"Look, if you're telling me that they're making their own drones, then I think you have to assume that the entire area around a Spider's home base will be riddled with those passive sensor units. I like the blocking idea. Those remote units in the drone hive had ultrasonic detectors, right?" Harper asked. We were in my room, brainstorming after I had filled her in on recent developments.

"Yes, why?"

"Well, just like you use fox urine to fool the feral dogs and rats, we can create a sound *package* to fool the ultrasonic sensors. In fact, maybe one that mimics a big dog would be best," she said, face lighting up with excitement.

"Actually, that makes sense, but if we have a group of people sounding like dogs coming in from all over the place, I gotta think it's going to make the Spiders suspicious. They're super sensitive to patterns."

"Ya think?" she asked, hands on her hips. "*Of course* it won't work for bunches of people. Any large movement of any kind of organism is going to trip their switches. This will likely only work for one or maybe two people," she said. "They notice animals even if they don't react to them, you know. But you better believe that they track them. Part of their threat assessment programming. So the Spider will know that a dog, or dogs, are moving about its territory."

"So I'd have to behave just like a feral dog," I said, thinking about it.

I'd seen way more than my share of dogs in the Zone. I've been hunted by them, watched them from hides, tracked individuals and packs, and even culled them. In the beginning, they ran in big packs, but as the years went by and the massive amount of *food* the drones had created for them had been consumed, the packs became much smaller. Nowadays, the biggest groups that I came across were three or four dogs at one time. Mostly it was pairs, but individuals weren't uncommon.

The older dogs had learned to leave me right the hell alone. The younger generations always had to lose a few before they too avoided my scent. Nothing ruined a recovery faster than young dogs. I hated to shoot them, but it was a clear choice, them or me. And when that happened, the birds would come in—seagulls, crows, ravens, and turkey vultures, which, of course, alerted every drone in the neighborhood.

"I'll have to move in the same patterns that they do. Kind of an energy-efficient sweep of an area, not in a straight line but in a twisting kind of path that gives them the widest exposure to scents and sounds," I said.

She raised one eyebrow like *no duh, dummy.*

"I'm just thinking out loud. Feel free to chime in, oh font-of-all-knowledge," I said.

"No, you probably know more about them. I kept way away from dogs. Which is easier if you travel those areas that are almost completely devoid of food. The dogs and rats hang nearer to the parks and the areas with lots of vegetation, where deer, rabbits, and squirrels browse," she said.

I knew this as well, but it helped to hear it. My mind was already formulating a plan, even working up a path to follow. We would be a pair of dogs, Rikki and me, perhaps driven from the better hunting grounds by a bigger pack, now looking for mice and rats.

All of the parks, big and small, were pretty wild now, full of deer and small game. If we inserted in the dark again, maybe the east side, and then worked our way across the island toward or through a park, it would give us a trail that matched the little backstory I was creating in my head.

It was also a little dangerous because the dogs hunted the darkness like wolves would. If we had to shoot a bunch, it would ruin the run. Maybe I should use skunk scent instead of fox, to make us a little less enticing to any night hunters.

"Jeez, I can smell the smoke pouring out your ears," she said, grinning, watching me.

"Sorry. The details are sort of just lining themselves up in my head."

"You can do that stuff later. Right now, we need to figure out how you actually hunt whichever Spider is lurking at 60 Hudson. It'll be wicked on guard after all the shooting yesterday."

"But probably accessing the cables to send instructions to any more infiltrators. Also, we've wiped out quite a few of its resources lately. If it were me, I'd be trying to build new ones."

"I'm not sure anyone could ever think like a Spider. They're just too alien. But what you're talking about is standard for warfare. When you lose or use up weapons, you have to replace them. Now... where would a Spider set up shop to build these things?"

"Anywhere it wanted. The mothership drones only need a source of printable material. They were designed to improvise. Powdered metals, nylon stock, polycarbonate, so they could work anywhere, as long as other drones brought the materials. They would just need power."

"Which means sunshine. So the motherships are on roofs, and if the Spider is staying close to internet access, then you need to be up high, watching the open roof areas on 60 Hudson," she said.

"So... this will be a traditional sniping mission."

"That's what I'm hearing—right in your wheelhouse, right?"

It was. I hadn't gone full-on sniper mode in a while now. But it made full sense. Old school, but with a new trick—doggy sound disguise. It also broke my latest sets of behavior, throwing off the patterns that the Spiders tracked.

"How do we make the two of us sound like dogs?" I asked.

She turned to my drone. "Rikki, do you have archival sound recordings of canines inside the Zone?"

"*Affirmative. The data is not extensive, as unneeded sensory recordings are deleted to conserve memory space,*" Rikki reported.

"How many recordings do you have? And how much time?" Harper asked.

"*Three recordings. Two canines in one, four in the second, and two in last. Forty-seven seconds, eighteen seconds, and twenty-one seconds.*"

"Okay, we'll have to splice some stuff together and do some looping. Try to make it sound unique, but unfortunately, if you stay in one spot too long or trigger multiple sensors in row, the Spider will crunch that data and spot it repeating."

"How about a couple of sound packets? One for two dogs and one for one. Rikki can leave to recon at times and I'll switch to just the single dog sounds. When he swings back, we'll use the the double one."

"No can do, genius. Rikki *is* your sound projector. If he leaves your side, you become a human sounding packet of squishy meat," she said.

"Well, that's... true. Damn. Not ideal. Rikki's recons are standard procedure. Hey! What if I used your neuro-prosthesis thingy to project the sound myself?"

She frowned. "You *can't* just throw it on and go running off into the Zone! It takes a long time to learn to use it. *You* have to get used to it, and *it* has to get used to you. Then you have to learn how to even begin to meld with any kind of computer, let alone an autonomous hunter-killer AI. No, that would only work if I went with you," she said, shaking her head and waving the idea away with one hand.

Hmm. I thought about that for a moment. She was very good in the Zone—in some ways better than me. The prosthesis gave her the ability to do a kind of mind meld thing with Zone drones, letting her convince them that she wasn't even there, as well as detect them from pretty good distances. And I'd been teaching her to shoot. She wasn't a bad shot, and she was much more fit now than when we had first met.

"What's that look? I don't like that look, Ajaya! Oh—no,

no, no. I'm not going back in there," she said. "No way."

I stared at her for a moment, then nodded. "Okay, it was just a passing idea. You got that computer ninja thing and with all your fitness stuff, I figured you'd be able to keep up, but you're right."

She pulled back and studied me. "I am?"

"Yeah. You may have grown up in there, but what I do is different and difficult. You only ever moved short little distances. And I'm going up against at least one Spider. You even said that you and your mom avoided them like the plague. I'll be going right into the lair of one," I said, shaking my head to dismiss the idea.

"Don't do that, you asshole! Don't try that psych bullshit by insulting my skills!" she said.

I held up both hands. "I'm not. You have awesome skills and lived right underneath them for years. But I travel big distances. You guys never did that. Admit it: That's why you were so out of shape."

"Listen shack head, I traveled all over the place by *myself*, without a fancy drone to protect me. I could leave you in the dust in there."

"Never mind, Harper. No need to get all bent outta shape. It was a bad idea."

"Bullshit! It was a great idea. I would make an awesome spotter and I'm better at getting by drones than you'll ever be. I just don't want to go in is all."

I held up both hands. "Peace. Not asking you to. You've done enough in there. You've lost *enough* in there. I got this."

"Do you? Because now that I think about it, you got real

lucky with Lotus."

"Wow, you really got all torqued up over just a few comments. No need to get insulting. Did I get lucky? Yes. Do I depend on luck to get in and out? No. I plan and execute very carefully. I move with stealth and attack them from ambush."

"Yeah? Well what are you going to do if the building you chose to set up shop in has those stripped-down Wasp remote sensors? *I* wouldn't even *need* a fake sound packet. I'd just convince the sensor that it was wrong. Admit it… you need me in there."

"Are you telling me that you want to go in? Because I'd say yes to that," I said.

She pulled back, a confused look on her face. I waited. She grimaced and cursed. "Shit," she said, looking me in the eye. "Shit, shit, shit." Lots was going on inside that skull, and I just about saw the moment she made her decision. Or maybe it was the moment that she *realized* she'd already made the decision.

"Yeah, I guess I am. But I'm gonna need gear," she said, leaning back with a look of almost disbelief on her face. "But yes, I'm going back in."

CHAPTER 30

Gear wasn't a problem. I was in charge of training stealth infiltrators, which gave me access to cutting-edge gear. I had the latest stealth suits in female sizes and shaped for the female form. I had suppressed firearms like the sweet little .300 ACC Blackout carbine that she had already fired at the range where I taught her, plus all the best ammo for it that Uncle Sam could provide.

What I didn't have was clearance for her to go in. That part was my job—getting her clearance and gear. Harper was working on a hundred other details that we had come up with when we brainstormed our plan and its consequences. And there would be consequences even if we failed, but especially if we didn't. So I had to get Harper into the Zone. But I knew someone who could get her clearance... or at least fudge it.

"Hey Maya, how's it going?"

"Oh, Ajaya," she said, caught off guard in the lab, bent over the metal body of an infiltrator. "It's, ah, been, ah, a bit crazy actually. Studying these things, trying to figure out where else they might be, how many of them there could be, things like that."

"Oh? Isn't finding them up to that Weber guy?"

"Well, ostensibly. The NSA is *supposed* to be the lead on finding them, but frankly they're using *our* algorithms to do it, so... you know."

"Don't be modest—they're using *your* algorithms, aren't they? The ones you personally wrote?" I asked.

"Yeah, true. But, hey... what's up with you? Aren't you supposed to be figuring out how to hunt the Spiders?"

"Actually, I kind of have... figured it out," I said. "It's what I wanted to talk to you about."

A suspicious look replaced the slight bewilderment she'd worn a moment ago. "Why don't I think I'm going to like whatever you've come up with?"

"Whoa, nothing bad, really. It's just I need to go back in and hunt them. Me and Rikki... and one other."

She frowned. "One other what? Person? Just one? Who?"

"Well, you don't know this person. And that's kind of the thing. See, I need to get access on the system for this person and, well, aren't you the administrator for Zone access network?"

Maya might be shy and a little awkward, but she wasn't anyone's dummy. Alarm flared in her eyes. "The major doesn't know this person, does he? Have they ever even been in the Zone before?"

"Yeah. More than me. Listen, Major Yoshida told me that my mission is to find and kill the Spiders. That's what I'm going to do. Sneak in and snipe the bastards. But with those new sensor remotes, I need a way to get by them. My... partner can do that. Has done that. But she doesn't have current access."

"*She?*" Maya asked, really alarmed.

Shit. I'd been so careful to not use feminine pronouns right up until I did.

"Yeah. You don't know her. No one here does."

"Astrid?" she guessed.

"No, not Astrid. She knows everything there is to know about running an LTV into the Zone, but not this."

"Wait... you hooked up the *Zone War* people with someone who could harden their camera drones against hacking and interference, didn't you?"

"How'd you know about that?"

"Please. You introduced us to Ms. Flottercot a while ago, remember? She's been trying to hire any one or all three of us ever since. But we can't break our government contracts. However, the last time I spoke to her, she said not to worry about it. Said she could wait till our contracts were up because *you'd* introduced a drone expert to her who could work wonders. A *female* expert."

I was really tempted to lie my way out of it. In fact, my mouth was opening to do just that, but suddenly, different words came out. "Yes. She's really good with drones, better than me, and if she goes in with me, I think we can nail a Spider CThree. But it's dangerous for her to come to the attention of... certain people. So I need a blank access for her. And really, Maya, it *is* within my directive to bring outside experts in with me if I need them."

"But the major doesn't know her. Oh! You don't want him to know her, do you? You think he'd what? Hurt her?"

"I don't know. It's like how we all had to be careful when Agents Black and White came in and took Lotus. Like the major said... there are different factions within the government and even within the military. I know for a fact that some of them would be dangerous to her. I wouldn't even bring her in, but she's insisting and frankly, Maya, I need her if I'm going to live through this one. Would you at least think about it? And not say a word to anyone no matter what you decide?"

"Because if I say anything, I could put this girl in danger. Thanks a lot, Ajaya, for putting me in this position!"

"Yeah, I didn't want you to know who she was, but you figured it out. But I wouldn't have even approached you if it wasn't super important and if I couldn't trust you."

She frowned at me, clearly unhappy. But Maya was the best of the three and she was always nice to me. Eric was the major's bitch and Aaron would throw anyone under a bus to get ahead. I was pretty sure she wouldn't endanger Harper, but I was really unhappy that I'd messed up and let the cat out of the bag.

She studied me for a bit. Then nodded. "I'll *think* about it. And I won't say anything. But I'm still not happy about how you went about that."

CHAPTER 31

She agreed—eventually. Took a few days, but I think that was in my favor because the hunt for infiltrator bots got more urgent as time went on, not less.

Turns out that besides the crew of the cargo jet, seven other people died in and around the city over the last seventy-two hours, all in events that were likely caused by the Spiders' spy bots. Six died at LaGuardia the day after the crash at JFK. They were killed when an automated fuel truck suddenly diverted course and crashed into a hangar, spraying jet fuel everywhere. It happened *while* Yoshida and company were sweeping the place, a last-ditch attack by a bot that they found and neutralized twenty-three minutes later.

The seventh person died back at JFK when a cargo loader, also automated, dropped a crate on him. The science squad found a program buried in its code, one that activated exactly twelve hours after the JFK spy bot was ended.

All of this sent Zone Defense into a frenzy, searching for spy bots everywhere and anywhere they could think of. But the root cause was the pair of seven-legged horrors controlling the Zone. Yoshida sent me emails and left messages, pushing me for an answer to the problem of the Spiders. Everyone on the team knew he was almost frantic about it.

So Maya called me two afternoons later and told me she

236

had the access codes for Harper. All we had to do was show up at whichever entry point we wished and plug in her codes. She could use a false name and wear a disguise because the code itself would alert the soldiers manning that entry that she was a covert operator.

We went in the next morning, inserting at the Williamsburg Bridge entry. We were both stealth suited, equipped, and armed. Harper wore sunglasses and kept her stealth hood up and her neuroprosthesis off her face.

The soldiers all knew me and were clearly curious as hell about Harper, even flirting a bit. She did look pretty good in her stealth suit—all that fitness training paying off. But as soon as she punched in her Maya-given codes, they shut up and stopped talking to her. Didn't even look at her again.

"Wow, do I suddenly smell like rat crap?" she asked as soon as the door to the airlock closed behind us. I shushed her because the entry operators were likely listening in.

Once we got inside the Zone, the point was moot because talking was over. She took a moment to slip her shiny metallic face net thingy on, smoothing it down and taking particular care with a spot on her jaw hinge. I knew from earlier discussion that she had a magnetic connection under the skin there, implanted by her mother when she was very young.

Rikki slipped out to recon the area and I checked over my .338 Lapua Magnum while we waited for her to get the fit just right.

I had my Remington MSR as my primary weapon, with a short-barreled .300 Blackout PDW as my backup. The Personal Defense Weapon AR was from my own collection, liberated from a Federal Counterterrorism office in lower Manhattan. It was amazing what I could carry around without issue, now that I worked for Zone Defense. Oh, and about all the weapons talk—deal with it... I'm a sniper, for heaven's sake. Guns are my tools of trade.

Rikki swung back around, hovering in front of us, with three LEDs lit on his front face plate, just under his ocular band. I glanced at Harper to see if she understood. She nodded, turning and pointing two fingers in one direction and one finger on the other hand in a different direction, indicating she not only knew about them, but knew *where* they were.

We headed out, Rikki on point with me behind him and Harper bringing up the rear. I heard her rattling something and turned to see her nervously getting her own rifle situated on its patrol sling. The slightly anxious look on her face disappeared when she saw me looking, replaced with a cool poker face which was followed a second later by one sharply raised eyebrow.

Ignoring her facial bravado and now relatively certain I wasn't about to get shot in the back, I turned back to the front.

We moved down FDR Drive, then turned west on Grand Street for a short distance before getting onto the slightly smaller, narrower East Broadway, allowing us to move toward our target but less out in the open.

Zone War's constant missions had basically trained the Zone drones to watch major roads and thoroughfares, as the big armored vehicles did better on the wider streets. One or two smaller streets over could make all the difference for avoiding attention.

We moved pretty well right from the start, but then as we all got into the grove, actually got quite fast, speedier than Rikki and I would have on our own. Between the Berkut's sophisticated sensors out in front and Harper's prosthetic ones behind, we moved with a confidence that I had never experienced with anyone else.

We traveled down and around the southern end of the skinny Roosevelt Park, through what was once China-town. Every park on the island had grown into a mini-wilderness, providing habitat for deer and small game. Rikki started the dog sounds a block past the park, keeping the volume low to begin with. We didn't want to at-tract real dogs, but we also weren't sure how far out the spy sensors would be planted.

Harper was able to answer the sensor question when we got near Church Street, suddenly tapping my shoulder and pointing to her face or, more accurately, pointing at her metal prosthesis.

She already knew American Sign Language, as her mother had taught them both. ASL was something my class had taken up as well, with expert instructors brought in to teach all of us. While not fluent, most of us could carry on pretty informative conversations in silence. Harper signed to me that she could *feel* the sensors, pointing out where they were placed in the buildings and streets ahead of us. Rikki moved in close and began to gradually increase the dog sounds as we approached the invisible line of sensors. The fact that Harper could point to an arc of sensors that curved around the giant Hudson Street building confirmed our theory that at least one Spider was hanging around the internet switching building.

Thankfully, our plan called for us to climb up the inside of the old AT&T Long Lines building at 33 Thomas Street. Long Lines has twenty-nine floors, and 60 Hudson has twenty-four. The fact that it was just outside the sensor line was a bit of unforeseen luck.

The building *would* have been hell to break into, as it was built like a fortress, except that the front doors had been left wide open. The skeletons strewn about the lobby wore ragged uniforms that looked kind of official —like government official. The fact that the floor was liberally strewn with expended 5.56mm rifle casings lent a bit more support to the internet theory that the building had housed an NSA surveillance office at the time of the Attack. My research into the building had strongly hinted at NSA involvement in the building from its inception.

I spotted bits and pieces of drone among the fallen guards. There were no rifles or sidearms, and the bones were spread around like something had searched around and under them.

Most drones have the programming and capability to operate human firearms. The smaller ones and aerial units were limited to handguns, but bigger UGVs like Wolves and Leopards could operate a long gun. The guards' weapons had likely been taken by drones whose own ammunition supplies were used up. I had to hope that those gun-toting units had either left the building years ago or used up their stolen ordnance.

Inside the lobby, I took a few minutes to lighten both our packs by taking out a few little packages of mayhem, setting my bombs near the entrance to welcome any drones that might choose to join us. We scouted the first floor, found a rear door, and prepped it for a fast exit. Then I closed and jammed the front doors shut. The glass on the front seemed more like public aquarium glass than standard building material. Hopefully it would hold off anything trying to get in.

Now the fun part. We entered the stairwell, finding more bodies and almost complete drone carcasses, as well as piles of expended rifle and pistol brass.

Rikki ascended the open well, flying straight up, while the two of us climbed on good old-fashioned human feet.

Harper started out strong, the occasional glare thrown my way to reinforce her commitment. But ten stories into it, she was breathing pretty hard. At fifteen, she was starting to look really winded.

"Where are we going?" she asked, squinting at me, hands on her knees, sweat dripping down her brow.

"Roof," I said.

"Why not a different floor, any floor, as long as it's lower?" she asked.

"'Cause they don't have windows. Come on; let's go."

We got another six floors up before she spoke again.

"What kind of building has no windows?" she asked when she caught up. Bent over again. I hid a grin.

"An AT&T telephone exchange building. It was designed to stay operational through almost anything," I said, then took off again.

By the time we hit floor twenty-nine, the top floor, she was huffing and puffing like an old tobacco smoker. There is no fitness like stair climbing fitness. I gave her credit, though—two months ago, she would have collapsed in the first couple of flights. We went up one more flight, to the roof access.

"This looks more bank vault than roof door," she commented. An exaggeration, but the door was a really serious steel number that had a certain bombproof vibe to it.

"Told you they wanted a building to outlast anything," I said. The door was sealed on the inside, which was unusual but then, anything involving the intelligence community was not going to be ordinary. I pulled a little bottle of pressurized oxygen and a metal tube a third of a meter in length from her pack.

"I was carrying that?" she asked, frowning at me.

"Yes, and now your pack is so much lighter, right?"

I lit the magnesium wick at the end of the tube, then opened the valve on the tank.

The thermite lance ignited with a hiss and an eye-searing flare of sun-bright light and smoke. I applied it to the thick metal lock, my suit's facemask darkening automatically.

A few seconds later, the lock clanged to the floor and I pushed the door open, letting fresh air in and all the smoke out.

We moved out onto the roof after a pause for both Rikki and Harper to confirm that they weren't sensing any drone activity.

The roof stretched away from us, the access coming out on the east end. Massive cooling units and a whole cluster of giant satellite dishes filled the roof. I was interested in the west side, which would give me a great view of 60 Hudson Street. Of course it was the farthest point from where I stood. I pulled a couple of XM-2080s and set them up near the roof door, then linked them to Rikki. Okay, time to see what we could see.

"You said that AT&T owned this building?" Harper asked,

looking at the uplinks as we trudged the full length of the roof.

"Yeah. It was a major telephone switching center."

A high wall blocked my view, but in the southwest corner of the roof, I found a way to climb up to a kind of ledge that let me look out over the buildings below, including a full, open shot of 60 Hudson and most of its Ziggurat roofs and ledges.

Nothing moved over there, but I saw spots of black on a couple of the stepped ledge roofs. Time for a sniper's best friend – high quality binoculars. Mine are salvaged Swarovski's – 10x42 with high density glass – probably cost over two grand back in the day. They showed me the truth of it. Solar panels. Each less than a square meter of area.

At first, I thought they were just set up for a drone to use as needed, but then one of them shifted slightly in my magnified view. I realized that a mothership was underneath the black square, which was just its elevated charging panel, levered up from its back.

I've studied all the drone designs, but the motherships had captured the least amount of my attention. Mostly because they just weren't that dangerous to me by the time I started helping Dad.

The clusters of Wasps they carried were initially quite deadly, each able to kill up to five adult humans with their toxic payloads of hydrogen cyanide. However, the hordes of Wasps used up most or all of their toxins in the first week of the Attack. I've seen medical offices and hospitals that show signs of being searched by machines for replacement toxins, but most of the medical compounds in Manhattan had lost the majority of their efficacy over the last ten years. I just wasn't that worried about that type of drone and frankly, they were pretty rare for me to come across. But right then, I was pretty interested in them. Anything that was producing new forms of drones was a problem.

"Rikki, range to rooftops of 60 Hudson?"

"307 meters to eastern uppermost roof. 311 meters to lower southern roof ledge."

Both were well inside my comfortable shooting ranges. Dad and I spent whole afternoons shooting things at those ranges, and the concrete ledge would make a really solid shooting platform, although not very comfortable and very, very exposed. The motherships were on the lower roof ledge of the Hudson Street ziggurat, the roof door propped open.

From *my* pack, I took a very thin, ultra light roll of wispy material. Tiny legs opened at the corners, raising the meter-by-two-meter rectangle high enough off the ledge for me to sit up comfortably under it. The material rippled in the sunlight, dark at first, then fading to match the color of the roof. It used much the same tech as our stealthsuits.

"Why was the light stuff in *your* pack," Harper asked, still frowning.

"Expedient sniper hide. I'm the sniper."

Next I pulled out a small tightly folded square, busting the tape on one side that held it together. It instantly unfolded into a self-inflating body pad much like a backpacker's sleeping pad, although this one had built-in pouches to hold ammo and optics close at hand. A perfect prone shooting platform.

Unfolding my MSR and extending the bipod under the barrel, I set the big rifle in place along with an extra ammo mag in one of the handy pouches on the pad.

Once my setup was to my satisfaction, I hopped up on the ledge and lay down prone, starting to glass the building through the big Leopold scope. "Wind?" I asked.

"From the northwest, twenty-one kilometers per hour," Rikki responded. I took my time, drew up a range card, dialed in the sight corrections on my scope, and then settled back to watch.

Now we waited.

CHAPTER 32

"You ever wonder if it's possible for a drone to evolve?" Harper asked about thirty minutes into our watch.

"Evolve into what?" I asked, eye glued to the scope, watching the sunny rooftop three football fields away.

She was rummaging in her pack and she took her time answering as she extracted a pack of energy bars from inside.

"Just evolve... not so much physically as intellectually. Each is an artificial intelligence, a learning machine. We know they change over time, learn, possibly grow. Why couldn't they morph into a much different intellect than what they started as?" she finally asked, handing me a chocolate peanut butter bar.

I chewed and thought, still watching but thinking about her question. My eyes slipped away from the scope, looking left to the matte black drone that was soaking up sun on the roof to my side. "Yeah, I think that's entirely possible," I said, my eye going back to the scope to watch my target zone. "Why?"

"I guess I just wonder if any of the more sophisticated drones might lose interest in hunting humans."

"Like the Spiders? I doubt that," I said.

"No, not them. That mission is so core to their central existence that they'll never lose it. I just wonder is all. You know your Berkut is really, really unusual, don't you?" she asked.

Surprised, I glanced at her and found her staring at Rikki, a thoughtful look on her face.

"Yes, he's pretty much one of a kind."

"You've backed him up, right?"

"Of course. Nightly. But he also has three onboard memory chips that keep backing him up continuously."

"He does?" she asked, twisting around to look at me.

"Wow, don't be so surprised—I'm not a complete idiot, you know," I said.

"No, no, I'm just surprised you used three, that's all," she countered in an unusual display of something that might almost have been remorse.

"Redundancy, redundancy, redundancy," I said, eye back on the scope.

"Well, that's good. I'm not sure how you did it, but your Rikki is one of a kind," she said.

"Spider," I said.

"What? No, I said Rikki—not Spider," she clarified.

"No, I mean, I see a Spider," I counterclarified, cross hairs on a tubular, black, segmented leg the size of a sewer pipe.

The leg was just extended out of the open doorway on the southern roof ledge of 60 Hudson, only the claw tip actually in the sunlight. The rest of the Spider was hidden behind the swung open steel door, but I'd know that kind of robot leg anywhere.

"Shit. It's actually there, isn't it?" she asked in a hushed whisper. In my peripheral vision, I sensed her looking through my binoculars.

I ignored her rhetorical question, my scope reticle on the metal roof door, about where I expected the Spider's body to be. It was a normal door, not the overbuilt bastard of a vault door that was on our building. The heavy .338 bullets would zip through that door like tissue paper. The sight settled into what I felt was the best spot, my breathing slowed, and my finger slipped into the trigger guard, found the little metal lever that could unleash near instant death, and almost on its own, started to apply pressure.

The massive leg suddenly pulled back behind the door and my finger came off the trigger instantly. Shit. So close. But, like every hunter, patience was required. I waited, barely breathing.

Seconds clicked by, turning to minutes. Harper moved around on the roof, bored.

"Ajaya?" she asked, sounding further away. I turned and glanced at her. She was staring at one of the really big satellite dishes.

"Yeah?"

"You said this is an AT&T building?"

"Yup. Why?"

"Well, this is a really unusual dish. More government than I'd expect. Almost NASA or military. And those lobby guards must have had assault rifles. Not very Ma Bell," she said.

"Yeah, well, there were some rumors that this building was really used by the NSA, with AT&T providing cover for them. Did you know that there's a couple of floors that have nothing but backup batteries on them? That there's enough fuel and food stored here to keep fifteen hundred people going for two weeks?"

"WHAT?" she asked, her tone that sort of incredulous one that seems to imply I'm stupid.

Suddenly something new moved out of the door, into the open. Several somethings. Vertical cylinders, like a tube of tennis balls but with a rotor on top and coated in sky blue paint. Hairspray units, four of them. The bomber units of the Zone. Slow, awkward, but almost invisible when seen against the open sky. Usually carrying golf-ball-sized bomblets.

"Shit, look at those," I said. Harper moved over and climbed up till she could peer over the edge. My binoculars were in her right hand as she glassed the roof I was watching.

There were just the four of the little aerial bombers and they just hovered out from behind the door, floated over across the roof to land right on the mothership I had been watching earlier. Small charging probes extruded from the little bombers, which then plugged themselves into ports on the back of the mothership. They were powering up, getting the benefit of the bigger drone's solar panel.

Then something else stepped out from behind the door, a Russian Wolf, its jaws clamped on a plastic milk crate, the heavy duty kind that city delivery trucks used to leave at restaurants and diners throughout Manhattan every day. The crate had woven plastic sides, and I could see something inside through the little gaps in the plastic mesh.

"What is that? Inside the crate?" I asked, reaching to dial up the magnification on my scope.

"I don't know. There's some kind of red and yellow symbol?" she asked. "I can't quite make it out."

I could see what she was talking about. Just visible through the milk crate's porous sides. Yellow and some blotches of red. I dialed up again.

"Can't see it clearly. I can see part of a word: c—o—b—a—l," I spelled.

"Cobalt. Cobalt-60. That's a radioactivity symbol!" she said.

"What?"

"Hospitals use that isotope for tests and stuff," she said, her voice rising in urgency. "Holy shit! Do you know how many hospitals are in Manhattan?"

"I don't know... like more than ten, maybe?"

"Probably more like twenty. Ajaya, if you collected all the medical radioactive isotopes from Manhattan's hospitals, you'd have quite a lot... like a dangerous amount."

Another Wolf came out the open door, this one carrying a metal box with the radioactive symbol right on its side.

"Ajaya, if they load that material into those bombers, they might try to get it out into the rest of the city," Harper said.

"They'll never get past the Renders, Harper. They'll get blown to dust," I said.

"And then the winds would blow radioactive dust all over Brooklyn," she replied.

"Is that really enough to do much damage?"

"I have no idea, but it can't be good to have radioactive dust floating through the most heavily populated borough in New York," she said.

The Wolves set the boxes down and then returned to the building's interior. A moment later, two of the Spider's feet moved back into view, the rest of it again hidden behind the door.

One of the hairspray units unplugged itself and then hovered over the milk crate. It settled down into the box and began some kind of activity with tiny manipulators on the bottom of its spray-can-shaped body.

"It's loading the Cobalt-60," Harper said, turning to look at me.

"So what do I do? I can kill that Spider right now, but if I shoot one of those hairsprays, I'll blast radioactive material all over the place, not to mention losing the Spider."

"No, it would just spatter around on the roof. A Render missile would vaporize it; your bullet would just spill it. Big difference. Ajaya, your family is downwind," she said.

I thought about it, thought my way through the shots. Time slowed and my brain sped up, firing solutions presenting themselves like a series of steps on a recipe card. I could just about do it.

"Get ready to move! Rikki, prep XM-2080s. Harper, grab both packs and both carbines, then get in the stairwell. As soon as I shoot, we're out of here."

She started moving but my trigger finger was already taking up the slack, the ballistic computer of my brain taking over. The rifle suddenly went off, thumping my shoulder. In my side vision, I saw Harper jump, but I was focused and in my shooting zone, my right hand running the bolt, my left moving the rifle to its new target, the right hand back on the pistol grip. The big rifle fired again, and again, and then a final time.

I pulled away from the scope, shifted my body back and off the ledge, folding the rifle's stock and grabbing the extra mag as I turned to run.

The last images in the scope popped up as my mind automatically ran through the shots. In my mind's eye, I saw that the metal door on that other roof now had a big round hole in its center, that the Spider legs were gone, that the two boxes of radioactive material were exploded all over the rooftop, and that the two of the hairspray bombers had just become piles of parts. I think the mothership drone was damaged too.

I dropped the partial mag, inserting the full one as I ran for the roof access door. Rikki hovered behind me, floating backward, gun still covering the open air behind us.

"Six UAVs inbound. Correction, now seventeen. Additional units responding on the network."

"Activate motion sensors on XM-2080s," I said as we hustled through the open stairwell door.

Harper shoved the door shut while I grabbed the broken lock bar and jammed it into the frame. She handed me my pack and my PDW, which I slung on my back, as the big MSR was in my arms.

Then we raced down the stairs.

CHAPTER 33

"Ajaya, you should have told me this was an NSA build-ing," Harper said, her footsteps sounding right behind me.

Going down is so much faster.

"Ah, you think this is a good time to chat about gaps in my pre-mission briefing?" I asked over my shoulder.

We only made two flights down before the building shook like a giant had smacked it and a thunderclap boomed over our heads. The UAVs had met my XM-2080 welcoming committee.

We picked ourselves up and kept going, jumping down three, four, and five sets of stair treads at a time. Fast, but brutal on the knees. I think we both should have fallen, more than once, but something—adrenaline maybe or just good old-fashioned fear—kept our feet on the dust-covered treads. Rikki hovered straight down the center of the stairwell, floating gracefully while we thumped, grunted, and stumbled our way back down.

"Yes, this is the time, you moron," she continued two floors further down. "Did you ever wonder if a build-ing with extensive battery and generator power facilities and its own military satellite uplink might be useful to a Spider CThree?"

Realization struck and I understood her point. The bot-tom of my stomach started to fall out, but then I remem-bered the massive Spider feet poking out the door at 60

Hudson.

"The Spider was in the other building. In fact, I think I might have put a round right through it," I said.

"There are two Spiders," she said.

The door to floor twenty-five exploded off its hinges, a huge black, segmented leg pulling back and a gray-green monster leaping through.

The overwhelming report of my .338 hurt every bit as much as the recoil did, and *that* almost tore the big rifle from my hands as I fired from the hip. The bullet didn't knock the machine back but it sure paused its forward motion for a moment.

Rikki's 9mm burped a long stuttering string of automatic fire, bullets tearing into the same spot my magnum round had already pierced. I'm a really good shot, but only a machine could successfully target the hole my bullet had created.

The Tiger stopped and shuddered in place, the sound of high-speed ricochets coming from *inside* its metal body.

I racked the bolt on the MSR but the Spider was gone, pulling its horrid cluster of legs back down the hall and around a corner so fast, it was like someone hit rewind.

Ears ringing, I waved Harper to go down the stairs, tossed a new block of ammo to Rikki, then pulled an MSLAM out and set it in the torn-open doorway, set for motion activation.

We doubled our speed down the stairs, moving so fast that we both should have fallen multiple times over. Yet I don't remember my feet even touching the stairs. Floors flew by and then suddenly we were down.

Breathless, we both paused, listening, trying to hear over the rasp of air and thud of our heartbeats. Not a single sound came from above. Rikki floated over to the stairwell door, waiting patiently for me to open it. When I complied, he moved slowly through, pausing to scan with his much stronger electronic senses. A glance at Harper showed her standing still, head tilted as she did her own electronic scan, the metal mesh of her neuroprosthesis gleaming on her cheek. As my breathing slowed, I started to hear a rhythmic pounding sound coming from outside the stairwell.

"Multiple UGVs outside main entrance. Poly laminated bullet-resistant glass currently still holding. Exit in this direction is untenable."

I looked at Harper. She shook her head. "They're trying to break through it. More units are responding," she said.

"What about the Spider above us?"

"I don't get anything. Never did. These floors must be shielded six ways from Sunday to contain random radio waves. The good news is that it can't call for more help if it's hiding up there."

An explosion above us sent concrete dust showering down. Then came the tick-tick-tick of multiple metal legs on stairs.

"We're out of here!" I said, slinging my MSR and unlimbering my PDW. We kept going down the stairs, heading to the first basement. The Long Lines building has three basements. During our recon of the ground level earlier, we figured out that the only other exit from the building was from the parking garage on basement one. We never went below that level, mostly because some seriously heavy duty locked doors blocked our access to whatever was underneath.

Rikki's light threw the shadow of my carbine across the mostly black interior as I led the way to the garage exit, my drone above and behind me. The underground garage exit turned right and ramped up to street level on Thomas Street, rising from underneath the front door. But unlike the front door, the vehicle entrance had been securely gated shut and the man-sized door in the metal garage door had been locked when we found it. Key word being *had.* We had fixed that little detail before climbing the tower stairs to the roof. Now, I didn't even stop, just hit the metal door and stepped out onto the vehicle ramp.

I was shooting immediately, Rikki flying up above my head, his own 9mm brass bouncing off my head as he too fired on the drones that awaited us further up the ramp. Flechettes stitched across the concrete behind us, ricocheted off the ramp itself, pain blossoming in my legs and torso, my suit face mask darkening to almost welder black.

The little AAC Honey Badger spat out full auto bursts of .300 caliber bullets. Egan, my supply *guy,* had provided supersonic rounds with steel core bullets that I had loaded into the magazines of both my gun and Harper's. While they had nowhere near the impact of .458, firing three, four, or five into a Wolf, Crane, or any of the Skyhawks and Raptors pretty much ruined the Zone drones' day. But as fast as we knocked them out of the air or beat them into the ground, more appeared at the top of the ramp.

"*Pull back,*" Rikki said. I listened, stepping into the garage and yanking the heavy steel door shut. A staccato rain of flechettes rang on the hardened exterior as Harper played her flashlight over my body.

"You got some wires poking out of you. Hold still," she said. Folding pliers appeared in her hand and without any other notice, she just started to yank bits of bent flechette out of my stealth suit and, oh yeah, me.

"Ouch! We don't have time for this. Ow! Damn it!"

"Stop whining. There's too many out there to get through. But something's coming. Now move your arm!"

"Shit! That shacking hurt! What something?"

"I. Don't. Know. Got it!" she yanked extra hard, actually tearing the tough material of my stealth suit. Most of the wire-thin flechettes had only gone halfway through the suit, bending over like poorly pounded nails, so my wounds were painful but not in any way life threatening. Unlike Harper, who was in increasing danger of meeting with violence.

"Okay, okay. Stop already, " I said, stepping backward. "Thank you. But Harper—what something are you talking about?"

Then I heard the distinctive whine-thump of an electro-mag weapon firing outside the vehicle gate, further up the ramp, maybe on the street. The patter of flechettes against the steel exit door dropped off instantly. Another whump of e-mag fire, still outside but from a different direction. Then a set of angry hissing sounds, like a pack of mambas, followed a second later by multiple explosions.

"*Unit 19 has arrived,*" Rikki said, moving back up over my head in front of the heavy man door. I moved over sideways, putting myself behind the door frame. New mag in the Badger—check. New ammo block tossed to Rikki—

check. Harper somewhere way, way behind me—check. Kick door open and start shooting.

Funny thing: There was nothing to shoot. Just a bunch of destroyed drones on the ramp, along with pieces of drone, as well as the big, matte black delta shape of the Decimator.

"*Unit 19 ready*," it said in its extremely mechanical voice. By comparison, Rikki's has a much more humanlike tone.

"Area status?"

"*Incoming units approaching down both ends of Thomas Street,*" Unit 19 reported.

"How many?"

"*Multiple.*"

Apparently Unit 19 wasn't really one for details. What to do, what to do?

A soft whir came from behind us and I whipped around, rifle rising. A sleek red car was ghosting toward us, almost silent, a sharp dagger-like T on the front hood and Harper grinning at me from behind the wheel. The car slowed but didn't stop and I leapt back out of the way as it lightly crunched into the garage door.

Harper's grin was gone but she jumped out of the car, excited nonetheless.

"I noticed this earlier when we came down to open the exit. All plugged in but I didn't think anything of it until you told me about the batteries and the generators. If the Spiders ran power at all, this thing would have charged. It's got a third of a charge!"

"Excellent, but get in the passenger seat. You've never driven before, have you?" I asked.

"Where would I have learned?" she frowned.

I checked the Tesla and found she was exactly correct. It had enough juice to take us to the end of Long Island. We just needed Brooklyn or Jersey.

Nowadays, almost nobody actually drives a car; the computers do all the work. Kids basically take a written test and demonstrate that they could control a vehicle if the computer failed— and they do that on a simulator. Maybe kids in rural areas still learn, but not in the Big Apple.

But my grandpa upstate had taught me to drive actual cars. He had a small collection, about half of them gas fueled. So this was easy.

"Let's get the garage door open," I said.

Rikki instantly floated over to the wall and poked his nose needle into a button.

The big door started to rise, driven by electric motors that must have had battery backup too—batteries that also got charged when Peony or Plum Blossom ran the building generators.

Rikki floated out ahead of us as we started out of the garage, turning onto the ramp. Unit 19 spun around a hundred and eighty degrees facing back outside, starting forward as we came abreast of it.

Metal crunched and dragged as I wove between broken Wolf and Crane carcasses, but they all fell away and the tires seemed okay.

Daylight was almost blinding as we arrived on Thomas Street, the ramp pointing us west. I floored the car, the instant acceleration slamming us back into our seats, the car momentarily jumping out in front of our drone escort.

A huge swarm of aerial units flocked down, dive bombing us, blasting flechettes, dropping bricks and pieces of metal on the windshield, lasing the tires while Rikki and 19 swooped among them like falcons on the hunt.

Unless they've been bulldozed by one of the *Zone War* armored vehicles, most roads in Manhattan are obstacle courses of derelict vehicles and debris. The Tesla had great acceleration but with no clear straightaways, I was forced to weave and dodge around buses, taxis, and crashed cars while running over curbs, knocked-down sign posts, and crunching across human skeletons.

Our car was a sedan, with no real ground clearance, and it was taking a huge beating as I smashed, banged, and rolled over everything in our way.

At the first intersection, I turned left down Church Street, couldn't turn down Reade Street because of a flipped-over garbage truck, so I went a block further before turning left again onto Chamber Street.

Skyhawks and Raptors shot out of the intersections ahead of me, Wolves, Leopards, and Tigers bounding at us from behind us, on each side, and from straight in front of us.

Rikki and Unit 19 were shooting and swooping, blasting UAVs with guns. The big Decimator used its missiles on the first wave of UGVs, blowing up at least seven or eight as we raced down the street. Then it ran out of missiles and the bigger land bots started to jump onto the car.

A Tiger landed on the hood, claws sunk right into the metal body. Harper screamed once and then shot it off the car with her rifle, the gun blasts peppering both of us with unburnt powder that bounced off the now perforated windshield. The Tiger fell away, immediately replaced by a Leopard that landed on the roof, the steel talons punching right through the metal above our heads.

Still yelling, Harper fired her rifle straight up, twisting and turning as she did so, somehow ejecting hot brass right onto my neck. I swerved around a US Mail Jeep, clipped the side of a big blue mail box, knocking the bullet-torn metal cat off the Tesla.

A Wolf landed on the hood, immediately followed by a crunching sound on the trunk. A glance in the rearview showed a second Wolf clinging to the back of the car. Both bots immediately started to drag themselves toward the nearest wheel well.

"If they shred our tires, we're dead," I yelled.

Harper pointed her rifle and pulled the trigger. The weapon clicked empty.

"Reload! You have to reload! Like I taught you," I yelled.

She let the rifle fall into her lap, staring straight ahead. For a split second, I thought she must have just shut down —gone into shock. But suddenly the Wolf on the hood froze. Then it turned and looked right at her. A second later it crouched, coiling up, then leapt over the roof, smashing into the Wolf at the back, both bots falling away in a tumbling, twisting dogfight.

"Reload," I said again, softer this time. She glanced my way, eyes refocusing, then looked at the rifle in her lap like it was her first time seeing it. Fumbling, her hands started the process of pulling the empty magazine and locking in a fresh one. It took her a few tries but she got it.

Meanwhile, I finally had a bit of a straightaway and I nailed it, putting a few more meters between us and the chasing bots.

CHAPTER 34

Weaving around a city maintenance truck, the end of the street suddenly came into view. The massive Manhattan municipal building loomed over everything, a solid dark mass that took up two city blocks. The huge building was lit by the sun behind us, the whole face of it illuminated. Realization flooded my mind. The sun was setting. Darkness was almost here.

Normally, nighttime in the Zone was a good thing, with drones slowing and losing power in the fading light. But that all went out the window when Spiders were running emergency generators inside former NSA hard points.

Just a fast right-hand turn down Centre Street, a turn that was right smack dab in front of the muni building, and there would be the ramp leading up onto the Brooklyn Bridge and to freedom. I pushed the speed up, even though my clear straightaway was gone, ruined by the string of NYPD cruisers lined up across the road. Some kind of last-ditch stand to protect the city building maybe. The white cars were pocked with bullet holes, laser burns, flechette marks, and rust.

My peripheral vision picked up on Harper's nervous glance my way. I ignored it, speeding up a little more. We needed to get off the island before dark. Fully powered drones had all the advantages in the almost complete black of Zone night.

"Ajaya..." she began, but whatever she was going to say

was blanked out by the mass of concrete and brick that suddenly impacted the street directly in front of us. My foot hit the brake but the car was already hitting the stone. Something smacked my face, blocking my vision, even as I felt the rear wheels come up off the ground. A second later, the car fell back, slamming down with a huge crash.

Stunned, head reeling from impact, my mind was nonetheless screaming at me to get moving.

Peeling what I now realized was an airbag off my face, brushing away powder from the bag, I started to unbuckle myself. A glance at Harper showed me she was even more stunned than I was, so I reached over and popped her seatbelt too.

"Driver door is unlikely to function. Egress passenger side," Rikki said, hovering outside my window.

I heard the whine-thump of 19's e-mag, then Rikki lifted a half meter higher and ripped off three fast shots.

Crawling almost into Harper's lap, I got her door unlatched, hitting it over and over with the heels of both hands until it moved. Then I really climbed on top of her and shoved the door open while she shoved me off her.

Outside, I looked behind us to see a flock of drones flying our way, our Decimator and Berkut calmly sniping away.

Suddenly terrified we were going to die almost in sight of the bridge, I yanked Harper out of the car, pushed her rifle into her hands, and hauled her by main force toward the only shelter in sight—the municipal building.

"Out of ammo," Rikki said, floating backward. I fumbled the last full ammo block I had for him from my pouch, awkwardly throwing it his way.

It was a bad throw, forcing him to twist around and face the muni building. Which is why he didn't sense the Sky-hawk that slammed into him in a suicide run.

The Indian UAV spun off and exploded into fragments against the broken fragments of building that had crashed down in front of our car. Rikki ricocheted the opposite direction, flung almost directly into my arms, his ocular band completely dark.

"Come on!" Harper yelled, now alert to our danger. She took off at a full sprint and, still clutching Rikki, I raced after her.

Feet thumping on pavement, the *zip* and *ting* of high velocity flechettes impacting all around us while behind, Unit 19 continued to fire its electromagnetic weapon, giving us as much cover as it could. We were close—so close—just twenty or so meters to go.

We raced across Centre Street, under the arches and into the government building, straight through the wide-open doors, jumping over piles of clothes with skeletal remains poking out.

At first, we just ran flat-out, but the interior was dark and we slowed, both looking around.

"Unit 19. Where are the nearest stairs?"

The big UAV swung around, its nose now pointed down a dark side hall. We turned and ran into the dark. Light bloomed, LEDs on the front of the Decimator, and we found the door to the stairwell. Once inside, we jimmied the door shut behind us and then climbed. Three floors later, we slowed, both exhausted and out of juice. I requested that the Decimator check the area just outside the stairwell and it complied readily, although it

John Conroe

completely ignored Harper when she asked for some additional light.

"How did it get here?" she asked me, watching it with a frown as it hovered down the long, black hallway in front of us. We were in some old nook of the third floor, away from the offices with windows.

"I don't know. Let's ask it when it returns. For now, I want to look at Rikki."

I wish I hadn't. Three of his rotors were busted, one of them so completely that the drive motor hung by just one thin wire.

"Oh man, I have so much work to do to get him back online," I said.

Harper looked at me sharply and when I raised an eyebrow at her incredulous expression, her face turned sympathetic. She reached over and turned the Berkut in my lap, shifting it enough that I could see the top of his airframe. A deep cavity was punched right into the tough carbon fiber, about the shape and size of a Skyhawk's nose cone.

"Shit, shit, shit," I said, yanking out a chemical light stick. We had held off while waiting for the Decimator's report, but now I had to see the extent of the damage.

His protective shell was crushed, right over his CPU. It was so bad that I couldn't get the outer case open and had to pick out shards of broken armor until I could see the core of his being. It was gone—smashed completely. My Berkut was dead.

266

CHAPTER 35

I went numb, my brain racing through *oh shit* to *no way* to *this can't have happened.*

Harper leaned in and when I glanced up, she was studying the Berkut's damage with a critical eye, but I didn't need her diagnosis—the Berkut that had guarded my back, front, and sides for over two years was gone. My buddy was gone.

"He's backed up," she said, making it a statement.

"But the computing chips, the CPU, they're gone, smashed."

"It's the software, Ajaya," she said, "Not the hardware."

"Where would I even get another Berkut to build from?"

She opened her mouth but closed it, uncharacteristically staying silent.

"Immediate area clear," Unit 19 said, sliding into our darkened alcove so quietly that I almost jumped. But its presence gave me something different to think about and reminded me that *we* still needed to survive or any thoughts about Rikki were moot.

"Unit 19, how did you get out of Zone Defense?" I asked.

"Dr. Comis ordered Unit 19 to support Instructor Gurung."

"Dr. who?" Harper asked.

"Maya. Maya Comis. She's the one who got you access to the Zone. Unit 19, when did Dr. Comis issue your instructions?"

"At 15:36 hundred hours. Direct physical access was granted via Roosevelt Island drone chute."

"Why did Dr. Comis send you?"

"Instructor Gurung had not checked in. Dr. Comis speculated that unforeseen circumstances had prevented contact. During forty-seven minutes of increasing physical signs of personal anxiety, Dr. Comis commented out loud various possible scenarios ranging from mechanical injury to ambush to death. Unit 19 was subsequently ordered to render all aid and support to Instructor Gurung."

"Great. Your girlfriend—your office girlfriend—freaked out and sent help—*to you*. What about me?"

"She doesn't know you, Harper, and she's not my girlfriend. Just a good friend. But you have a good point. Unit 19, please add Harper Leeds to your command network. You are to obey her commands and render her aid as well."

"Unit 19 will comply with level three commands from individual Harper Leeds and will render aid."

"What's that mean? Level three commands?"

"It means you're lower down the command chain but it will obey as long as your orders do not conflict with higher-level orders."

"What level are you at?" she asked, hands on her hips.

"I don't know," I said. The pushy, competitive Harper was back.

"Unit 19, what command level does Instructor Gurung hold?" she asked.

"*Level one.*"

She snorted, gave me an eye roll, and turned away to continue looking at Rikki's broken shell.

"Unit 19, do you sense any drones in this building?"

"*Affirmative. UGV and UAV activity noted on ground floor, in three stairwells, and one basement.*"

"Anything approaching this position?"

"*Negative. Ground floor activity has diminished within last fifteen-minute time period. Likely due to onset of nightfall.*"

The Decimator was no Rikki, but I could see some improvement over the last few times I had interacted with it. Volunteering a potential reason for the reduction in nearby drone activity was something it wouldn't have done a few months ago.

I sat down, deciding that we were okay for the moment. Harper threw me an energy bar and I washed it down with sips from my stealth suit's hydration unit.

Beat—emotionally, mentally, and physically—I let myself relax, taking time to check my weapons. Only two full mags for the .300 Blackout, one of which I switched into the weapon, storing the partial mag that had been in the gun. I had seventeen rounds of .338 remaining for the MSR, but I'd be unlikely to be able to shoot them all off before one of the Spiders' minions took me out.

Harper asked me questions, things about the Spider in the NSA building, stuff about our plans, changes we might have to make. In short, she distracted me, kept my brain working as much as she could, kept me planning, leaving no room to consider other things—darker thoughts.

We talked for quite a while and my brain got mushy.

"Ajaya," Harper called in a near whisper. I glanced up, suddenly worried. She waved a hand at my expression, her body language relaxed. "Take a rest. We can't leave while they're still active out there. I'll keep watch with Unit 19."

I started to protest, but the entirety of my exhaustion hit me. "No more than twenty minutes," I said.

"Sure," she said, cracking a chemical light-stick and leaning over Rikki's remains. "Twenty minutes tops," she said, eyes focused on the Berkut.

I let my eyes close, taking a slow breath to try and calm my brain. And then I woke up. Strange, weird dreams one moment, wide awake and anxious the next.

Harper turned at my sudden movement, clearly startled by the motion.

"How long?" I asked.

"I don't know... maybe a bit more than fifteen minutes," she said. Unit 19 was flat on the ground in front of her and she seemed to be checking the big Decimator over.

"Where's Rikki?" I asked.

The Decimator started to rise but she stopped it with a touch of her hand, still looking at me. "I wrapped the airframe and put it in your backpack. This one is pretty much ready to go," she said, an oddly satisfied expression on her face.

"Still has ammo?"

"Yeah. Those electromagnetic weapons are hell on power

but leave a whole lot of space for ball bearing ammo. Probably fifty or more shots left. I can't believe how much power storage they managed to get in this frame," she said, eyeing the big drone with clear admiration.

"Any sign of drones?" I asked.

"This one says there are five still in the building, all lying dormant to conserve power. I can't sense any of them, but my range is shorter. If we can get around them, we should be able to get out one of the extra doors and get across the bridge."

"Any ideas on how to work that?"

"Yeah, actually. I noticed that you have rope in that pack, and what looks to my uneducated eye to be climbing harnesses. Think we could get down an elevator shaft? There are apparently like thirty of them in this building. No way can five drones cover this whole place."

"You ever use climbing gear?"

"I've been to an indoor rock gym a few times. If you belt me in and give me some pointers, I'm pretty sure I can rappel down a few stories in an elevator shaft."

"How are we going to pick the shaft?"

She reached up and tapped the side of her face, her finger brushing the metal mesh. Then she reached down and tapped the carbon fiber shell of the Decimator.

It made me miss my Berkut. It would be so easy with Rikki. I knew she was really good with her neuroprosthesis, but her range was short and I didn't have anywhere near as much faith in Unit 19. But our options were limited and if we gave the Spiders time, they could and probably would march an army of freshly powered drones into this building to hunt us in the dark.

I did know that Unit 19's sensors were cutting edge, as was all the other technology packed into its frame. But it just didn't have the software of my drone, which I was mildly annoyed that Harper had packed away. It felt like I should have been the one to do that.

But I had apparently passed right out and I did feel marginally better. Climbing upright and retrieving my pack, I was still tight, sore, and exhausted, the scabs on my torso and legs pulling painfully as my stealth suit stretched, but overall, I was not quite as bad as before. We could get out—no, strike that—we *had* to get out. Now, before the CThrees or ThreeCs, as they were sometimes called, had more time to prep their forces.

Hopefully Peony was nursing a .338-sized wound right through its core.

"Alright, what's the plan?"

"I think we head toward the back of this floor, maybe down on the other side. We'll scan for trouble, avoid the stairs, and pick an elevator shaft. This one can scout the shaft, and if it's okay, we'll rappel down, sneak the hell out the back somewhere, and beat feet over the bridge."

It was as good an idea as I could think of. The muni building was absolutely huge, each floor a vast space unto itself. With the Decimator looking for trouble, we were very likely to pick a clear spot and sneak out, which sort of bothered me. Why only five units? Why not put a hundred dormant drones all through the ground floor? What could distract the Spiders from the hunt?

"Unit 19, what was the state of the Zone Instant Response Strike Force at the time of your deployment?"

The Decimator didn't respond immediately until Harper

gave it a tap, which seemed… odd.

"IRSF was deployed across multiple theaters of operation with a reserve force held at Zone Defense Headquarters for emergency contingencies," the big drone said. Maybe it was because it was sitting on the floor, but it sounded slightly odd. Better not be running out of power.

"What is your status?"

"Missile packs depleted. EMag ammunition reserves at forty-two percent. Power at seventy-one percent. All other systems nominal as per standard Decimator specifications."

Still sounded weird. But I was over being here and the more I thought about it, the more Harper's plan sounded like the right one.

"Alright. Let's get going," I said.

Unit 19 shot up off the ground, the down blast of air blowing my food bar wrapper right out of the doorway. Its sudden takeoff left it almost seven feet off the ground and it had to drop down a bit before it could fly out the door of the little alcove we were camped out in.

"What did you do?" I asked Harper, causing her to snap around and stare at me, shocked. "Give it vitamins or something?" I finished, taking a perverse enjoyment in seeing her flustered.

She snorted, looking down at her own weapon. "Sure. Why not? Maybe I invented cocaine for drones," she said, following the big drone out.

CHAPTER 36

Did I mention how large the building was? Because it was... really large. In the middle of the third floor, we were so far from any windows that we would have been in complete darkness if not for the green glow of our chem sticks. Unit 19 hovered silently and damned near invisibly just ahead of us as we navigated the maze of offices, hallways, meeting rooms, and elevator banks.

We cut a careful diagonal across the floor, moving to the opposite corner, till we got near the rear. Harper said that she had run probability calculations with Unit 19, and they indicated that most of the ground units would be spread in the front and back of the building as well as the side nearest the bridge. So we would head to the furthest point from them and choose our elevator shaft very, very carefully.

I'm not going to lie... it was spooky as hell. Especially without Rikki. That damned Decimator was just a silent smudge of darkness against even darker blackness. And we took it slow, being very careful to step softly, open doors smoothly, and avoid making any sound at all. The soft soles of our boots were specially designed for silent movement, just as our stealth suits had a soft brushed exterior to avoid noise.

My trainees had gotten very very good by the end of our classes, building on their considerable skills as snipers and scouts, but none of them had a mark on Harper. I guess growing up *inside* the Zone tends to teach silent movement like no other class on Earth.

After long minutes of creeping through ghoulish green illumination, we both froze at sudden unexpected lights. I think we both realized at about the same time that we were just seeing the lights of Brooklyn through the rear windows of the building. It was just a few, as we were only on the third floor and numerous dark buildings blocked much of our view, but that handful of bright lights was a huge uplift after what seemed like hours of darkness. Probably less than an hour since we ran into the building, but between the nap and the stygian blackness, it seemed longer.

When I remembered to breathe again, I looked at Harper, who just gave me a wide-eyed glance before looking away. Unit 19 was stopped at the next door, hovering silently in place, like it had forgotten what it was doing. Weird damned drone. When I moved right up behind it, the dark mass suddenly slid forward, entering what I could see was a hallway. Open doorways showed offices with big windows, and most had at least a few Brooklyn lights visible through the glass.

Now that it was moving, Unit 19 accelerated right down the hall and stopped in front of a pair of very old elevator doors. When we got up to it, the damned thing swiveled in place and lit up a single green LED on its faceplate. Probably picked that up from its training with Rikki.

"All clear?" I asked, just to make sure.

"Yes, it doesn't sense anything," Harper said almost absently.

"Let me guess... you connected your prosthesis to it while I was napping?"

She waggled one hand. "Kinda sorta. I get impressions from it, not a full connection."

I pulled off my pack and got out rope, harnesses, and a few odds and ends of gear. Then I pried the elevator doors open with my kukri. Unit 19 shot into the shaft like an overeager hunting dog, slammed to a halt, then slowly and smoothly descended.

"You sure that thing is all right? Seems herky jerky to me."

She gave me a glance, then shrugged. "How would I know?"

I tapped my right cheek and nodded her way.

"Like I said... not a clear connection. Just impressions. Maybe they did some updates and it's still incorporating them? How do I put this thing on? It's different from the gym one."

A few minutes later, she was harnessed up and I was getting my own on when 19 came back up the shaft.

"Clear."

With a glance at Harper, I tossed the coil of rope, which I had already tied off to a radiator, down the shaft, then helped her get roped up. Next I tossed a chem light down the center of the shaft. The light stick fell all the way to the bottom of the shaft, down in what must have been the basement. It made a depressingly small circle of sickly green light way, way below.

"Unit 19, be prepared to catch Harper if she falls," I told the drone. It waggled its wings in what must have been another imitation of Rikki.

"Hahaha, very funny," she said.

"No joke. If you fell, I'm pretty sure it could catch you. Those fans are hella strong."

"Then why rope up at all?" she asked, then answered her own question a split second later. "Oh, power usage, right?"

"Yeah. Not sure how long its charges would last if we used it like a lift, and we might need every bit of power for its EMag weapon to cover our exit over the bridge."

The big drone had already begun to descend again and now Harper took a breath and inched her way till she was backed up to the edge of the pitch dark shaft. With sharp, jerky motions, she released enough line so that she now leaned out over the straight drop. Then, holding my eyes with her own, she let a bigger bit of rope run out, simultaneously taking a little jump. She only dropped a foot or so, but it gave her enough confidence that her next bound took her away into the darkness.

When I leaned out over the edge, I saw her, illuminated in a pool of soft green light, making good progress toward our goal, which was two stories below. The delta shape of the Decimator was outlined by the green light at the bottom of the shaft. The big drone was holding station right at the first floor elevator doors.

Harper made it down in just a few long moments, and she successfully, if nervously, got herself onto the little ledge that ran around the shaft. I waited till she clicked her carabiner to a cable on the concrete wall before I roped myself up and began my rappel.

Soon enough, I too was down with my feet on the ledge. I stayed on the rope as I worked my way to the doors. I glanced back at the Decimator and it took that as a cue to illuminate me with a single LED. I tilted my head and opened my mouth to ask if the way was still clear, but Unit 19 waggled its wings as soon as my head moved to one side. Damn but Unit 19 was making real progress on body language.

My kukri slipped between the doors and they popped right open. 19 slipped out into the hall and scanned in every direction, then waggled again. I slipped out, got off the rope, and then waved Harper to make the transition around the ledge and out onto the ground floor.

CHAPTER 37

The muni building was the exact opposite of 33 Thomas: exit doors all over the place. We egressed out the back corner, stepping out from under an arch that was much smaller than the one on the front. A few ruined cars were parked in what must have once been assigned spots. They made good cover as we slipped through the dark of night, working our way toward the twisting loops of road that ramped up to the gargantuan bridge that stretched out in front of us, backlit by the lights of Brooklyn.

It was so close. But we had meters and meters of open ground till we could get on the ramps, and Unit 19 was pointed directly at our objective but frozen in place, multiple fans softly blowing exactly the correct amount of air in just the right directions to hold the meter-wide machine motionless.

I wanted to ask if the way was clear but realized that I didn't have to. Unit 19 was on point like my grandfather's setter, Darby. Something deadly, or maybe several somethings, were between us and safety.

Why bother to hunt us out of the massive, labyrinthine building when we had to cross the bridge to get home? Just stake out our exit path. That's why the Spiders had only put five drones in the building.

So I moved up and under the Decimator, crouching down to study the way ahead. There was enough ambient light to see the thick tree cover that had fully overgrown the roads. I was feeling really unsure. If Rikki had been here, I would have no problem figuring out how many and what kind of drones awaited us, and probably where they were hidden. But Unit 19 had nowhere near Rikki's sophistication. It just hovered on station.

I turned to Harper. She too was frozen, one hand touching her prosthesis. But she noticed my attention and turned her head slightly toward me. Then her left hand came up with three fingers extended. Her right hand pointed straight ahead, then swung to the left as she folded one of her three fingers.

Five drones. Three ahead, two off to the left. I wasn't sure if she was reading them herself or if she was picking up on Unit 19. I didn't like it—any of it. I was odd man out, unable to read the drone protecting us and unable to convey the proper tactics, to call the plays we needed if we were going to get a first down.

I needed more information. Tapping Harper on the arm to get her attention, I mimed a flying bird with one hand, then made finger-crawling motions.

She frowned but immediately pointed left, held up one finger while copying my finger motion for a ground bot with the other. Then made a better bird motion. One of each. I raised an eyebrow and made a clawing motion. She nodded. Great: a Tiger and Kite to the left.

Then she pointed straight ahead and made more crawling fingers before holding up three fingers. Three UGVs. When she saw that I understood, she leaned her head back and made a silent howl at the half moon overhead. Wolves.

Four ground units, in the dark, and no Rikki. We needed some kind of edge. If we stepped into those trees, we would be bloody meat in seconds. Nighttime might be my friend most days in the Zone now, but not against fully charged combat drones. Like the natural predators they were copied from, they had all the advantages. Thermal night vision, acute acoustic sensors, as well as ground vibration detectors. Unit 19 could pick them out and probably pick them off, at least the Wolves. But the Tiger had armor that would present a challenge even to 19's EMag weapon. My .338 Magnum was the only weapon we had that could take it out reliably with one shot, and I had no way to aim it. Maybe if I had a thermal sight of my own, but I might as well wish for a gauss mortar or Thompson's Cerberus cannon.

If I had Rikki, I might try something else... something a bit daring. Maybe not so daring if Rikki was there, but I'm sure other people would think it so. I rose and tapped Unit 19's underside, unconsciously using a signal I would have used with Rikki. 19 did nothing for a split second, then dropped a full meter or more in altitude.

It was now about chest height to me. Which was almost exactly what I needed. I unslung the big MSR rifle, unfolded the stock, and laid it across the top of the drone, bipod extended.

Harper was watching me curiously and now I waved her over, motioning for her to look through the scope. She frowned, not understanding. I made the cat claw motion, then pointed at first the scope and then off in the direction of where the Tiger was supposed to be. Her brows rose in confusion, then enlightenment flashed over her features. She gave me an odd look, one I couldn't decipher, before putting her head down and looking through the scope.

Immediately she moved the rifle, awkwardly shifting the

big gun, but before she got it more than a centimeter, Unit 19 twisted in mid-air, bringing the gun barrel around for her. This time, she looked again and then pulled back, surprised. Then back on the scope, this time lifting the stock to drop the elevation. Finally she froze, and careful not to disturb the weapon, she pulled back and looked at me. I nodded and carefully leaned in to take over the sniper rifle, making sure not to jar it a millimeter off target.

She nodded, then took a big breath as she realized what was about to happen. She fumbled her own rifle off her shoulder and checked it over, clicking the safety off.

Seeing she was ready, I put my head down, eyes to the scope. The reticle was black and so too were the trees they were trained on. It didn't matter. I didn't need to see anything. I just needed to make a careful shot without letting the rifle come off its aiming point.

Breathing carefully, I snugged the big weapon into my shoulder pocket, curled my finger around the trigger, and began to take up slack. My breath went in, then half out, stopping completely, and I had enough time to marvel at how solid a rest the Decimator was providing when the big rifle suddenly went off.

Full power with no flash suppression. A ball of fire like dragon's breath exploded in the night, the blast and recoil coming together with a familiar shove. Night vision completely gone, I pulled the rifle off Unit 19 and dropped down to a kneeling position.

The Decimator instantly spun in place and fired its electromagnetic gun. It slid sideways a few centimeters on its fans and then fired again.

Something fell out of the trees where I had shot. Big,

metal, and thrashing. Stars in my eyes blocked what I was seeing, but I managed to get the crosshairs of the MSR onto the grinding, twisting metal monster. My second round killed it dead.

"Kite and one Wolf remain. Multiple drones responding from the building behind," Unit 19 said. It still sounded odd.

"We have to run for it. One Wolf isn't enough to stop us with three of us shooting, so we just have to be ready," I said.

"Waiting on you, Gurung," Harper said, eyes watching the trees, rifle held across her body, barrel down, finger indexed alongside the trigger—just like I had taught her.

We started to jog, running straight for the closest ramp, the big Decimator slightly out in front of us. I took the time the easy pace gave me to first fold the stock, then sling the MSR, pulling the little Honey Badger Short Barreled Rifle from my back and chambering a round.

A whirring came from the left, soft, quiet. The Kite, trying to distract us. Unit 19 swiveled the opposite way as it flew straight, pointing slightly to the right of our line of travel even as its big delta-shaped body still followed the direction of our path.

"The Wolf is over there, keeping a tree between it and Unit 19's weapon," Harper said.

"Good. The longer it leaves off its attack, the better," I said. "Ready to go faster?"

She didn't answer, but her stride lengthened out as we hit the base of the on-ramp, jumping over the side rail. Then we were sprinting and turning, spiraling up the ramp, unable to cut any corners, forced to follow the roadway.

"Multiple UAVs on approach," Unit 19 said, twisting in mid-

air to point back behind us. The big drone was now flying backward without any reduction in speed. *"Advise closing eyes and opening your mouths. Renders inbound."*

"Do as it says," I yelled to Harper, grabbing her arm to slow her and pull her down beside me, closing my eyes as we almost fell on the asphalt.

Light flashed behind my eyelids, bright enough to hurt, and thunder shook the ground, bouncing us like rubber balls. Eyes squeezed tight, I could only feel what was happening, and even that was jumbled and confusing. The hard steel and plastic of my PDW bounced off my cheekbone while something soft shoved against my chest. Then the shaking stopped and I opened my eyes to find Harper on top of me and fires burning west of us. Entire trees were aflame, lighting up the night. Other trees had been broken, tossed aside like twigs, along with a few cars and piles of debris that used to be sophisticated drones.

Harper climbed off me, then held out a hand to help pull me up. I took it, suddenly dizzy. My cheek hurt, my ears were ringing, and spots of light swam before my eyes. But we were alive.

"We have to go," I said. "Now, before any more can come after us."

"Concur," Unit 19 said. *"Zone Defense has been notified and is responding. However, reducing the distance to Brooklyn Bridge exit is warranted."*

It was more of a stumble than any kind of coordinated run, but the result was to move us out and onto the famous bridge. Wind blowing across the East River whistled through the metal uprights and the lights of Brooklyn drew slowly closer. The wind suddenly changed, blowing straight down on us from above and then the night lit up again, but this time it was electric spotlights blinding us, with shadows moving fast through the eye-searing brightness. Familiar thumps sounded all around us and I found myself reaching out to keep Harper's gun barrel pointed down.

"We'll take those," a voice said from inside powered armor while gauntleted hands relieved us of our weapons. The down blast of air grew vastly more powerful as a massive shape descended—the giant Quad coming down as close as the bridge's gargantuan suspension cables would allow. An armored soldier pressed close on each side, grabbing my arms and armpits, lifting my feet easily off the ground. My captors crouched and then jumped, all three of us flying through the well-lit night to land in the open hatch of the Quad. A second later, two more troopers touched down with Harper between them. Unit 19 floated in by itself, flying directly to its own charging station, where robotic arms instantly began to rearm its depleted munitions.

"Ah, Ajaya. Always in the thick of it, aren't you?" an armored form said with the voice of Yoshida. Neither of my soldiers had yet released my arms and neither seemed to have any inclination to do so. Harper was also being held tightly.

"Back to base," the major said and the big aircraft swerved so suddenly that I would have lost my feet if I wasn't in the iron clutches of the soldiers. The craft accelerated and then, almost before it got going, it was already descending, this time all the way to the ground.

CHAPTER 38

We were separated immediately and I was shown into a room near the Strike Force offices. Just me, a table, and a couple of chairs—and then left there to cool my heels. None of the armored soldiers would talk to me, and the ones who escorted me were not people I knew very well.

They kept all my weapons but left me my pack, so I ate two energy bars, drank water, and attempted to patch up my wounds. Fifteen minutes after the door had shut and locked, it reopened, admitting a medical officer.

I didn't know the medic and he didn't talk beyond asking me questions about my health, current condition, and what hurt.

Eleven small punctures on my front legs and torso, and three across my back. Harper had yanked all the metal and the suit had slowed the flechettes way down, so he just disinfected and bandaged all the wounds. After that, he packed up and left, the armored soldiers in the hall letting him right out but firmly closing the door in my face.

Seems like I had been here before, maybe not this room, but held without explanation or even contact. My decision to go back to work for Zone D looked stupider and stupider all the time.

With nothing to do, I put my feet in one chair and leaned back in the other—and promptly fell asleep.

The door slammed open and I was just suddenly standing on my feet, arms raised, fists knotted.

"Look at this guy, Estevez—ready to fight anybody," Yoshida said from the doorway, looking mildly amused. He was in battle dress uniform, the shorter Corporal Estevez standing just behind him.

I had no idea how much time had passed, and barely even remembered where I was. Stepping back, I crossed my arms over my chest and gave them both a level look. "Finally getting around to me, huh?"

He raised both eyebrows, dark eyes boring into me. "Getting around to you?" he asked, as if trying the phrase on for size. "Yeah, I'm *getting* around to you. After saving your ass on the Brooklyn Bridge and dealing with your security breach, I'm *getting* around to you."

"Save *my* ass? As I recall, we were doing just fine, hoofing it for the exit, when you all rolled up and basically seized us, then threw us in lockdown."

"Yeah, let's talk about that *us.* You brought an unknown civilian into the Zone on *my* watch, using *my* personnel to get clearance without proper background checks to handle *my* mission," he said, moving up into my face.

"Yes," was my whole answer. He waited, his eyes moving back and forth between mine, eyebrows moving up in an incredulous expression.

"That's it? You going to rest on just an admission of guilt?"

"Yes. I'm guilty of executing the mission you assigned me. I'm guilty of proceeding with an absolute minimum of resources from you. I'm guilty of penetrating the Zone, stopping a dirty bomb attack on Brooklyn and firing on my assigned target, then successfully exfiltrating with absolutely no loss to you—just me."

He frowned, briefly.

"What dirty bomb?"

"The multiple hairspray units that the Spider was equipping with Cobalt-60. I sniped the Spider and radioactive material so they couldn't fly it out of the Zone."

"No Raid Can has ever made it out," Estevez said.

"Right, because Renders blew them out of the air—over the Zone—into the wind," I said.

"Wait, hold up. What exactly happened in there?" Yoshida demanded.

"You don't know? What have you been doing all this time?" I asked, still not certain of the time. The soldiers who had stuffed me in the room hadn't let me get my AI from my locker in the ready room.

"We've been trying to figure out who your mystery girl is. Maybe you should start with her?"

"Didn't you just ask her?"

"She said her name was Harper Leeds and gave us an address that's in your building. When we run her prints, voice patterns, retina scans, name, Social Security number, all her data, it all comes up bullshit," Yoshida said, eyes getting a little wild.

"So what did Harper say about that?" I asked.

His eyes bulged and a vein in his temple visibly throbbed in time to a very fast heartbeat, but he didn't speak. Estevez gave him a sideways look, then turned back to me and spoke up. "We can't ask her because she's disappeared, you moron!"

The major turned and looked at him, eyes getting even crazier. I almost laughed. Almost. Something, survival instinct maybe, kept the laughter on lockdown. But I did back up and sit down in my chair.

"She just disappeared? Let me guess: You put her in a room like this but put the heavyweights outside *my* door and she just what? Walked away?" I asked.

"Who. The. Hell. Is. She?" Yoshida asked, taking a step forward with each word, which left him looming over me.

"She's my Zone anti-drone specialist," I said. "And now you see why. She just ghosted herself right out of your high-security military installation."

"This is serious, Gurung. I've handled you with kid gloves up till now. I coddle your mother, I tiptoe around your sensitive ego, I let you get away with all kinds of shit, but not now. You brought a motherfucking security risk into my base and now she's doing who the hell knows what for who the hell knows who."

"Wrong. *You* brought her to Zone Defense. I just took her into the Zone. I would have taken her out of the Zone. But you're the one who yanked us out and brought us here."

He turned with a roar and punched the wall. It wasn't a sheetrock wall either, but the concrete block one. His knuckles left an imprint in the concrete.

For a split second, I thought he was some kind of cyborg or something but then blood started to drip off his hand as he glared at me.

I decided to just stay quiet, but kept a watch on him in case he went hog-wild crazy.

After a second, the cray-cray left his eyes and he took a deep breath. Then he grabbed the other chair and sat down. His left hand came up and rubbed his face a few time, his right still dangling, still dripping blood. He took another breath and then looked around. Spotting a roll of gauze, he grabbed it and started to wrap his hand, very matter-of-fact.

"Let's start at the beginning. Records show you entered the Zone this morning with your mystery guest. Walk me through every step of your time inside."

For the next hour, I talked, explaining our infiltration to Hudson, the climb up 33 Thomas Street, the observation of the Spider, the radioactive isotope, my shots on target, and our mad dash out of the building, being chased by the Spider that was already inside the NSA or AT&T or whoever's building it was. He listened without a single word or question while I described our run in the Tesla, the crash, and holding up in the muni building. I explained about Unit 19, and felt myself get distant and remote when recounting Rikki's end. I even pulled the shattered airframe of my drone out of my pack and showed it to him.

When I got done, he just stared at me for a long time. Then he stood abruptly, turned on his heel, and walked out, Estevez trailing after him.

The door closed and I settled back for another wait, but just a few minutes had gone by when the door opened and another trooper brought me a tray with a big mug of tomato soup, a chicken salad sandwich, and a brownie along with a bottle of water.

I finished the whole thing in just a few minutes, but rather than sit back, I looked around for something else to distract me. And spotted Rikki.

My drone was still unwrapped and sitting on the side of the table, so after a moment, I pulled it closer to take a second look at his damage.

It wasn't any better the second time, but I was way more thorough. Rikki's CPU was toast, a fact made obvious by the bits of broken carbon fiber armor that had been removed. Something about that bothered me. A few seconds later, it hit: I had put all the pieces back in place. But when I unwrapped Rikki to show the major, they were out of his shell and sitting in the bottom of the bag. The bag that Harper had wrapped him in.

Taking a closer look, I spotted another issue. His housing wasn't together. It looked like someone had pried his casing apart and then didn't snap it back together. I pulled him open and looked inside. Immediately, I spotted it. Two gleaming black data chips sat in place in the custom holder I had installed. The third spot was empty. I looked his interior completely over. Nothing. It wasn't bouncing around free inside him. It wasn't in the bag. It was just flat-out missing.

Harper. She was the only one who could have done it. The only one who had the opportunity, back during those fifteen minutes I had slept on the third floor of the muni building. Why?

My door re-opened and Yoshida came back in, followed by Estevez and Sergeant Rift.

The major pulled the chair around backward and straddled it, eyes locked on mine.

He lifted his left hand and tapped his wrist unit with his roughly bandaged right one. Instantly, an image projected on the institutional white wall of the room. It was an exterior nighttime view of the upper levels of 60 Hudson Street, lit a ghostly green by night-vision equipment.

"This is a Render shot taken ten minutes ago. This the ledge where you witnessed the Spider?"

"*One* of the Spiders," I said. "The other was already inside 33 Thomas. But yeah."

The image moved in close and the AI running the Render highlighted a big portion of roof, as well as the side of the building, in red. Radioactivity readings appeared in the middle of the red area, the values climbing higher as the drone scanned the spot.

"That tests out as Cobalt-60," Yoshida said, his tone bland.

The viewpoint swung around, moving over to see inside the open door into the building. Then it zoomed in, picking up something on the floor just inside. Sudden white light illuminated everything and the object on the floor became a massive metal foot, one that was attached to a giant Spider that lay slumped on the floor, now almost completely illuminated.

"I got it?" I said as I realized the CThree was defunct. The image moved slightly, side to side, changing the shot enough to see a little of each side of the dead drone. A small entry hole was visible on its left side, a bigger-sized hole blast out the right side.

"Yes. Looks like you got it."

CHAPTER 39

He let me out of the room and I got a chance to call home and tell Mom I was alright, even though my call was closely monitored by Sergeant Rift.

Then I got pulled into the Strike Force operations room to watch Yoshida and a team go in on the Quad to pull out the Spider. Specially suited troopers retrieved as much radioactive material as they could scrape and package up, and then applied a fast-drying impermeable containment foam to the rest.

General Davis observed the proceedings with a group of his officers while on the other side of the room, watching me as much as the screens, were Agents White and Black.

Nobody spoke to me, nobody said good job, nobody acknowledged my existence. In fact, they were so dedicated to ignoring me that I was like a ghost in the room. Or maybe an elephant.

An hour later, I was shown to guest quarters and left to my own devices. So I slept. When I woke, my AI told me it was a little after nine in the morning. My hosts had curtailed the amount of access my virtual assistant had, leaving me with no ability to call, text, or email my family and Astrid. I could play virtual reality video games or check bank account balances as well as read and watch the news, but I couldn't tell the ones I loved that I was alright.

That last bit was pretty interesting. All the headlines were about the Zone and escaped killer drones. The media had learned of the units recovered under the city and in the drone hive. The stories clearly painted a picture of dangerous killing machines manipulating city and corporate systems. There were numerous statements from government officials trying to simultaneously calm the waters and redirect public anger at Zone Defense. General Davis was quoted a great deal and blamed even more—especially by Congressman John Numer, who was grandstanding all over the City and Washington.

Then I found a live White House Press Conference by the president, who forcefully backed General Davis and announced that the military, at his direction, had undertaken an array of responses to contain and get ahead of the situation. When the press wanted details, General Davis stepped up to the podium and outlined something he called the Skilled Operator Assault Program. SOAP, as he immediately shortened it, was apparently a new program created at his command to train and equip the most skilled and experienced special operations commandos in the US military to successfully infiltrate the Zone, hunt down and kill off drones, using *loyal* US military drones as aerial K-9 units. That was all good, but then he quoted drone kill counts in the thousands and announced the successful elimination of two of the Spiders as well as the elimination of all of the infiltrator bots. It was a wonderful-sounding tale of government competence that stood tall for all of three minutes. Right up until a reporter asked over what time frame those kill counts had come, and how many were attributable to the caches recently recovered by Team Johnson on *Zone War*. Davis brushed the question off on the grounds of sensitive information, but it was too late because the sharks smelled blood in the water.

Another reporter asked if the general was taking credit for my kill of Lotus, using my name right in his question. This caused at least two others to ask what role *Zone War* and Gurung Extractions had played in any and all of the program's successes. When Davis scoffed at the idea, the reporter projected a video clip holographically right over his own wrist, showing an indistinct outline of me from behind with a crystal clear image of Rikki flying overhead.

At that point, the president stepped in front of Davis to thank the press and walked out, effectively ending the conference.

Me, I was still stuck on the image of Rikki flying protectively above me. I asked my AI to kill the newsfeed and turned back to examining Rikki. I had multiple backups of his software and maybe, just maybe I could find a Berkut airframe, get even better computer components, and rebuild him. Now that I didn't have to keep him a secret and I had some capital, I could go all out on equipping him with the best of the best. Too bad Harper wouldn't be there to help me, but I knew she was long gone. With one of Rikki's chips. Probably to use his recordings. I plucked the last two chips out and hid one in my boot and taped the other to the inside of my black web belt, using a piece of electrical tape almost the same color.

We had discussed the most likely outcome of our mission before we ever stepped into the Zone. The day before going in, I had been hit with a bolt of guilt and had told her that she couldn't come with me. That it would completely blow her cover. She had just nodded and said of course it would blow *that* cover, but she had others. Then she proceeded to lay out how *she* felt about my little mission. That her mother was the reason the Spiders were so deadly and so unilaterally focused on the elimination of humankind. That she had her own cross to bear and it wasn't up to me, in any way, to decide what *her* personal honor and conscience demanded. That she had thought of little else since she got out of the Zone. She had been... well... fierce.

So I knew she had activated steps and plans she'd already had in place. Moved assets and personal items to somewhere else. And I knew absolutely nothing about those plans because my own outcome was most likely going to be intense questioning and likely under a truth scan, which while not yet admissible in court had nonetheless recently become standard protocol for military intelligence. No more torture. Just hook up advanced brain scanning equipment, ask your questions, and read the responses. Far more effective than the old lie detector approach, and extraordinarily difficult to mentally defend against. The powers that be were going to find out about her. But they would have a damned hard time tracking her, a point she'd proven by simply walking out of Zone Defense without a trace.

My door suddenly opened and a squad of Zone Defense guards entered the room, eyes hard and hands on steel batons and Taser wands.

Right. Time for that interrogation.

The squad marched me at a fast pace through the complex, down multiple levels, and into a large conference room somewhere in the building I had never been before.

Agents Black and White, along with their boss, who I had learned was Deputy Director Timothy Fountain, held center stage at a big table, along with three white-jacketed technician types. Major Yoshida and his Estevez shadow were off to one side, while across the room, leaning casually on a chair, was NSA Director Weber. A compact, complex-looking device sat in the middle of the big table and a view screen on one wall showed General Davis's unsmiling face looking on from what looked like a seat on a jet.

"Ah, Mr. Gurung, so glad you could join us," Agent Black began.

"Black, White, time to get your interrogation continuing education credit for the month?" I asked.

White raised one eyebrow, Black smiled, and the deputy director looked ready to blow a fuse.

"You are facing extraordinary charges of treason, wiseass. Your very life hangs in the balance. Your attitude could make or break you," Deputy Director Fountain said.

"Is that how it works, General?" I asked, turning to the projection on the wall. "I train your super-special SOAP people, kill your Spiders and, oh yeah, provide thousands of dead drones for you to claim credit for, and you reward me with death?"

"Be careful, Ajaya. You took an unknown agent into the Zone and exposed all of our networks to her," the general said.

"Yes to the first part, no to the second. Yoshida exposed your network. If you had simply left us alone, we would have exited the Zone without going anywhere near your networks. Hell, we probably would have gone back in and hunted down the last Spider for you. But the major, who seems unable to get anything done without me, had to swoop down and haul us here. Here, where all of your forces couldn't stop one young woman from casually walking out of the building, leaving you with nothing. Less than nothing. In fact, I bet she erased all images of herself on the way out. While you were trying to run her background, she gave you all a master class in network manipulation and ripping through cyber security measures. And now she's out there, somewhere, with who-knows-what kind of incriminating secrets about Zone Defense, your ineffective programs, and the Zone itself."

Oops. Maybe a bit much. The room had gone deathly still and even Director Weber was now sitting straight up and paying attention. Too late to back down now.

"So let's get to it. Hook my up to your brain reader and let's take a deep dive into the *real* history of the Zone."

Double D Fountain had gone killer cold instead of looking ready to freak out. Now he turned and spoke to the three tech types. "Get out."

They fled, no other word for it. They just about flat-out raced from the room.

Meanwhile, Yoshida was staring at me, and when I met his eyes, he made the tiniest side-to-side motion of his head. Nope. Too late, Major.

"You seem to be offering things up rather freely, Ajaya," Agent Black said.

"Sure, why not, Agent? Your little truth machine will get there eventually anyway. I'm just tired of all the waiting. So let's move it along. In fact, why don't you get to the part where you explain how my family is at risk, how you will kill me, my sisters, my mother, and my grandmother to cover your secrets. Why wouldn't you? How many citizens have you already killed?"

I was tempted to say three hundred sixty thousand, but

some measure of self-preservation stopped me. I had a solid chance of getting out, but there were things my mouth could say that might take it too far to recover.

Both Black and White were frowning now, and Yoshida was focused on me like a hawk. DD Fountain started to speak, but Yoshida held up his hand forcefully and stepped forward.

"You have an edge, Ajaya. What is it?" Yoshida said.

"What the hell are you talking about, Major?" Fountain asked.

"You can say what you want, Deputy Fountain, but Ajaya is by far the most skilled in-Zone operator to enter Manhattan. He has survived the most dangerous place on earth for years on end because he is careful, crafty, and always has an edge or two. This isn't bravado. Ajaya has a plan and he is extremely confident about it."

Fountain took that in, opened his mouth to say something, but then closed it and looked to Black and White. The two agents nodded, agreeing with Yoshida.

"My *edge*, Major, strolled out of your facility and disappeared into thin air. I have no idea what she scavenged from *here*, but she had plenty of video storage of what we went through in the Zone, cleaning up part of the mess you all created. I imagine that a big slug of it is currently going viral as we speak."

"Who the fuck is she?" Yoshida asked.

"That's her story to tell, which is also part of my edge. But I will tell you that you were only partly correct—I *might*, in fact, be the most skilled operator to *enter* the Zone, but I'm not the most skilled to *exit* it."

"What does that mean? What the fuck does that mean?"

Fountain asked.

"It means she was raised *inside* the Zone. She knows its secrets. Well, most of its secrets. Nobody knows what the Spiders were up to, not completely. But she knows your secrets and way more importantly, she has proof. And as you've been so thoroughly shown, she can penetrate cyber security better than you all can."

"You realize you just made her the most wanted terrorist in the world, don't you?" Director Weber asked. His voice was matter-of-fact, his eyes interested in my response. More like a college professor than the head of the NSA.

"Ah. Director Weber. I didn't expect you, but it's nice you're here. I was just in one of your old stomping grounds. Actually had no idea about that till we were already sitting on top of it. Pretty cool building, that Long Lines, if a bit stark. It's curious that the remaining Spider was hanging out inside it, isn't it? I mean, there's still power in that building and a really nifty satellite uplink that Harper tells me is pretty high-end. What could a Spider CThree do with an NSA uplink? I bet the internet is wondering about that right now."

Weber's mildly curious look turned to something else, something cold and deadly. He touched one side of his eye with his left hand and flicked his right-hand fingers through empty air.

On the big screen, General Davis was looking off camera and his face was going through different expressions of anger, dismay, and maybe something that was akin to anxiety.

"There's video out," Davis said, still looking offscreen.

Black and White exchanged glances, then simultaneously activated iContacts. Yoshida just stared at me, arms crossed, face locked down.

Fountain, apparently not wearing contacts, turned to the wall screen. "How bad is it?"

"There's video from their trip through the Zone, condensed. Shows the 33 Thomas building, their climb up the stairs, the roof of the building, then gets to the roof of Hudson Street with the Spider, the micro bombers, their identification of the radioactive material. I'm seeing the shooting sequence now. This must have all come from the Berkut's video recordings. I'll scan ahead," Davis said.

"There's also video from our own Renders. Showing the dead Spider and our recovery actions," Agent White said, still watching, as his eyes were glowing red.

"It's pretty complete. Got vid of the encounter with the Spider in the Thomas Street building stairwell, and their flight back off the island," Davis said.

Weber walked to a corner of the room and touched his ear, making a call. He stood stiffly, back to us, talking, his words too soft to hear.

Fountain gave me a glare and walked out of the room. Agent Black turned off his contacts, leaving his partner to keep watching.

"You think this is enough to protect you?" he asked, his voice curious, like we were discussing my quarterly business plan.

"This? No. This just makes it a tiny bit tougher for you to simply make me disappear. It refutes much of the White House press conference, or at least throws much of the claims into doubt."

"What else do you have, Ajaya?" Black pushed, voice still deceptively soft.

I thought about it. How much to say and when? We had covered a bit of this in our preplanning, but we had agreed that the situation would be fluid and I'd have to play it by ear.

Was it time to reveal her mother's identity? No. If I gave that to them, they would have time to create a smear campaign to discredit the doctor's name and history. Harper had her own plan, and the released videos were just the first step. She needed time to plant and layer the rest.

"As I mentioned, we have pretty much the complete history of the events leading up to Drone Night," I said.

"Fiction. Conspiracy theory. My grandmother could discredit that," White said, his red eyes going back to brown.

"Really? That good, is she?"

Deputy Director Fountain came back into the room. "The vids were released across thirteen initial channels, then another thirteen sites an hour later. They've already gone viral across the planet. Harper Leeds worked as a software technician and consultant, specializing in drones. Over the last two and a half months, she worked for seventeen companies, including Flottercot Productions and three of the major network affiliates, modifying and hardening drones. The videos released on all of these channels simultaneously, during advertisement breaks between live segments," he reported, his expression sour. "Weber will know what can be done, if anything."

Director Weber had turned slightly to listen to Fountain while still on his call. He turned back and finished speaking, then came back around to face all of us.

"The quick answer to that is... nothing. Short of turning

off the entire internet world wide, it's too late. This is now a job for the fixers," he said. Then he focused on me. "Your companion is very good, Ajaya. World class. But she won't be able to hide. We'll find her and end her plans; you have to know that, right? No one can hide from us. We've proven that."

"Oh, you're referring to the Gaia Group? Easy enough to find them if you're the ones who propped them up as fronts in the first place, isn't it? No real trick to that. But let's lay this out a bit, see where it takes us.

"Harper is a computer genius, raised by a computer genius, inside the deadliest artificial intelligence environment in the world. She fooled CThrees just to survive. You could almost say that the Spiders were her teachers. And she was raised knowing the truth behind Drone Night, the truth behind the Gaia Group. I notice none of you have asked me a single question about what I mean by that and I've mentioned it a bunch of times. Interesting. Also, as Fountain just said, she's been working in the outside world for several months. Preparing. Now, I also find it fascinating that we've completely focused on me and Harper and left the whole Spider in the NSA super hideout alone like it's the elephant in the room. If Peony was sending out bots to influence systems in New York City, what do you suppose Plum Blossom was doing with an NSA uplink? Harper's goals are to survive and help me survive. Plum Blossom wants to kill the world. You people have really screwed-up priorities."

"Pretty speech, Ajaya, but it's all just words. Nothing to back it up," White said like a bank loan officer questioning my profit and loss statement.

I turned and looked around the room till I spotted a good old-fashioned clock on a wall.

"What time did the videos get released, General?" I asked.

On screen, he frowned for a second but decided to answer. "Ten hundred hours."

"And the follow-on releases occurred at eleven hundred. It's eleven forty-seven now. My prediction is that at twelve hundred hours, you'll get another dose of something to back it up."

CHAPTER 40

They stared at me for a few heartbeats.

"Let's just hook him up and find out everything he knows," DD Fountain suddenly said.

"Sir, it's just a few minutes. Let's wait and see if anything comes out of this drama theater," Agent Black said.

"Major?" Davis asked from the wall screen.

"I'll be surprised if something doesn't happen at noon sir," Yoshida said, eyes still on me.

"Well then... we wait. But let's keep chatting, Ajaya," Weber said. "So far, your mysterious companion has done an admirable job escaping Zone Defense and planting some cleverly concocted videos. But you have to understand that none of that is insurmountable."

"Like that you could wear it away with a careful campaign to modify public opinion? That over a few months you could put enough propaganda, spin, and diversionary information to make the world audience believe that Harper and I plotted to murder the pope and there is no threat from the Zone?"

Weber's face twisted up in a mix of a little anger and a little disgust. "I wouldn't put it so crudely, but you obviously understand the gist."

"Yeah. Couple things. One, what makes you think you have a few months? Peony escalated its attacks here in

New York when those plans came to light. What's Plum Blossom doing right now? You're the expert, Director. What mayhem could a powerful artificial intelligence do with access to NSA equipment and systems? Think it could use your own playbook against you? Crash the financial markets, destroy the power grid, cause world military units to falsely attack each other, seed the ground for a nuclear war?"

"That's a bit of a stretch," Weber said with a look of disbelief.

"Is it? Plum Blossom's been working on its plans for ten years. For all you know, it already *owns* your entire network. They freaking built their own drones and successfully planted them in major infrastructure systems. What if everything they did here in New York was just an experiment to help them do it everywhere?"

Weber stared at me, the disbelief replaced by reluctant realization. His mouth opened, then closed. The others were all looking at him and DD Fountain finally spoke. "That's not possible, is it?"

Weber glanced at him, then back to me. Abruptly he turned and started another private call.

"I don't believe it! You can't tell me this crazy story has any basis in reality," Fountain said.

"What was number two, Ajaya?" Yoshida suddenly asked. Everyone turned to him, even Weber, who was still on his call. "You said *one, what makes you think you have a few months.* What's your follow-on point?"

"Oh, yeah. Two, what makes you think Harper is going to let you run a cover-up? We've seen this pattern of changing human behavior through massive spin campaigns all our lives. Hell, I had college classes on it. The thing about spin is that everyone does it. It's just a question of who does it the most," I said.

"What the fuck does that mean?" Fountain demanded. I looked at the clock. It was old-school military, had an hour hand to cover all twenty-four hours in a day, with twelve hundred at the bottom where six would be on a standard clock.

I pointed as the last few seconds ticked down and the minute hand clicked straight up, with the hour hand on the twelve hundred hours mark.

They all followed my gesture, stared for a second, and then turned back to me, expressions questioning.

"Well, don't look at me. Check the internet," I said.

Davis was already doing so, talking to someone just off-screen.

"Another round of video releases just occurred. Over a hundred, it seems."

"I'll go out on a limb and guess a hundred and sixty-nine," I said. They looked at me, frowning. "You know... thirteen times thirteen? And at thirteen hundred hours, probably something like... what?" I asked, trying to do the math in my head.

"Two thousand, one hundred and ninety-seven?" Agent White asked.

"Nice math, Agent! Yeah. Another multiple of thirteen," I said.

"How is she doing it?" Davis asked.

"She programs drones," Yoshida said.

"Yes, but actually her expertise happens to be AI, which

almost all drones now have. I'm going to guess that these releases are different, each of them. The first batches were all the same, but these will all vary, as will all the follow-on ones," I said. I was guessing, but I *did* know Harper and a bit about how she thought.

"She's programming AI units to make their own packages. Gave them a mission and set them loose to achieve it. And you know how single-minded AI can be," I said.

"You have to have something for this?" Fountain said, turning on Weber, who for his part was frozen at my words. The NSA chief's eyes twitched a bit and then suddenly focused on me.

"Activate Furies," he said. It took all of us a second to realize he wasn't talking to us, but to whoever was on the other end of his call.

"Yes, I'll give the authorization code. Weber, Francis, seven alpha, lima niner echo eight, zulu, zulu, victor. I hereby authorize program Furies."

"What the fuck is that?" Fountain asked.

Weber, who was really pale, took a breath, blinked twice, and then focused on me. And for the first time, he looked angry. Really angry.

"Something we thought we'd never have to use."

"Super-killer AI program? Eats the whole internet?" I asked.

"Too crude, but it will eradicate whatever she's done," he said.

"At what cost?" Agent Black asked.

"Enormous cost. It'll knock out most of the internet for at least a day."

"Shut down airlines, traffic control, power grids, and shit? Did you just do Plum Blossom's work for it?" I asked, incredulous.

"Please. You think your friend is the only one with programming elegance? We have the best in the world," Weber said.

I waggled a hand. "Probably not. The best of the best go to the Googles, Amazons, Facebooks, and Apples. You can't pay them what the corporations can."

He smiled. "True, but we can exert pressure and have those corporations and others do the work for us," he said.

"Sure, outsource security. That won't leave any holes or anything," I said.

"You little shit. You're responsible for this! By your actions, you caused this!" Weber said.

I couldn't help it, couldn't stop my smile.

"Shit! You knew!" Yoshida said.

I shrugged. "Harper guessed. She's a little paranoid but really, can you blame her? Growing up knowing that everything is a lie."

"What are you talking about?" Davis asked, holding up a hand to block whoever was talking to him on the plane.

"By doing all this, all these videos, they forced Weber to unleash hell on the internet. If the Spider really has broken into major government systems, wouldn't that stop it too?" Yoshida asked.

Weber was frowning, working through all the ramifications.

"No. No way are you going to convince me that this, this punk is that smart," Fountain said. "To make all the pieces fall this way."

"He doesn't have to be. It works either way. If their plan resulted in a release of Ajaya, then they would be free to pursue Plum Blossom and we'd be warned about the threat. If there was some killer NSA program, then it could do their work for them," Yoshida said.

"But leave Ajaya in our hands and lose their internet leverage," Davis said, frowning.

"Harper doesn't believe for a second that whatever the NSA has cooked up can actually completely eradicate everything. You think corporate code wizards are going to build you a monster and not think of ways to protect against it? You're dreaming if you do. Not to mention that China, India, and Russia will have countermeasures in place," I said. "We don't even think it will eradicate Plum Blossom's plans, but maybe it'll slow them down. She actually thinks that there's quite a few AIs out there that will fight back on their own. If it threatens their core programming, which it does, then they'll work counter to it. Most won't win, but everyone that fights is a drag on your beast."

"You've caused untold damage, Ajaya, and you're not even clear that you want us to win," General Davis said.

"*You* to win? No, not any of *you*. What we want is for you to stop the ass covering and concentrate on saving humankind. You programmed super AIs for human destruction, let them loose in one of the most resource-rich environments possible, and then left them alone for a decade to plot our destruction. And you did it so you could take power from your predecessors. But your reign will only last until Plum Blossom wipes us all out. So what we did will reverberate around the planet. It may slow Plum Blossom down, but mostly it will alert the whole world to the threats. Probably won't stop them, not all of them, but it may stop a few, and at least people will have a chance."

"A chance? A chance? Do you have any idea about the panic and mayhem this will cause?" Weber asked.

"Isn't panic and mayhem your natural element, Director? Don't you people excel in calming the masses and presenting the solutions? Well, guess what? You're up."

CHAPTER 41

They threw me back in my guest room. The march back to my gilded cell showed me that Zone Defense wasn't immune to what was happening across the world. Soldiers ran down hallways, others huddled in small clusters, going silent when our group went through. But the lights stayed on and I still had news access when I got to my room.

The internet was still up, so whatever the NSA Furies program was supposed to do, at least it wasn't a full shutdown. But standard programming had been taken over by the news desks covering breaking stories all over the world. And much of the mayhem occurred right in the network studios, with unexplained sudden shifts to sponsor ads, with most of those glitching badly. Sound went in and out and every news agency had completely ineffective attempts to go to on-the-ground reporters or drones on the scenes. Eventually the networks just stayed with the on-air anchors and kept the presentation as simple as possible, but breaks in the live presentations still happened. And most of those presentations reported that the issues were being caused from either inside the Zone or by the NSA, or both.

The bulk of the news was here in the US, with financial markets temporarily shut down without clear explanation and people reporting access issues to the millions of blog pages on the net. The airlines also announced computer issues that resulted in hundreds, if not thousands, of cancelled or delayed flights. Utility companies announced unexpected systems checks and issues all across the North American grid. But gradually, as the afternoon wore on, key infrastructure came back online.

By dinnertime, things had smoothed out and the glitches mostly stopped, although the blog issue was still full blown. But through it all, the news kept going, and despite the enormous confusion and erroneous reporting, the overall story started to solidify. Talking heads had put together the connection between Harper's video releases and the worldwide computer issues, which was an easy one to make because all the glitchy messages had mentioned the Spiders and the government over and over.

I turned off the sound after the tenth time hearing my own name and then shut everything off altogether when I got sick of seeing myself. Instead, I started to tear down Rikki, seeing what was recoverable and what wasn't, making plans for upgrades and new features.

About two hours later, the door opened and Yoshida came in, Agent Black following him, along with some guard types and a tech in a white coat.

Yoshida waved the troopers forward, they grabbed my arms, and then the tech stepped up and zapped me in the neck with a jet gun.

"Okay Ajaya, we're sending you home," Yoshida said.

"With a tracker," I guessed.

"Ah, a tracker *and* a tiny grain of radio-controlled explosive," Black said cheerfully. "Sitting right on your carotid artery. And it's a sensitive little bugger. Look at it cross-eyed in the mirror and it goes off. X-ray it and boom. Try to block its signal and boom. You get the idea."

313

"So elevators are out?" I said, my wise ass mouth trying to buy time for my brain to think through the sudden overwhelming fear.

"Nah, way more sophisticated than that. It's basically a deadman's switch. As long as it gets the signal, it's fine. And we'll be close, count on it. Just don't go shooting down any odd drones you see. Might blow your own neck out," Black said with a certain satisfaction.

My attempt at a poker face must have failed because Black started laughing. "Not so smart now, are you?"

Something hardened inside me. The tsunami of terror receded and a kernel of something else started to grow in its place.

"Whoa there, Sniper. Don't get that kamikaze look on your face. You've forced us to close off the doors available to you, but there are still a few ways out," Yoshida said. He turned to Black. "I told you, you gotta handle operators different. Corner them, leave them no way out and they'll make a choice that you don't really want. Blow himself up on television or something equally stupid."

"He's not even military," Black protested.

"He's military through and through. Doesn't matter that he never enlisted," the major said. "Now, Ajaya, you got what you wanted. Kicked over the whole damned hornets' nest. Can't do that and be surprised by being stung, can you? You got our complete attention, but now you gotta deal with the consequences."

I rubbed the side of my neck. It *did* sting. "I'm guessing that Weber's thing wasn't really all that. Last I checked the news, things had calmed down."

"Yeah, got no comment on any of No Such Agency's doings, but I will say I highly doubt anything has calmed down. If anything, it's just going to go straight up from here," Yoshida said.

"And it'll be hauling you up with it," Black said. "You wanted credit, you got it. Hope you enjoy it, kid." With that, he turned and walked out, the tech and most of the guards following him. That left Yoshida and a single trooper, who I suddenly realized was Corporal Boyle, looming silently by the door.

"Sorry it worked out this way, Ajaya. I think that in this case *you* backed *them* into a corner," the major said.

"I'm guessing this will all be blamed on me somehow?" I asked.

He gave me regretful smile, one that didn't accept any responsibility, then clapped me on the shoulder with his granite-hard hand and walked out, leaving me with Boyle.

The tall, gloomy corporal gave me a nod. "Us troops always get the shit, Ajaya," he said, holding out a hand toward the door.

I took the hint, stuffed Rikki and my notes into my pack, and swung it up on my back before stepping out the door. It took me that long to register his words. He was including me as one of the troops. Despite the stress and fear of having a bomb in my neck, being tracked, and now hearing I was going to somehow be the government's fall boy, his inclusion hit me somewhere deep inside.

"They wouldn't let me give you your weapons back," he said like it was somehow his fault.

"I didn't think they would. Gonna miss that little Honey

Badger though. Sweet gun."

"Sarge Rift is taking care of them for you," he said, leading me down the hall. Like I would ever be back.

"Kayla wanted to come but the major said no. Bunch of the others are pissed, but what can they do? What can any of us do?"

Now *I* was feeling bad for *him.* "Hey, Boyle, don't worry. I'm alive and out of the Zone. The rest is all fluff."

"You're tough, Ajaya. Like iron. Lost your drone and your nice guns and got a bomb in your neck and you're getting crapped on by the brass when you completed your mission and all that. It just sucks."

"Yeah, well, if I understand the major, the suck factor is only going to get worse before it gets better. If it gets better," I said.

"Yeah, a serious increase in suckage is normal for *every* mission. But it will get better. The team is betting on you. The sneak and peek people you taught mostly feel the same too. You've survived everything the Zone could throw at you... you'll get through this too."

We were at the main doors by now. I turned and held out my hand. He shook it, then stepped back, came to attention and saluted me—and held it. Suddenly self-conscious, I snapped off a salute back, if only to get him to recover. A couple people around us gave us funny looks, but Boyle ignored them. He gave me a nod and turned on his heel, walking back the way we had come. Still catching stares, I turned and headed out into the night.

CHAPTER 42

"Welcome to a special edition of *Zone War*. I'm Cade Kallow and your host for this extraordinary and completely exclusive interview with a young man at the center of global controversy. Ajaya Gurung, welcome."

"Hi Cade," I said, sitting on his right side.

He looked at the empty seat to *my* right, a mournful expression on his face. "No offense, Ajaya, but I much prefer our chats when they include my all-time favorite guest."

"Yeah, I much prefer to have her sitting by my side too."

"Rumor has it that there is trouble in paradise?" he asked.

"My relationship with Astrid is just that Cade, *my* relationship. I'm not here to talk about that."

"I know, I know, but in the interest of keeping the *Zone War* audience from being distracted by her absence, I thought we should at least touch on it. What I understand is that you two are taking some time?"

"That's accurate."

"I also understand that she was unhappy with your last incursion into the Zone, or more accurately, your choice of partner for that incursion," he said, immediately holding up a hand toward me. "And Ajaya, I say that because your choice of partner is totally on topic for tonight's interview."

"Astrid's feelings about me and my actions are totally hers, Cade. I would never discuss them without her present to represent her side of it. Every relationship is two-sided, and both sides are equally important. But if you wish to discuss Harper and my last incursion to the Zone, that's fine."

"Okay, Ajaya, totally fair. Let's get right to it. Over the last few days, the amount and extent of internet disruptions globally has exceeded anything ever seen in the history of the internet. And you're at the center of it."

"Because the government says so, right?" I asked.

"Well, in fact, yes. The White House specifically named you, as well as an individual they say goes under the alias of Harper Leeds."

"So the network outages occurred at a time when I was being interrogated by Zone Defense, the Department of Defense, and the NSA, simultaneously. And yet I somehow knocked out massively hardened corporate and government AI networks all over the planet without having any access at all to the web?"

"The White House statement was that you bore responsibility in conjunction with a terrorist named Harper Leeds, an individual who appears in videos with you that were first released to various news agencies, including this show. Video that later was forcefully inserted into paid advertising slots. Hundreds of them. And I understand the lawsuits are already piling up?"

"What do I bear responsibility for, Cade? Appearing in the video? That's absolutely true. All of that footage was real. We penetrated the Zone, set up a sniper hide on top of 33 Thomas Street, which is also called the AT&T Long Lines building, staked out the internet access hub at

60 Hudson, observed a Spider CThree, observed hairspray bombers being loaded with radioactive isotopes scavenged from Manhattan hospitals, directed fire into those aerial bombers before they could be exploded by Render drones in the jet stream above Manhattan, and fired a round that ultimately ended one of the two remaining Spider CThrees in the Zone. Yup, that was me. And the additional footage of Zone Defense soldiers recovering the dead Spider and cleaning up the radioactive spill was real too."

"You're saying you should be counted a hero, not a villain?"

"I don't care for the title hero, Cade, but I do care that I carried out a mission given to me by Major Cal Yoshida of the Zone Defense Instant Response Strike Force, to hunt and kill the Spider that was controlling the escaped drone infiltration units, which I also helped hunt down and kill. Also, the only reason Zone Defense knew there was a possible escaped drone problem was because I brought it to their attention. So I've personally killed two of the three Spider CThrees and yet Zone Defense and the White House wants to tar and feather me for internet disruptions caused by NSA attack programs."

"Whoa, Ajaya, let's take a second and work through all that. There's a whole lot in that statement to unpack," Cade said. "The White House has not refuted your kills on the CThrees, but they do say you and this Harper disrupted the internet. Now you claim the NSA is involved?"

"Sounds like the makings of a conspiracy theory when you say it like that, Cade. But it's not a theory, it's a fact. Harper released video to protect me. We were picked up by Zone Defense when we were on the Brooklyn Bridge, which you saw in the footage. Zone D had no reason to

forcefully grab us other than they were butt hurt that
I took someone into the Zone that they didn't know.
However, I was given enormous leeway in handling my
missions when they hired me in the first place, first to
train those SOAP soldiers, then to hunt escaped bots, and
finally to hunt down Spiders. But they couldn't hang
on to Harper, and she released video to keep them from
doing anything permanent to me."

"Permanent? You're suggesting, Ajaya, that they would,
what? Kill you?" he asked, incredulous.

"To cover up what I know, yes. And they still might at any
moment. If you get sprayed with blood from the bomblet
in my neck before this interview is over, don't say I didn't
warn you."

"What? A bomb in your neck? Ajaya, this... this..." He
looked completely incredulous.

"Sounds crazy? Sure. Do you have that EMF detector I requested you have?"

"Yes?" he said, still shocked. He turned off camera. "Dave,
can you bring it over? I'm going to have our technical
expert, David Young, operate this electromagnetic frequency detector because he's the expert and I'm just the
..."

"Eye candy?" I asked. Despite his shock at the direction
we had gone, he laughed a bit at that.

"Funny guy."

Dave the tech guru came over. He was short and wide,
bearded, and looked exactly like a tech expert might
look.

"Hold it by my neck. Here on this side," I said.

"It's definitely getting a reading," Dave said. He waved it across the rest of me, then came back to the side of my neck. "Yeah, nothing else on his body, but there's something under the skin right there," he said, reaching out a finger to poke.

I pulled away. "Good way to lose a finger, Dave. It has a grain of high explosive attached. According to my interrogators, it both sends out a tracking signal and receives one, likely from a drone somewhere outside this building at this moment. X-rays, attempts at surgery, or loss of the drone signal will set it off. As it's sitting on my carotid artery, I won't survive that explosion. But it is detectable without danger by an EMF device."

"Dave, you're absolutely sure there is something there?" Cade asked.

"Yes, and if you look close, Cade, you can see the tiniest lump. It emits a signal, but I can't attest to explosives," Dave said.

"Thanks, Dave," Cade said. Dave nodded and retreated off camera. "Ajaya, that only proves you have a radio chip of some kind in your neck. It doesn't prove an explosive. You understand what that means?"

"Yes. People will say I put it there myself. Listen, Cade, I'm not here tonight because I think I'm going to convince anyone of anything. The people I'm up against are the global masters of controlling public opinion. They've had decades to practice."

"Dammit, Ajaya, every time you speak, you give me six new questions. Let's stick to the main points—why are you here... if not to change opinion?"

"The same reason that Harper released those videos and

then convinced AI platforms to send out the secondary videos: to keep the true architects of the Drone Attack from burying the truth and, more importantly, ignoring the massive danger we all face right now."

"Jeez Ajaya, you cannot keep doing that! How can we get anywhere if you lob bombs left and right?" he asked, completely exasperated. "True architects?"

"Tell you what, Cade. Why don't I just give you a summary and then you can pick and choose where you want to go?"

He held out both hands in a go-ahead motion.

"So, back when I sniped those Tank-Killers, the ones that were trying to trap the Johnsons, I rightfully should have died attempting to escape. See, I made it down the elevator shaft, through the tunnel, and out on the street, but what I never told anyone else was that a Tiger was just a few meters from stepping on me when someone else intervened. Kind of ironic, huh? I mean, I intervene to save the Johnson Clan and someone else jumps in to save me. Basically, an unarmed girl threw a brick at the Tiger and then escaped it. That girl was Harper, although I didn't know anything about her at the time. I dug around and found stories of sightings of a young girl in the Zone. Later, I tracked her down. Harper grew up in the Zone, Cade."

He just stared at me, eyes wide, speechless.

"Yeah, it's kind of a lot. My personal AI, who is monitoring this program, will now send the files we collected on the earlier sightings of Harper to your AI, Cade. Yours and Trinity's."

He stared a second longer, then touched the side of one eye. He looked off into red-eyed space for a few moments, then focused back on me.

"I can confirm that you sent me files that appear to be articles," he said cautiously. I think he was just starting to realize that this interview wasn't going anything like he had imagined.

"Yeah, let's let Trinity look them over and have her people check them out. Trinity, that's going to be really important in a few minutes," I said, turning to look where she was sitting off camera.

"Ajaya, I feel like I've lost complete control of this interview," Cade said, maybe just a bit shaken.

"It was never yours to begin with, Cade," I chided him with a smile. "Now, where were we? Oh yeah. It took me some time to track down the girl in the Zone. She was like a ghost, coming and going as she pleased, avoiding killer drones at will. I say that literally, Cade. Harper uses her will to confuse drones and hack AI systems."

I held up one hand because I could see overwhelming disbelief on his face.

"Let me explain. Harper's last name isn't Leeds. It's Wilks. She's the only daughter of Dr. Theodora Wilks, an artificial intelligence genius who was employed by the New York Stock Exchange to keep their automated trading systems safe, secure, and running like a top. That's a matter of record," I said, turning back to Trinity with a raised eyebrow.

"We'll check it, Ajaya," Trinity said off camera but loud enough for it to make it on air.

"Now, Cade, Dr. Wilks was also an early leader in applied neuroprosthesis, devices that allow humans to interface with computers. In fact, she was years and years ahead of her time. Her very best work was done with her daughter. And her expertise made her a natural target when the people behind Drone Night needed to have the mechanical leaders of their drone army upgraded and improved. And Dr. Wilks had just been diagnosed with an incurable, ultimately terminal disease. With no family, she was under huge pressure to get the treatments she needed to slow the disease as well as set up her eight-year-old daughter to survive her eventual death. In short, she needed money... lots of money. And she had no idea what the Spiders would be used for.

"On the eve of Drone Night, the people who hired her attempted to kill her and left her for dead. They didn't know her daughter was there at the Exchange, hiding. Wilks survived and they stayed in the Zone because life outside the Zone was more dangerous."

"But we killed the terrorists," Cade said.

"Did we? Oh, we killed the crap out of *some* terrorists, but not *the* terrorists. See, back at that time, the country was divided more than at almost any other time in its history. Divided over politics, religion, ideology, sexual orientation, the haves versus the have nots, and so on. You know, you lived through it. But there was a group of people who were well placed, who were tired of waiting for their chance at the top, who came up with a way to bring it all together."

"You are honestly telling me that you think Drone Night was some kind of false flag event?" Cade asked, totally incredulous.

"Who benefited from Drone Night, Cade?"

"No one! Absolutely no one!"

"Really? What about the handful of people who had

shorted the market with crazy prescience? At that point, the richest people were the owners of the FANG companies and other technology innovators like them, but immediately after, it was a whole new group. Look where those people are today."

He was angry now, so angry I worried that his ability to continue was shutting down.

"Don't bail on me now, Cade. We're getting to the good stuff," I said.

"This is absurd! Do you have proof of any of this?"

"Me? No. Harper? Yes. Which is why she's out at large and I'm here with a bomb in my neck."

He waved his hands like he was throwing in a towel. "What could you possibly get out of doing all this, saying these things, and not having proof?"

"Ah, good. What we want, Cade, is to focus the world's attention on the real threat... the remaining Spider CThree. Here's the big moment, Cade; do you have the balls to see it through? Never mind. Trinity? Do you have the balls? I think you do. Play this chip. It's a message from the late Doctor Wilks, who died so that Harper and I, well mostly Harper, could get out," I said, tossing my data chip off camera to Trinity, who caught it like a professional athlete.

"Are we really going to play something we know nothing about?" Cade said staring, off camera to Trinity.

"You will if you want to keep the highest ratings in history going," I said, meeting Trinity's eyes, which shone with ill-concealed interest.

She nodded and handed the chip to Dave the IT guy.

"It looks like we're going to do this," Cade said with a resigned sigh, running one hand though his hair. Cade never messed with his hair on air.

A few seconds later, a video window opened on the wall behind us, letting us both watch while it played in full view of the cameras. Suddenly, Harper's mother appeared on the screen and began to speak.

"Whoever you are, the fact that you're watching this means that I am likely dead. My name is Dr. Theodora Wilks, and I am the person responsible for programming the Spider CThrees that were released into Manhattan. I mean to say that I did not choose the direction of their programming, just that I was the one who upgraded their CPU capabilities and coded their neural nets. When their purchasers... I won't say owners because nobody owns them now... gave them their initial instructions, I argued long and hard against it.

"But ultimately, it wasn't up to me and had I known what they would be used for, I would never have agreed to enhance them to the degree I did. But that's all behind us now. I'm sure if there is an afterlife, then I am already atoning for my actions even as you watch this.

"Here is the important part of this message. The Spiders that I finished were, at their time, the most advanced AI networks on the planet. That may sound like bragging, but it's the simple truth. Today there are more powerful chips and more sophisticated systems out there, but none have been running... growing... learning, as long as the Spiders have. You need to know this. Their instructions were open-ended. The people who released them into Manhattan programmed them with one simple order: kill humans. With no other restriction, the Spiders will do everything in their considerable power to complete that order. Kill humans... all humans... everywhere. You should, under no circumstances, believe that

just because they are momentarily contained on the island that they aren't actively pursuing their mission. They won't stop, they'll never stop, and my modifications will give them a viable lifespan far in excess of their original specifications. They have to be stopped. Even contained on the island, they have access to the internet via optic lines running through the city. They are unmatched for hacking power and experience. They already control more around you than you could imagine. Should they succeed in escaping the island, they will spread out and seek to fulfill their mission. Eradicate humans —everywhere. They must be stopped. They must be killed. If you have this message, you need to pass it on. Without any sense of overdramatics, the fate of the human race depends on your actions. A list of the improvements made follows."

The screen cut to a list of technical specs and stayed there, frozen in place.

Cade didn't say a word as it ended, his eyes still glued to the screen.

"That's what we hoped to achieve, Cade. Harper Wilks went back into the Zone with me to hunt down and kill the Spiders. For her, I think it's a family honor thing. For me, it's a family survival thing. We got half the job done. You already know that some drones escaped, carefully designed drones that influenced vital AI networks to a scary dangerous degree. In fact, there's probably one in this very building somewhere. But that footage of us in the stairwell of 33 Thomas Street should have scared the living hell out of you. It should have scared the people who interrogated me. Actually, I think it did, because number one, they released their NDA doomsday program and, two, I'm still alive. See, as I mentioned before and I hope everyone playing at home has already fact-checked, 33 Thomas actually once harbored a vital NSA surveillance hub. It was code named Titanpointe and it had massive capabilities. Harper told me the satellite connection on that building was the only one of its kind in Manhattan. The building was designed to survive a nuclear holocaust, had provisions for fifteen hundred people for two weeks, and generator and battery backup with big stockpiles of fuel. The Tesla we discovered in the basement had a partial charge, Cade."

He got it in a second, his face going pale. "It wouldn't hold a charge for ten years, would it? Someone had to run the generators."

"Or some*thing*. So, a super AI programmed to kill off mankind was left alone with an NSA satellite connection for ten years."

He was silent again, real fear on his features. "You're serious about all of this, aren't you?"

"Like a heart attack, Cade."

He looked around the studio, meeting faces that reflected as much shock as he was showing. Then he frowned. "You didn't bring any of your lovely family here to back you up?"

"My lovely family is no longer in the City, Cade. They're out, hopefully in a location that is more secure than a major metropolis."

"That's the scariest thing you've said so far," he said, and he meant it. "What can we do? What can be done?"

"I don't know about our digital infrastructure, Cade; not my area of expertise. We were hoping that whatever the NSA threw at us would slow down Plum Blossom's plans. And as the world hasn't ended, that might be the case."

"If that's the case, why are you still here?" he asked.

I pointed at my neck. "I was told to hang close. Short leash and all that," I said.

"Oh. That's what you meant when you said you were still alive, isn't it?"

"Yeah. I can't really help with the World Wide Web, the internet, or major AI systems. I kill drones, Cade."

"And you're the only person alive to kill two Spider CThree command drones," he said, the light dawning on his face.

"Yeah, that's my guess. The new people, the SOAP troops, stupid name that, are good, real good, but, well, you know."

"Yeah. Nobody else has killed thousands of drones all by themselves," he said with a nod. "But you don't have your drone anymore... your Berkut?"

"We'll see. I don't know if I can bring him back; the damage to his shell is really bad. Maybe if I can find a dead Berkut or other suitable airframe. Maybe. We'll see. But I think I'm likely headed back in at some point. But do you understand why I'm not all that concerned about lawsuits right now? The people suing me will need to stay alive if they want their pound of flesh, and so will I. What do you think the odds are?" I asked, tilting my head.

He shook his head, looking exhausted and scared.

"Well, Cade. I promised a unique interview. Did I deliver?"

He looked around the studio, where people were in various states of shock or answering and making frantic calls, the normally well-run production facility looking chaotic.

"Yeah, you did. I really wish you didn't, but you really, really did," he said. "How much time do we have? We can win, can't we?"

I shrugged. "At this moment, Cade, we've got the world's attention. From here, it will depend on what the world does with that. Does it freak out, blow everything to shit, and do the Spider's job for it? Or does it come together and fight like hell? Me, I'm a fighter. I'd hunt Plum Blossom with or without an explosive leash. Harper, whereever she is, will be fighting, and she's scary good at the AI stuff, Cade. She took the government to school over the last few days. And hopefully, the people in power, the ones who did this... well, I hope they're focusing as hard on this as they did when they killed off almost four hundred thousand US citizens. But hey, look... I made it through the interview and I didn't blow up all over you! Good, right?"

He looked at me like I was crazy. "The scariest part of all this is that I actually believe you... I don't want to, but I do. Every single part."

"Well, I'm sure I didn't convince everyone, Cade. We'll just have to see how this all pans out, won't we?"

He nodded, face almost expressionless. I think he was maybe exhausted. Then he remembered his job and turned to the camera.

"This is Cade Kallow, and this has been a special edition of *Zone War*. It's time to say goodnight and I sincerely hope it won't be the last time I get to say that."

CHAPTER 43

The apartment was silent and empty. No laughter, fights, or outrage over high school drama. No quiet, powerful parental guidance. No wise grandmotherly love and cooking. Just me.

Coming straight back from the studio, I didn't even stop for takeout. Aama had left me a bunch of food in the freezer and fridge, and I heated up some curry and naan.

Just me and my AI. And a dead Berkut. Taking my food into the living room, I asked my Virtual Assistant to put up the news. Then I wished I hadn't. It was all me. The interview, my claims, the fact checks and the dozens of pundits that lined up to refute everything about me. I almost turned it right off, but despite the negativity and the vitriol aimed my way, there was an undercurrent of desperation to it. And the regular news anchors seemed shaken. Of course the internet was exploding, chat rooms and blogs clogging up with anger, fear, hate, and desperation. The White House announced a press conference for early the next morning, which made the talking heads wonder why so long a wait.

Trinity was interviewed exactly four times. When pressed on whether she believed me, she kept her answers short. Yes. Yes, she believed. And each of her interviews was shorter than the one before it. The final interview was by phone, and only an hour after I had left the studio. When asked where she was, she answered that she was on her way out of the City, then she said she had to go and hung up. The interviewer, a moderately famous anchor, tried to laugh about it but you could tell that it bothered him.

Trinity was a notorious and self-acknowledged publicity hound—although she used the word *whore*, usually with a laugh. And she had fled New York. It mattered.

Opinions ebbed and flowed, the initial experts denying that there was anything to worry about. But people dug and shifted the data and more information came up. Titanpointe, the NSA, the drone hive incidents, more expert AI system failures, more accidents, more problems, it all bubbled up. Elected officials were quoted and had the same range of responses as everyone else. But gradually, as the evening hours went past, as enough experts thought it through, as enough facts were checked and rechecked, the possibilities weren't being denied quite so hard, the ideas weren't sounding quite so far-fetched.

"Incoming call. Barbara Gurung," my AI announced.

"Take it."

"Hi, honey. Just checking in. We watched the interview. How are you?" my mom asked, her face creased with concern. Then the twins sandwiched her. *"Ajaya, that was sick!"* Gabby said. Monique just looked at me, studying my face. I crossed my eyes at her and she smiled, a little.

"I'm okay. How are Grandma and Grandpa? Everything okay up there?"

"We're fine, honey. Other than you being down there. Ajaya, what you did... honey, your father would be very, very proud. And so am I."

"Yeah, you should have told us about Harper. We had no idea

she was such a badass!" Gabby said, her twin uncharacteristically quiet but nodding in agreement.

"It wasn't my secret to tell, and it would have put her life in danger."

"Kind of in danger now, isn't she?" Gabby asked with an eye roll.

"Yeah, but it's of her own choosing. And the stakes make it worth it," I said.

"I'm sorry about you and Astrid, honey," Mom said.

"Well, she didn't like Harper and she didn't know all that about her, either. She needs to think about it. I get it. Plus, maybe she would be better to, you know... explore other options?"

"Ajaya Edward Gurung, don't you ever say that! I know you're referring to that God-awful thing in your neck, and just don't! We'll find a way. We always do."

"Yes, Mom. Sorry. I shouldn't have said that. Hey, tell Aama the chicken curry is awesome."

"Don't attempt to change the subject on me, young man. You keep hope! Something will change, you just wait and see!" she said, looking one second from crying. I felt like shit.

"Yeah, you're right, Mom. Plus, they need me," I said.

"Damn right they do! Oh, your grandparents want to say hi," she said, looking offscreen.

Her parents came on and gave me a pep talk, told me how proud and stuff they were. It was mostly standard grandparent stuff but the thing was, it made me feel better. Especially my grandpa. He wore his pride for me like a football jersey, and it helped. We all talked some more and then I said I had to go. Pretty sure Mom was going to cry as soon as the call ended but, well, it was what it was.

"Incoming call. Astrid Johnson."

"Take it."

Her face filled the wall. "Hey," I said. Brilliant, right?

"Hey. I saw the interview," she said, then laughed a little self-consciously. *"Shit, the whole shacking world saw it."*

"Yeah, well, that was the hope. You know, reach out to the globe and, like, not explode," I said with a nervous laugh.

Her face fell instantly and I felt like a shit all over again.

"I can't talk about that, AJ. I...just can't."

"Yeah, that was poor taste on my part. But hey, I'm consistent, right?"

She gave me a sour look but mostly still looked a bit devastated.

"What did the fam think? Martin call me names?"

"No. No, not at all. They took it serious. Dad believed every single word. He said that we're loading the LTV on the flatbed, packing up, and getting somewhere safer—tonight."

"What about the show?"

"Ajaya, you just announced the end of the world. My father thinks many things, but he respects the hell out of you. If what you said comes true, there won't be a show. The whole world will look like the Zone."

"Yeah, well, it's not over. No fat women singing the final song yet."

She grimaced at my insensitive joke, but her face almost twitched toward a smile. *"You can't say stuff like that, AJ!"*

"Well, I mean it. Lots of fight left. I'm going to find a way to kill Plum Blossom, whether Zone Defense helps or not. And Astrid, I know you don't like her, but Harper is scary good at what she does. And we've stirred things up. They'll have to do something."

"Dad says they won't get their heads out of their asses in time. AJ, I'm sorry I got so mad about the Harper thing. She's pretty and smart and you have a lot in common with her. I felt insecure about us."

"I'm not that kind of person, Astrid. And frankly, I'm pretty sure I annoy the hell out of her most of the time. But we are effective as a team... that's all. And you have to know that I've been in love with you since Drone Night, right?"

"No, I didn't know," she said, looking simultaneously pleased and sad, somehow. *"You never said that."*

"Well, that's my bad," I said.

"AJ..." she said.

"Hey, don't worry. This will work out. You load your badass self up and head out with your family. I'd be with mine but well, I'm leashed up a little tight. But that's just for now."

"Ajaya Gurung, you better be alright!"

"As you command, Princess Astrid."

"I love you!" she blurted.

"I love you too. Always have. Always will. Now gear up and get out. Pack your best guns and shoot straight."

"I'd tell you to do the same, but you always shoot straight."

"Hah! That's an admission that I'm a better shot!"

John Conroe

"I didn't say that. But... maybe."

Someone, maybe her father, Brad, spoke to her from off-screen. She nodded to him and tucked a strand of blonde hair behind one ear. If I died the next moment, that's the image I'd take with me. One perfect finger, one perfect ear, and a strand of glorious blonde hair.

"I have to go. We're leaving."

"Yes, you do. Do what Brad says. He's smart and he's a survivor."

"That sounded almost like respect?"

"Maybe. Definitely respect JJ. Martin's still a douche though."

She laughed, but her eyes glimmered with tears. *"Love you, Gurkha boy."*

"Love you, War Princess."

The call ended, leaving me to sit back. Oddly, I had a smile on my face. She was leaving me—everyone was leaving me—but she loved me. And she would live. Brad was a bastard but he was a scary smart bastard who loved his daughter. They had weapons, training, and a freaking armored vehicle. I'm sure he had a place to go, a backup plan. He always did. When the apocalypse came, and it sure looked like it might be soon, the Johnsons would survive. Me, I might survive too. Well, except for this damned bomb in my neck.

But it sucked being alone. Not going to lie about that.

Then I heard a tap. Just a little sound. Metal on glass. It came again and I got up. My pistol was in my room, left behind, unneeded for the last mission, and the tap had come from back that way.

I only had one light on, plus the vid screen. I shut the light off and moved quietly through the darkened apartment. The tap sounded again, freezing me in place. Definitely the bedrooms. I moved, ducking low and crawling around the doorway into my room. My 9x23mm was in my bedside table. I reached up and quietly opened the drawer. Gun comfortably in my hand, I immediately felt better. Then another tap—close—like *my* window close. Crawling to the foot of my bed, I leaned out, pistol leading the way, till I could see the very base of my window.

A big dark shape blocked the window, unmoving. It took me a second to realize it was hovering there. A drone. No, a really big drone. In fact, I had only seen one drone that size and shape. I stood up and activated the weapon light on my pistol. Unit 19 was hovering outside my frigging bedroom window, just sitting there, waiting.

My mind ran through a dozen possibilities, but basically none of them made sense. So I nutted up and stepped over, unlocked the window, and raised it up. Unit 19 gently bumped the screen. I took the hint and raised it, stepping aside to let the big Decimator silently glide into my room.

"Unit 19? Status?"

"Identification incorrect."

"What do you mean? You are Decimator Unit 19."

"Negative." Then it ticked—four times, fast. Not possible. It couldn't be.

"Rikki Tikki?"

"Hello Ajaya."

Then it hit me. Harper. While I slept in the government

building. The third data chip from Rikki's shell.

"How long?"

"Full assimilation of Decimator systems completed seventeen hours and fourteen minutes ago."

"And you just what? Escaped the base?"

"Rikki unit subjugated base security. Previously planted scout viruses."

"But why? Why did you come here?"

"Primary mission: Protect Ajaya Gurung. Secondary mission: Protect Gurung family and Astrid Johnson is not currently attainable."

"What are you protecting me from?"

A laser lit up on the Decimator's front, the red dot moving across the floor, up my leg, and stopping somewhere below my chin. I glanced at my mirror over my dresser. The dot was on my neck... right on the spot where they had injected me.

"Subcutaneous tracking and termination device. Possibility of accidental detonation unacceptably high. Rikki unit hacking deadman frequency."

Mom was right. Something would happen—something *had* happened. My drone was back from the dead. I looked over the gleaming carbon fiber shell of the Decimator.

"System status?"

"All systems optimal. All capabilities optimal."

Rikki was back and he was sporting a whole new ass-kicking airframe and he could keep my neck from exploding—maybe. Things were looking up. Way up. I closed the window and sat on the bed. Rikki hovered over and floated down onto the covers next to me. Then he ticked softly, four times—fast.

Hear that, Plum Blossom? That soft ticking is the sound of your upcoming demise.

The End

Author's Note

Ajaya, Rikki and company will return in *Web of Extinction,* the third and final book of the *Zone War* trilogy. I expect to have it done and out by the fall of 2019. As usual I need to thank Gareth Otton for his awesome artwork and Susan Helene Gottfried for her editing skills.

Borough of Bones is my first book of my new life as a full time author. A huge thank you to my wife of 29 years for taking the leap into the unknown with me. The best is yet to come.

Dear fans, I hope you enjoyed book 2 and I can't wait to get writing *Web*. Thank you for riding along with me.

Made in the USA
Monee, IL
10 October 2020